The Bridge

Silvio Cadenasso

PublishAmerica
Baltimore

First printing

ISBN: 1-4137-4148-7
PUBLISHED BY PUBLISHAMERICA, LLLP
www.publishamerica.com
Baltimore

Printed in the United States of America

To my wife, Judy,
without whose support this novel
could not have been completed.

The creation of a novel is a time-consuming process and is not easily done alone. My thanks to the following people who assisted me along the way:

My wife, Judy, Anne Allen, Lorie Brallier, Barbara Duggan, Steve Figler, Earl May, CS Perryess, Anne Peterson, Sharon Seymour, Sidonie Wiedenkeller and three friends who did not live to see the completion of this novel, Al and Jay Leddy and Dr. Marty Rochlin.

1

A dam Knight cut back the throttle and descended to five
hundred feet. A carpet of green came up to meet him, and he
was soon skimming over a redwood forest, heading toward a
horizon hidden by fog. He glanced nervously at his silent passenger,
a man he'd met just two hours earlier. The man had spoken barely
two words the entire flight—said his name was Weatherly.

Adam had never shown a six-million-dollar property, hadn't
even come close. He'd only been in the business five months and was
barely hanging on. It didn't make sense that this Weatherly guy
would seek him out, since four other Realtors in the office had more
experience. He wasn't about to turn a potential sale away, though,
no matter how remote it seemed. Now that he had family
responsibilities, he needed the money more than ever.

He flew toward the fog hanging just offshore, banked right and
headed along the water's edge. Breakers washed onto the narrow
beach below.

Weatherly seemed engrossed as he scanned the scene. He didn't
seem to hear when Adam spoke, just kept staring down. "That cove
down there," he finally said. "It's on the property?"

"Yes. You could probably keep a little boat anchored there."
Adam did a one-eighty back to the cove and circled it a couple of
times. Then he made several passes over the property to check out the
runway. It appeared to be plenty long enough and in good shape for
a dirt strip—looked like it was recently graded. The faded windsock
at the far end barely moved. He circled around, sideslipped down as
he passed over the trees and glided in for a soft landing.

Weatherly climbed out, checking the surroundings through dark glasses. He stood slightly taller than Adam, maybe six-two, with a solid physique, close-cropped salt-and-pepper hair and a sun-creased face. Adam guessed his age at about fifty.

Adam tucked a notebook under his arm. "Shall we check out the cabin?"

"I'd rather go down to the beach first."

They headed toward the shore, taking a trail through a grove of redwoods so dense it blocked out the sun. Adam could hear breakers crashing in the distance, their volume increasing as they got closer to the beach. The smell of seaweed hung in the salt air.

Adam loved the Northern California coast. When time allowed, he liked to bring Carla here, but it took a good two hours by car, and he seldom had time. Since he'd gotten his real estate license, he'd been working six and seven days a week.

The trail ended at a small beach, and they continued parallel to the shore, toward a rock outcropping that sheltered a cove. Sandpipers ran in and out of the surf. Adam inhaled deeply. No matter how uptight he was when he got here, the ocean always mellowed him out.

A boat sat anchored offshore, a red flag with a diagonal white stripe fluttering from its mast. "Strange place to be diving," Adam said.

Weatherly glanced at the boat, then stepped off the distance around the cove. He silently paced back and forth around the inlet, finally looking at Adam. "You know how fast it drops off out there?"

Adam consulted his notes. "It doesn't say. I'll check when we get back to town."

"No need. I can find out."

They walked down the beach, with Weatherly stopping to write in a memo pad. He glanced at the dive boat and back at Adam. "Why don't you meet me at the cabin in a couple of hours? I'd like to walk the property alone."

"I should really be here to show you around."

"That's okay. I'll figure it out."

"You don't even know where the property lines are."

Weatherly removed his dark glasses. "Just meet me at the cabin."

Adam felt a chill as Weatherly's blue-gray eyes connected with his. He momentarily lost his train of thought. "All right," he finally said, glancing at his watch, "four-fifteen at the cabin." There couldn't be any harm in his nosing around here if it made him happy. It wasn't like there was anything he could steal. It was better not to alienate a client if you expect to make a sale, and Adam desperately needed a sale.

He followed a trail up the rise, across a suspension footbridge and through a meadow surrounded by chattering crows. What made this guy think *he* had all the answers? Adam had researched the property.

The man had just barged into the office that morning and asked for Adam. He wouldn't say who, or even *if* someone had referred him, just that he wanted to see this piece of property. Was it Adam's pilot's license? That was the only thing that made sense. But how did he know? Strange — really strange.

This seemed like a good property — about fifty acres with a two-bedroom cabin and a barn. Adam guessed that some of the redwoods were over two hundred feet tall. He had never been here before, but he would make up for his lack of knowledge while waiting for Weatherly to return. He retrieved a key from a lockbox and unlocked the barn door.

The odor of dust, hay and manure hung in the air as Adam squeaked the door open. Cobwebs coated the ceiling and rafters. Dust kicked up onto his shoes as he ambled across the dirt floor. It would take a lot of work to bring the barn up to code. Adam would keep this in mind when structuring Weatherly's offer — that is, if there *was* an offer.

The cabin looked fairly new, though. It had modern wiring and appliances, and a fireplace that covered much of the living room wall. Adam imagined himself here in the middle of winter, sitting in front of a fire. He plopped into an overstuffed chair to ponder his prospects.

Wouldn't it be something if he made this sale? He'd already figured out his share of the commission, $108,000, and couldn't imagine earning that much money at once. It would sure come in handy, as he and Carla were getting in over their heads.

He'd left a good construction job over her objections. But there just didn't seem to be any future in hanging wallboard for the rest of his life. Then he went three months with no income. After his only sale, he'd taken Carla out to dinner. High on success and Chardonnay, they became careless, and now she was pregnant. With their savings gone and bills mounting, he had to do something soon, or their creditors would eat them alive.

He should probably check in with his office if his cell phone worked out here. Adam opened his phone and checked the screen, but there was no signal. Maybe he'd have better luck outside, but with all the trees, he doubted it would be possible.

As he went outside, he noticed that the fog was poised to engulf the landing strip. If he and his client didn't leave soon they could be stranded overnight. He threaded his way toward the beach, calling out repeatedly to Weatherly, but there was no answer.

The fog covered the shoreline and hugged the hillside. No way could he find anyone in this. And the surf was so loud it wouldn't do any good to call out. He started down the length of the beach. Why hadn't he been paying attention? Without any cell phone service way out here, he couldn't even call Carla if they got stranded overnight.

The breeze sent a chill through his summer shirt, and he shivered, wishing he'd brought a windbreaker to stave off the dampness. Time was running out if they expected to fly out today. He had to find Weatherly, and fast.

Through the haze, Adam could just make out the gray silhouettes of people in the distance. He quickened his pace. As he got closer, he saw Weatherly talking to two men in wetsuits. They looked over Weatherly's shoulder at a note pad, and seemed to be getting instructions.

The men stepped back and hefted their tanks onto their backs as Weatherly pulled a small semiautomatic pistol from a leg holster, checked its clip and put it back.

Adam froze, then slipped behind a sand dune. He crawled to the top and peeked over. Weatherly pointed to the cove, seeming to chop it into imaginary sections with his hand. The divers nodded, then put on their masks and retreated into the water. Weatherly checked his watch and headed up the hill.

Adam was tempted to confront him. He'd had plenty of experience dealing with his type when he was stationed in Afghanistan, so that part did not bother him. But if he said anything, he might be kissing a sale goodbye. For now, he'd just wait and see.

He doubted that the pistol was more than protection for Weatherly. But why would he need it? And since it was a concealed weapon, he would have to have a license to carry it.

With the fog moving inland, the main thing was to get airborne before it was too late. He headed off the trail, cutting through a stand of trees.

Cops carried concealed firearms, but Adam doubted Weatherly was a cop. He just didn't fit the mold. There was something about people who were this secretive. A lot of them were nutcases, and this guy seemed to be in that category. Adam would bide his time for now. If it got to be a problem, he'd deal with it.

By the time Weatherly emerged into the clearing, Adam was seated and ready to fire up the plane. "Did you have a good look around?" Adam said as Weatherly climbed aboard.

"Yes."

"We have to leave before we're socked in. Sorry I won't be able to show you the cabin and barn."

"No problem."

The plane sped down the runway and lifted off through the encroaching fog, something he shouldn't have done, since he didn't have an instrument rating. But it was either that or stay here all night. At four hundred feet, he banked left and headed inland.

Weatherly scribbled notes on the twenty-five-minute flight back to town, meeting Adam's attempts at conversation with nods and grunts. What had Weatherly done in the time he'd spent alone? What were he and the divers up to? And the pistol—why did he need a pistol out there? Right now it didn't make any difference as Adam concentrated on his runway approach.

Heat waves radiated from the pavement as Adam landed and taxied to the hangar. It was almost 4:50, and he'd gotten the plane back just before closing time.

So far, he didn't have a clue if Weatherly was interested in the property. He had to find out. "Well, what do you think?"

"If I decide to do anything, I'll let you know."

"Do you have a business card?"

Weatherly nodded and winked. "I'll give you a call." He turned so quickly, Adam didn't have a chance to shake his hand.

Weatherly climbed into a silver Hummer and drove away. The commission check, already half-spent in Adam's mind, vanished.

2

Why did he let people treat him like that? If he was going to survive in this business he had to take control. Adam went to the office to settle up for the plane rental, then headed for his car.

The old Mazda coughed and clattered to life. Weatherly had used him. He knew he wasn't interested before they even looked at the property. He just needed a free ride to the coast. And that pistol— what was he, some kind of Rambo character? And why was he talking to the divers?

Cool air began streaming from the dashboard vents. The air conditioner was one of the few things that still worked on this clunker. The old beast probably wasn't going to last much longer. And if he couldn't afford another car, he'd be dropping Carla off at work and using the pickup. Driving clients around in it would even be worse than in the Mazda. So much for looking successful.

It was stupid to get bummed over Weatherly. This morning, Adam didn't know he existed. Besides, he was strange. He sure seemed interested in that cove. Those divers had to be checking it out for him. Could he be a drug smuggler? That was the only thing that made sense.

Adam headed onto the freeway. He should have seen through Weatherly right away, or at least not let him call the shots. But when you're in a sales slump, you have to take what you can get, and Adam had been in a slump since the day he'd started. He couldn't just blow the guy off.

Some day, he'd make it up to Carla. There was that authentic Tiffany lamp she'd fallen in love with at Wood's Antiques—$2,799.

Hopefully it would still be there when he had the money, and he'd buy it for her.

The Mazda rattled down the tree-lined street. Adam dodged a familiar pothole and pulled into the driveway, parking over the puddle of oil.

It would be better to tell Carla about the plane rental tomorrow — maybe even next week, picking just the right moment, when she was in a good mood. In fact, maybe he wouldn't even mention it. There was no way she'd find out until the bill came, and by then, maybe he'd have a house or two in escrow. Right now, he just wanted to put this experience behind him.

"Hi, sweetie." Carla leaned on the dresser as she pulled off her shoes. "Have a good day?"

"It was okay." Adam walked into the bedroom. "You just get home?"

"Yeah. I had to get some loan docs out at the last minute." She unzipped her skirt, and it dropped to the floor. "Well, at least we can use the overtime." She pecked Adam on the lips.

Adam put a hand around her waist. "You look pretty sexy for a pregnant babe." He nuzzled her neck and caressed her still-flat stomach. "How's Junior doing?"

"I don't even know he's there." She leaned back. "You need a shave."

"I need you." He pulled her close.

"Adam," she said, pushing away, "I need to unwind from work." She reached for a hanger in the closet.

Adam followed her, wrapping her in his arms and pinning her against the closet door. "I know a good way to relax."

"I'll bet." She pecked him on the lips and ducked out of his grasp.

"Okay, I'll just feel miserable, then." Adam emptied his pockets and peeled off his clothes. He grabbed a towel and turned on the shower.

"Shall we invite Craig and Cindy over for Scrabble?"

"Sure." Adam jumped into the shower.

"I'll give them a call."

Adam soaked in the steaming water. It shouldn't be much longer before he got in a groove. He had to. It didn't do his self esteem any good to have Carla supporting him. Most of his friends were doing well. Some had already bought homes. He seemed to be the only one who was struggling.

But he knew it wouldn't be easy getting started in a new profession. He just hoped he could hold out until it paid off, and the sooner, the better. He was tired of his father-in-law ragging on him about it. That was the worst part. Adam shut off the water and grabbed a towel.

Carla met him as he stepped out of the shower. "What's this?" She held up a credit-card receipt.

"Where did you get that?"

"I found it on the floor. What is it?"

"It's for an airplane rental."

"This was today? Why?"

"I had to take a client to the coast."

"Is he going to buy something?"

"I'm not sure."

"I thought we agreed not to put anything on the card. You know how much interest they charge?"

"I didn't have a choice. He wanted to fly, and I couldn't very well say no."

"You could have suggested driving."

"Come on, honey, that would have taken four hours out of my day. If I'd driven the Mazda, I'd probably be up around Ten Mile Road right now, waiting for a tow truck."

"Oh, sure." Carla sighed. "How is this going to look at the bank if we can't pay it?" She turned away.

"Sorry. I had to make a quick decision, and it seemed like the right one at the time. Look, I've been under a lot of pressure, and you're not helping."

"You don't think I'm under pressure? Mr. Williams said he'd charge us a late fee next month if the rent wasn't on time."

"He's all bluff."

"That's easy for you to say. I'm the one he always comes to when he wants money. Do you know how embarrassing that is when he comes in at work?"

"Hell, yes, I know. But can't you see that I'm trying? You don't know how frustrating it is, working ten hours a day and coming up empty."

"Yes, but that doesn't pay the bills. I'm scared. If you don't get something soon, we may have to ask my dad for more help."

"I'm not going through that meat grinder again." Adam wrapped the towel around his waist and went into the bedroom.

"Well, we just might have to swallow our pride and do it. What about the clients from last weekend?"

"I left a message on their machine this morning, and they should be calling me back." Adam hoped he was right.

"Daddy says you're just not cut out for real estate," Carla said.

"It's none of his damn business."

"I can't tell him that."

"I know. But every time I see him, he gives me a ration."

"He *did* say he could get you on with the phone company. You need to think about it."

"Then I'll end up just like him, fifty years old and still hooking up wires for a living. I want something better. Give me a little time. Everything's going to fall into place. I can feel it. I've gotten so close on some of these; it won't be much longer."

"I know." Carla snuggled up to Adam. "I won't bring it up anymore."

"Promise?"

Carla nodded.

Adam pulled her close, feeling the tightness of her body slowly begin to soften. He caressed her back as she relaxed, her head resting on his shoulder. He moved a hand under her blouse, and finding the clasp of her bra, he unhooked it.

"What are you doing?" Carla nuzzled his neck.

"Nothing." The towel slipped from around Adam's waist. He eased Carla onto the bed and slipped his hand under the waistband of her panties.

"Don't forget—Scrabble—Craig and Cindy."

"Okay, tomorrow."

"I can't believe we're getting our butts kicked by two pregnant women," Adam said as he searched the Scrabble board.

"Yeah," Craig said, "but they cheated—four against two."

Cindy rearranged the letters in front of her. "Don't be sore losers. We're just smarter than you are."

15

Adam shook his head. "I can't do anything."

Carla headed for the kitchen. "Anyone want anything from the fridge?"

"We have to go," Cindy said. "Justin is kicking up a storm. Besides, I'm beat." She put her last letter on the board. "I'm out."

Craig pulled Cindy's chair back and helped her up. She was so big, she could barely move.

"Let's hear it for the winners," Cindy said.

Carla slapped her upturned palm and then they hugged. "Next time it's at our house. Maybe Craig will have his contractor's license by then, and we can *really* party."

"I'm not playing Scrabble against you again," Adam said as he hugged her. He and Carla escorted their guests to the car.

Carla stopped. "Adam, is that the phone?"

"Yeah. The answering machine will get it." He opened Cindy's door and held her arm as she struggled into the seat.

Craig got behind the steering wheel and started the engine. "See you next weekend, if not sooner."

Adam and Carla waved as Craig backed out of the driveway. Then they walked, hand-in-hand into the house.

Adam spotted the light blinking in the dark living room. He pressed the play button on the answering machine and listened. "Weatherly here. Meet me at your office tomorrow morning at eight."

3

The office was dark when Adam arrived at seven-forty a.m. Normally, he slept in on Sunday mornings, but today was an exception. He measured three scoops into the basket and filled the coffeemaker with water, just as Millie had shown him. On his only other attempt, people complained that his coffee was strong enough to remove paint. He hoped he'd done it right this time.

Weatherly wanted this meeting because he was ready to make an offer. Adam was sure of it and could hardly believe his good fortune. If he handled it right, his money problems would soon be over.

The conference room—he'd better make sure it was clean. He switched on the light and glanced around, finding papers strewn about and crumbs and coffee stains on the table. Adam grabbed the 409 from the supply cupboard. He wanted everything to be perfect.

If he had been able to contact his broker, he'd feel more confident, but he tried both last night and early this morning, and got the answering machine each time. He couldn't even get through to his cell phone. Mike was probably gone for the weekend.

Adam saw the Hummer pull into the parking lot. Weatherly spoke on his cell phone as he got out of the car and marched up the sidewalk. Adam wondered if he had the pistol. It didn't make any difference, though. He just hoped his nervousness didn't show. Reminding himself that a hundred-thousand-dollar commission rode on the deal did nothing to ease his anxiety.

He arrived at the front counter and waited. What was keeping Weatherly? Adam saw him standing near the front door, cell phone to his ear. He didn't seem to care that he had an eight o'clock appointment—pretty inconsiderate.

Adam busied himself at his desk. He finally heard the front door open and returned to the counter. "Let's go into the conference room. Would you like some coffee?" It sounded like groveling and wished he hadn't said it that way. This was no time to screw up.

Weatherly shook his head. "I'm real short on time." He pulled out a memo pad and glanced at his notes. "Has the property been surveyed?"

Adam thumbed through the folder. "Yes, it has."

The cellular phone rang from the holster on Weatherly's belt. "Just a second." He turned and stepped outside before answering it. Adam waited as Weatherly talked for maybe five minutes. What could he be discussing that was so private? He finally folded the telephone and returned inside. "Okay, where were we?"

"I made sure that the property had been surveyed."

"Right. Could I see the parcel map?"

Adam pulled it out and slid it across the counter.

Weatherly frowned as he examined it. "I'd like you to run up there and find the boundary stakes."

"Is there a problem?"

"I think this map is wrong."

"That's not likely. What makes you think so?"

"I've just got a hunch."

"It says right here that the property was surveyed two years ago."

"Just check it out. It's important to me."

"Okay." Adam had to get a commitment from Weatherly. "Are you getting ready to make an offer?"

"I just need to know where the boundary lines are, for now."

"If you can verify the lines to your satisfaction, will you be ready?"

"Let's just see what you come up with."

If Adam let him walk right now, he might never see him again. "There may be some other interest in the property."

"Look, don't push me. If I decide to buy, I'll let you know."

Adam hoped his disappointment didn't show as he scribbled a Post-it note and stuck it inside the folder. "Where can I call you?"

"Leave the information at the UPS Store. They'll forward it to me." Weatherly glanced at his watch. "I have to go." He turned and headed out, pulling his cell phone from its holster as he reached the car.

Adam took a deep breath and slowly exhaled. What an asshole. Weatherly could have asked him to do this over the phone. The man was a control freak, a lunatic. Adam didn't like being jerked around, couldn't even stand the guy. But he'd continue to play along until he put the deal together. At this point it didn't look promising, though, with all the crazy demands.

He turned off the coffeemaker and lights and locked the door. He'd rather not drive the Mazda to the coast, but if he babied it along, it should make the trip all right. At least when his in-laws arrived for his weekly grilling this afternoon, he'd be gone. Maybe Carla would even go with him.

"How's this?" Carla spread a blanket on the sand. The fog was breaking up, and the warm sun radiated through Adam — perfect timing. And the ocean seemed unusually calm.

Adam set their ice chest down, and Carla began looking through the containers of food. When he asked her to come along, she decided to pack a picnic lunch. She called her mom and told her they wouldn't be home and not to drop by. Adam could almost hear Dixie whining.

The rhythm of the ocean had a soothing effect. It made Adam forget his tensions and worries. He could feel Carla unwinding, too, as he massaged her neck.

"Oh, that feels good," she said as she stretched her neck down and around. The sun reflected off her shoulder-length brown hair, giving it golden highlights. Adam ran his hands down to her shoulders and along her back. He'd been crazy about her since the eighth grade. She stood out from the rest of the girls, tall, with long legs and an easy smile. And she carried herself with athletic grace. He'd always gotten tongue-tied around her, but one day in the library, in their junior year, she'd asked him what he was reading and they began talking.

"That was relaxing. Let's go for a walk." Carla's voice cut into Adam's thoughts.

They started past the cove and around the point, where the beach ended at a rocky outcropping. Then they climbed over the top, to a second, smaller beach littered with driftwood. "Before long you won't be able to do this," Adam said.

"I know. It won't be long, and we'll be buying a crib and blankets and baby clothes."

"And if I make this sale we can buy a house."

"Do you think you will?"

"I don't know. He's so darned unpredictable."

"Well, whatever happens, we'll get by."

"I know, but I hate being broke all the time."

Carla stopped and facing Adam, took both of his hands in hers. "We won't be. You just have to believe in yourself. I do."

Adam held her close. If it weren't for her support, he'd probably go crazy. "Hungry?"

"I'm starved."

He took her hand, and they headed back toward their picnic.

"Did you find anything?" Carla yelled.

"No." Adam and Carla had walked the boundary lines for almost two hours. They found the stakes along two of the three sides, but the ones adjoining the property to the north seemed to be missing.

"I don't think they put any along here," Carla shouted.

"They had to." Adam threaded uphill through the redwoods. "If there weren't so many trees, maybe we could find them." He studied the map and scratched his head. "I don't know what to think. Maybe they *are* missing."

"What should we do?"

"I'm out of ideas. Let's go home." They returned to the car and headed up the road, passing a barely visible driveway.

"Adam, did you see that house back there?"

"I didn't notice."

"If it's on the next-door property, maybe they'll know where the boundary is."

Adam stopped and backed up until he could see a house between the redwoods, about a hundred yards off the road. He pulled into the driveway.

"What a neat place," Carla said.

Adam drove down a lane bordered by flowers, and stopped at a two-story Victorian house. A formal garden that burst with color surrounded them. Redwoods towered nearby.

A barking Labrador retriever trotted up as they came to a stop.

20

"Hush, Bruno." A man about sixty, dressed in jeans and a long-sleeved denim shirt looked up from his gardening and started down the sidewalk. He carried three apricot-colored roses in one gloved hand and shears in the other.

"Hello." The man smiled.

Adam got out of the car. "Hi." Bruno nudged Adam and got a head pat.

The man tilted the flowers toward Adam. "Ever seen roses like this before?"

"I don't think so. Nice."

"Developed this strain myself." He began snipping the thorns off. "What can I do for you?"

"I'm Adam Knight." He handed the man a business card.

The man stuck the shears in his hip pocket and took the card. "Real estate, huh? I'm Jack Kinney," he said, looking up. He removed his glove and shook Adam's hand. "We don't get many visitors. What brings you out here?"

"I've been looking for the boundary stakes along your south property line and can't seem to find them. I'm hoping maybe you know where they are."

"I might." He nodded toward the car. "That your missus there?"

"Yeah, this is Carla."

Carla rolled down the window and smiled.

A woman dressed identically to Jack came out the front door.

"Oh, honey, I'd like you to meet these folks. This is my wife, Elsa. Come on in the house, and we can talk about those property stakes. Would you care for a glass of lemonade?"

Adam glanced at Carla, and she nodded. "That sounds good." They followed the Kinneys up a sidewalk bordered with rose bushes. He hadn't expected to find such a nice home in this isolated place — white picket fence, groomed lawn and bright beds of flowers. A small shack, a ham radio antenna and a satellite dish, all encircled by a chain-link fence about fifty feet uphill from the house, seemed completely out of place.

Jack held the screen door open, and Adam and Carla followed Elsa into a living room with drawn shades. After being in the bright sunlight, Adam could barely see.

As Elsa continued into the next room, Jack pulled up the shades.

"The missus likes to keep it dark so the furniture doesn't fade."

"Your home is so nice," Carla said.

The room was filled with old furniture—looked straight out of a Norman Rockwell painting. Family photos were placed around the room, and a spinet piano sat against one wall.

"Carla's into antiques," Adam said.

Jack nodded. "As you can see, so's my missus."

The photo hung over the piano, one of a younger Jack shaking hands with another man as they stood in front of a bank of microphones. "Who is this?" Adam asked.

"An old friend."

"He looks pretty important."

"He was."

"Bring them out to the sun room, Jack." Elsa spoke with a slight German accent. She brought a tray with four frosty glasses and set it on a glass-topped coffee table. Then she returned with a pitcher of lemonade and ice cubes and filled each glass.

Adam and Carla sat on a white wrought-iron love seat with thick flowered pads. The floor was of Mexican tile. In the corner, a fountain trickled into a pond filled with koi. "Nice place," Adam said.

Jack eased into a matching chair and picked up his glass. "Thank you. We found the property when we were on vacation a few years ago. I was an engineer at Lockheed down in Sunnyvale. It was interesting work, but after thirty-five years, I was ready for something else. When I retired, we decided to get away. That's why we built this house."

"It's lovely," Carla said.

Jack refilled Adam's empty glass. "So why are you hunting for boundary lines? You got a buyer?"

"Maybe. My client asked me to locate the stakes. I found all of them except the ones along your property."

"They're out there, just hard to spot, with all the trees and everything." Jack set his glass on the coffee table. "Why don't you girls stay here and chitchat while I take this young man and show him where those stakes are."

Bruno trotted up as they came out the front door. Jack patted his head as he went past and headed toward the carport, with Bruno a step behind. "We can take the pickup. It'll be a lot quicker."

They climbed into an old, restored GMC. Bruno jumped in just ahead of Jack and reached Adam as he got in on the passenger side.

"What year is this?" Adam asked, leaning his face away as Bruno's tongue found its mark.

"It's a '48. Picked it up from an old farmer down in Booneville. He'd had it up on blocks in his barn since 1962."

Adam was surprised to see a red '56 Corvette parked next to a new Cadillac Escalade. He pushed Bruno back toward Jack. "Did you restore these yourself?"

"Yep. That's one of my hobbies. You know, when you get to be my age you've got to have something to do besides sit in a rocking chair or you'll end up at the undertaker's."

Jack fired up the GMC and backed out. "So what kind of guy is this buyer of yours?"

"I'm really not sure," Adam said, a little embarrassed that he didn't know his client any better. "I just met him." He certainly wasn't going to tell Jack that his prospective neighbor was a nut.

Jack pulled onto the road without slowing or checking for traffic. "We have to be careful who we get in up here, you know, with all the weirdos and dopers and stuff. We don't want the wrong people moving in."

Adam gulped. "I know what you mean."

Jack parked a short distance down the road and headed into the forest, with Adam and Bruno close behind. He walked about fifty feet and stopped behind a huge redwood. "Here's one of 'em," he said. He stood in front of a large bush that had grown around a two-by-two post with a piece of faded surveyor's tape drooping from the top.

Adam checked his map. "It's about fifty feet off. No wonder I couldn't find it."

They zigzagged downhill to the next stake, broken and lying on the ground. A third stood on the bluff above the shoreline and blended in with its surroundings. Adam scribbled some notes and stuck his clipboard under his arm as they headed back to the truck. If he hadn't had Jack's help, he would never have found the stakes. How did Weatherly know?

Jack let Adam off in front of the house and pulled into the carport.

As Adam waited for him, his gaze zeroed in on the small outbuilding behind the house. The gate had a padlock big enough for the U.S. Mint. "What's that building?" Adam asked.

"Oh, that? It's just a little storage shed." Jack opened the front door and followed Adam inside.

Adam and Carla thanked the Kinneys and headed on their way.

"Aren't they nice?" Carla said.

"Yeah, they are." Adam steered up the winding road toward home.

"Mr. Kinney's a sweetheart. He reminds me of my grandfather."

"A little, I guess." Adam thought about his client. He'd drop the information off. Then he could only wait until Weatherly contacted him. His boss always talked about client control and Adam had none in this case. He was completely at the mercy of a man he hardly knew and didn't trust. This deal had to go together. It just had to.

4

et's see," Carla said as she entered numbers into a hand-held calculator. "If we pay the minimum on our credit card, we'll have thirty-two dollars left over for groceries. How's your gas?"

Adam glanced at the gauge. "Just under three-quarters. That should last until Friday." The car behind him honked, and he realized the light had turned green.

Carla punched in more numbers. "Next Friday's check will go for utilities and a tank of gas. Hopefully we can set some aside for rent. Are you getting any closer with that couple you were working with?"

"They decided to hold off for now."

"How about the man on the coastal property?"

"It's been two weeks since I heard from him." Adam turned down the side street and pulled into Craig and Cindy's driveway.

"We may have to borrow a little from Daddy."

"No way. I'd rather look for some odd jobs. There's always some client at the office who needs a handyman."

"If you could come up with just fifty dollars a week, I think we could squeak by."

Carla trotted up the front steps and rang the bell. Adam followed closely behind, carrying a paper grocery bag under each arm.

"Hi, we're here," Carla said, opening the door. Adam went in behind her and took the bags to the kitchen, dropping them on the counter.

"Hi," Cindy said, waddling into the room. "Craig's out back." She looked as big as a house.

Adam went to the patio to find his best friend standing in front of the barbecue. "Smells good."

Craig looked up through the smoke as he stabbed a chicken wing, glanced under it and put it back. "That's 'cause it *is* good. Grab a beer."

Adam pulled a Sierra Nevada from the ice chest. "You find out about your test?"

"Just got word yesterday. You're looking at the newest general contractor in town."

"What did Bolton say?"

"Haven't told him. I'm not ready to burn my bridges yet." Craig dodged a stream of smoke as he turned the chicken over. "Besides, with the baby coming and all, I need the insurance. But you know, if some high-roller comes along and throws a bunch of money at me, I guess I'd consider it."

Adam popped the cap off his bottle. "I don't think you can miss as a contractor, which is more than I can say for my real estate prospects." He tipped the bottle and took a large swallow.

Craig set the fork down and picked up the beer at the end of the table. "Any more on that flaky guy?"

"Weatherly? No. If he was interested, he'd have gotten back to me by now."

"Why don't you just call him up and ask him?"

"That's part of the problem. He wouldn't give me his number. I don't know anything about him, where he lives, or even if he's married. Most people I deal with will open up a little, but this guy hardly said a word."

"I guess it wasn't meant to be."

"You got that right. I've already put him out of my mind."

Adam paced to the coffeemaker, filled his cup and then returned to the open folder on his desk. He stood, reading his notes, afraid to sit down, feeling as if he might burst if he stopped moving.

When he and Carla got home from Craig and Cindy's there was a message from Weatherly that he wanted to make an offer on the property.

Since he was too keyed up to sleep, Adam arrived at the office just after sunrise, hoping that this would give him plenty of time to review the file before Weatherly got there. Weatherly would expect him to make some recommendations and he hoped he was up to the task. How should he structure the contract? Five and a half million — maybe a little less — would probably be enough to get a good counter offer. He'd formulate his thoughts after interviewing Weatherly.

If only he could have consulted Mike. It seemed that lately, his broker was never available on weekends when Adam needed him. Besides, the last time they had talked on the subject, Mike said to kiss Weatherly off, that he was wasting Adam's time.

So all Adam could hope was that he could put up a good front and not stick his foot in his mouth. He saw the Hummer pull into the parking lot right on time.

Adam escorted him into the conference room. This would be strictly business — no small talk and no socializing.

"Let's get this over with," Weatherly said. He pulled a note pad from his pocket. "I'm prepared to offer four million, four ninety-five."

"That's kind of low-ball, isn't it?" Adam couldn't believe it — on a six-million-dollar asking price?

"I'll be paying cash. That ought to get their attention."

"Cash?" Adam gulped. Maybe he *was* a drug smuggler. He wrote $4,495,000 in the blank. "And we'll need an earnest-money deposit. How much do you want to give me?"

Weatherly thought. "I suppose five thousand."

"That's not much on a five-million-dollar offer."

"That's what I'm putting up. They can take it or leave it." Weatherly took Adam step-by-step down the page as he filled in the blanks. Adam could see he was no novice in real estate matters.

Adam's hopes sank. At this price, he doubted the offer would have much of a chance. If Weatherly really wanted this property, he'd be more realistic. Why was he wasting Adam's time?

Weatherly read the contract line-by-line, scribbling changes as he went and slid it to Adam.

"You need to put in your address and phone number," Adam said.

"That's optional. Just leave it blank."

"Okay," Adam finally said. What was Weatherly trying to prove? "Oh." He had almost forgotten. "I need your earnest money deposit and if this goes together, we'll need another $95,000 to open escrow."

Weatherly went out to the Hummer, taking a briefcase from the back seat. He opened it, took something from it and then put it back before returning to the office. "Here's five grand," he said, tossing a wrapped bundle of bills on the counter.

This was the last thing Adam expected. What was he supposed to do with cash? Is that what the briefcase was full of? Only drug dealers and the Mafia carried cash like that.

Adam rewrote the contract and Weatherly signed. "I'll take it over to Cascade right away. Hopefully, we'll have a response by the end of the day. And oh, I really *do* need your phone number."

Weatherly didn't react for a moment. He finally grabbed a pad from the counter and scribbled some numbers on it. "This is my pager. Call me when you know something." He wheeled about and left without another word.

Man, what a downer. Adam would go through the motions, but he was sure the offer would be flat-out rejected. Now he had five thousand in cash to deal with, and the banks were closed. He stuck the money in the back of the bottom drawer of his desk and hoped it would still be there when he returned. He didn't know what else to do with it. Butterflies kicked up in his stomach as he drove to Cascade Realty.

Henry Battles glanced up from a crossword puzzle when Adam marched into the storefront office. "Hello there, young man. I remember you. You're the new guy at Valley, aren't you?" He looked over the top of his glasses.

"Yes, I'm Adam Knight." He shook Mr. Battles' hand. "I brought you an offer on the coastal acreage."

"Well, let's have a look at it." Mr. Battles shoved his glasses up the bridge of his nose and reached for the contract.

Adam handed it over and sat down. He'd always felt uneasy around this grizzled old character. Mr. Battles was a legend in these parts. The rumor was that he'd been running a one-man office since Indians roamed these valleys. And bringing a low-ball offer like this would certainly not endear him to the old man.

Mr. Battles couldn't just kick him out, though. He was required to present any offer, no matter how unrealistic, but he could make Adam's life miserable if he wanted.

"Hmm." Mr. Battles skimmed the contract. He took out his pen and pointed to each filled-in blank as he scanned the first page and continued through each sheet until he finished. He scratched the tuft of white hair just above his forehead and looked over the top of his glasses. "Did Mike help you write this up?"

"No. My client and I worked on it together. Why?"

"Pretty good for a new guy. Not quite what we need to put a deal together, but it's the basis for a good counter. Let me talk to my client and see what we can work out."

Adam breathed a sigh as he and the old man rose from their chairs.

Mr. Battles smiled and pumped Adam's hand. "Good job, son."

"Carla, are you here, honey?" Dixie Rinaldi swooped into the house, wearing magenta-colored Spandex leggings. With her bird-like legs and plump figure, she reminded Adam of two twigs holding up a marshmallow. "Oh, hi, Adam. Where's Carla?"

"Out on the patio." The aroma of Dixie's perfume wafted in — gardenia — smelled like a goddamned funeral parlor.

He'd forgotten to lock the front door again. And invariably when that happened, Dixie barged in without knocking. Once, she'd found him in his Jockey shorts and it didn't seem to faze her. When he asked her not to come in like that she said, "We're all family. It really shouldn't bother you." That really pissed him off.

Today Adam and Carla would tell her parents about the baby. Adam didn't want to say anything yet, but Carla could hardly wait to break the news. They would eventually find out, so Adam supposed that he might as well concede this small point to his wife.

Al came in with a grocery bag. "Brought you some frozen chicken thighs from Costco and some day-old bread from the bakery. Dixie thought you could use them." A faint stale-cigar odor drifted in with him.

"Thanks." Adam continued reading the sports page. Every Sunday afternoon it was the same. Al and Dixie would come by and try to take over their lives. They'd bring groceries, implying that he couldn't afford them, and boss him around. Adam always found himself listening as Al gave advice on everything from time management to the proper way to mow a lawn. Well, that was going to change.

And then there was Al's job with the phone company. Christ, he was just a tech—connected little colored wires to screw terminals all day. But to hear him talk, you'd think he was the top dog at SBC.

Al sized Adam up. "Sunday's a good day to make real estate contacts, you know?"

Adam sighed. "I just wanted to be here for your visit, Al." A little lie was sometimes the best course.

"You want to put this stuff away?" Al set the bag on the coffee table and flopped onto the couch.

Adam bit his tongue and carried the bag into the kitchen.

Dixie and Carla came in, both talking. "I bought you these shorts at a garage sale yesterday," Dixie said. She pulled them from a bag and held them in front of Carla. "I don't know if they'll fit you, though. Are you putting on weight?"

"Mom, sit down next to Daddy. Adam and I have something to tell you." Carla eased onto the arm of Adam's chair.

"What. What is it?"

"Sit down first."

Dixie glanced at Al with a worried expression and then sat down beside him. "What?" She clasped her hands together and leaned forward.

Carla beamed. "We're pregnant." She grabbed Adam's hand.

"Oh, honey, I'm so happy." Dixie shuffled over and hugged Carla.

Al coughed. "Oh. Did you plan it or was it an accident?"

"Al..." Dixie shot him a cross look.

"That's all you can say? Daddy..."

"I mean, we're happy for you."

"You don't sound happy. Daddy, what's wrong?"

Al fidgeted and cleared his throat. "Well, how on God's green earth are you going to support a baby on what he makes?" He nodded toward Adam as if he were pointing out something that had fallen from a garbage truck.

"What's that supposed to mean?" Adam felt his blood pressure rising.

"Well, Christ, you're hardly getting by right now. Don't get us wrong. We're happy for you, but you should really have thought it out first. Couldn't you have waited?"

"For what?" Adam rose from his chair. "I should have known you'd find something negative to say." He grabbed his car keys off the bookcase.

"Where are you going?" Carla looked as if she might cry.

"I've got some things to do at work."

Carla followed Adam out the front door. "Adam, he didn't mean it."

"Yeah, right." He hugged Carla and pecked her cheek. "I won't be long." He didn't intend to come home until Al and Dixie were gone.

Al knew how to yank his chain, and Adam was angry with himself that he'd reacted. What really hurt him was that Carla was caught in the middle.

Why did Al think he was a loser? It wouldn't be much longer, and he'd be doing well. Al was probably pissed because Carla didn't marry a doctor or a CPA. He'd better get over it, though, because Adam and Carla were in this marriage for the long haul.

Being at the office was barely better than being around Al. Millie, the only one at work, insisted on showing Adam the latest pictures of her grandchildren. He was surprised to find himself smiling over the images of snotty-nosed little kids. He hoped his and Carla's baby was cuter than these monsters were.

Millie answered the ringing telephone. "It's for you." She handed it over.

"Adam, this is Henry Battles. Get out your pen and start writing. I've got a pretty good counter-offer here."

5

G ood night, Adam."
"Good night. See you tomorrow." Adam watched Millie lock the door behind her.

He'd been waiting at least a half-hour, and Weatherly still hadn't phoned. What was his problem?

The telephone startled Adam from his trance. "This is Adam." Please, God let him be cool about this, he muttered.

"Weatherly here. What have you got?"

Adam took a deep breath, glad that his client wasn't there to see his shaking hands. He was determined to have a strong voice and maintain control, although he felt anything but confident. "They countered at four million, nine ninety-five." Adam went through the changes and waited for a reaction.

Weatherly didn't hesitate. "Let's see what happens at four million, six."

Adam phoned Mr. Battles.

"I don't think that's going to do it, son. I'll call you back."

How long would this go on? Adam felt as if he might wig out before—or if—anything came of this. He looked at the clock. If he kept his mind occupied, it might help settle his nerves. He thumbed through his client list. It was pretty short—not much work to do here. Maybe he could figure out what to do with the commission if he made this sale. He had to do something to maintain his sanity.

If this deal went together it would pay him probably half again what his father-in-law made in a year. That should shut him up. Al was probably bad-mouthing him to Carla at this very minute. Adam would show him. His gaze drifted to the wall clock again. What was keeping Mr. Battles?

Adam couldn't concentrate. He thought about his mom, raising him alone. She'd be proud of him now. She tried to see that he had everything, even though she had a tough time making ends meet most of the time. When she died a few months after he graduated from high school, it almost killed him. He looked at the clock.

The phone finally rang. "Mr. Battles?"

"Hi, honey, it's me. They're gone. Why don't you come home?"

"I'm waiting for a call. It shouldn't be long." He hoped he was right.

The phone rang again right after Carla hung up. "Well, son, we're getting a little closer. Everything's fine but the price. He insists on four million, eight."

"I'll call my client." He phoned Weatherly's pager and punched in the number. The clock seemed to barely move as he waited.

The phone rang. "What did they say?"

Couldn't he have the decency to say hello? Adam could barely stand Weatherly's abrupt manner. "They want four million, eight."

"Doesn't he realize I'm going to cash him out?" Weatherly's voice had an edge.

"It's in the offer."

"Counter at four million, seven, take it or leave it."

Adam didn't like ultimatums. His boss said that they could kill a sale faster than anything. He wanted to tell Weatherly what a shortsighted moron he was, but the last thing he needed to do was piss him off. "I think it would work more to your advantage if you had some flexibility. You *do* want this property, don't you?" Adam couldn't believe he was being so blunt.

"If I didn't, I wouldn't be wasting my time."

"You give them an ultimatum like that, and you could be kissing this place goodbye. Leave some room for negotiation. We're close. I know it." Adam tensed as he realized what he'd just said.

There was a long silence on the line. Then Weatherly finally spoke. "All right. See what they come back with."

"I'll call you in a couple of minutes." Adam phoned Mr. Battles. "He'll go four million, seven, and he's firm on the price."

Henry didn't answer.

"Mr. Battles?"

Still no answer.

"Mr. Battles?"

"Oh, yes, son. I was just jotting some notes." Adam began to sweat as Mr. Battles took another long pause, then exhaled a loud sigh. "You know, my client came down quite a bit from his asking price."

"Yes, I know."

"I'll run it by him, but I don't think he's going to be happy."

The sky turned dark as Adam waited. What was taking so long? Would Mr. Battles call back this evening?

The telephone startled Adam. "Well, my client doesn't like it, and I had to do a lot of talking to bring him around. As a face-saving measure, if your buyer will come up another ten thousand, and if he'll make his deposit non-refundable, my client will go for it, but he won't budge another penny."

Adam knew it was up to him, now. "I know I can talk him into it. Stay where you are. I'll call you right back." Adam punched in the pager number. Thirty seconds later, Adam's telephone rang.

"Come up another ten grand and agree to forfeit your deposit if you default, and it's yours," Adam said, realizing his voice quavered.

"I told you my final price."

'What do you mean?"

"Four million, seven. Not a penny more. And I won't default if the seller holds up his end of the bargain."

"You're going to kill a deal worth almost five million over ten thousand dollars? That doesn't make sense." Weatherly was an asshole.

"You let *me* decide what makes sense. He'll come down. At least if he wants to sell it, he will."

"Why don't you meet him halfway?"

"You mean split the ten thousand? Hell no. Call him back and work it out."

Adam phoned Mr. Battles. "My client won't go any higher."

"I don't know. This will probably kibosh the whole deal."

"Over just ten thousand dollars? It could be a while before another offer comes in."

"These are the instructions my client gave me, son."

"Would you be willing to split the ten thousand dollar difference out of your commission?" Adam figured it was worth a try.

"Hmm. I don't know. I've put in a lot of work on this, and I deserve compensation."

"I know, but you'll still be getting a big commission." Adam waited through the silence on the phone line. It should be a simple decision. Mr. Battles would make more on this sale than Adam would, but if he had to, Adam would absorb it alone. He wouldn't let it get away.

"I suppose I can," Mr. Battles finally said. "When you stop to think about it, a short commission is better than no compensation at all. Well, son, I guess we can put a sold sign on it."

The next hour was a blur. Weatherly came to the office, signed the contract and pulled out a cashier's check for an additional $95,000. He'd had it with him all along.

Adam said he would open escrow the first thing tomorrow. What started as a hassle fell right into place. He hoped he looked calm, although inside, he was ready to explode.

Five thousand out of his commission was a small price to pay. After all, he'd still get over $75,000.

Weatherly wasn't so bad. Now that Adam was getting to know him, he could see he had some good qualities.

"I'm going to need a contractor," Weatherly said. "Know anybody?"

"Sure. Craig Hubbard. Hubbard Construction. Good builder." He scribbled Craig's number, glad he could steer some business to his best friend.

"I'll call him."

Adam watched as the Hummer's taillights disappeared around the corner. He wanted to turn cartwheels as he picked up the telephone to call Carla. "Put on your sexy black dress. We're going out to dinner."

6

"Adam, come and see this cute outfit Cindy got for the baby," Carla said from the dining room table.

"Just a second. Oh, go! Go! All right!" Adam watched a ball sail over the right field fence and into San Francisco Bay. He dunked a tortilla chip into a bowl of salsa.

"Barry Bonds is going to break the record again. I know it," Craig said as he set his empty beer bottle on the coffee table.

Adam took the empties into the kitchen, glancing at the baby's outfit as he stopped at the fridge. "Nice." He brought two beers back and handed one to Craig. "So how's things at Weatherly's?"

"Great. I met with him Thursday at the property. He has all the workers lined up. All he needs is someone with a contractor's license to oversee the job. This is going to be a piece of cake."

"Sounds like."

"He wants me to add two bedrooms and another bathroom to the cabin, and put a loft out in the barn to use for an office. The barn's going to need a lot of work, mainly a new roof. And it has to be completely rewired.

And he's going to put up a new building, too—just one large room and a bathroom with six stalls and a large common shower. It's real bare-bones—a corrugated tin roof and no heat."

"What's that for?"

"I wish I knew. I can't believe how much he's spending. Just what he wants so far is going to run over four hundred thousand. That's forty thousand for me. Do you know what I can do with forty grand?"

"Buy groceries for sure."

"Not only that, it'll give me some seed money to buy some property, and I can build that spec house. Thanks for the gig, buddy."

"No problem. When do you start?"

"ASAP. He's already got the permit ball rolling. I don't know what kind of connections he's got, but he has something on someone — says he'll be set to go in a couple of weeks. Between the county and the Coastal Commission, they usually hold things up for two or three months or more, depending on whatever endangered species or Indian artifacts they find."

Adam nodded. "Wouldn't surprise me if he's paying somebody off."

"You think?"

"Wouldn't surprise me. How is he to deal with?"

"Great. Just gave me the plans and asked me to build it."

"He's not hurting for money. Damn! Did you see that?" Adam leaned toward the television. "That's the second time he got caught looking at a third strike. I don't know why he brought his bat up there if he wasn't going to use it."

"Yeah, they ought to get rid of him," Craig said, as he pulled a spiral notebook from his pocket and began writing.

"Don't you ever give that notebook a rest? You probably even write down when to take a leak so you won't forget."

"Okay, asshole, laugh, but you should try it. Maybe your production would go up."

"Anybody home?" Dixie swung the front door open and barged in. She wore a low-cut pink blouse that showed about a foot of cleavage, and pants so tight, Adam expected her butt to bust out at any moment. And that perfume — what was it? Adam almost choked as he inhaled a whiff, an overwhelming pineapple — or was it banana? If he hadn't been paying attention, he'd have thought a tropical fruit salad had just arrived.

"Come in, Mom." Adam didn't know what else to say, since Dixie was already inside. Al and Dixie needed to get a life.

"Hi, guys." Al came in behind Dixie. "Who's playing?" He carried a cardboard box into the kitchen and plopped it on the counter.

"Giants and Padres."

"The Cubs and Braves are on TBS right now."

"Yeah, I know." The way Al pranced in, you'd think it was *his* house.

Dixie joined Carla and Cindy at the dining room table and began looking through the baby clothes. "When is your due date?" she asked.

"In three days," Cindy sighed, "and not a minute too soon."

Al sauntered to the fridge and looked inside. "You have any Bud?"

"No, just Sierra Nevada."

He helped himself to a beer, returned to the living room and dropped onto the couch. "You know, Bud would save you a bunch of money over this stuff. Besides, I think it tastes a lot better."

"If I'd known that, I'd have bought some." Adam felt the steam building.

"So, Mr. Rinaldi, what do you think of the Giants' chances this year?" Adam appreciated Craig trying to change the subject.

Al sprawled on the couch. "Oh, they'll probably fold down the stretch like they always do." A muffled belch escaped from his throat.

"They've been in the playoffs three of the last four years," Adam said. "That isn't exactly folding."

"Yeah, but they've never been able to win the big one."

It wouldn't do any good to argue with Al. He had an opinion on everything, and he was always right.

Al leaned back and drew a bead on Adam. "So when do you get your commission?"

"Next Friday." Adam continued watching the game.

"Don't forget you owe me two grand."

"I won't forget." Adam felt his face flush. He sensed Craig tuning in on the conversation. "Did you think I was going to stiff you?"

"No, but I just wanted to make sure you remembered."

"You know, I don't like that. I've never given any indication that I wasn't going to pay you. And it's inconsiderate of you to bring it up in front of Craig."

Al rolled his eyes. "Come on, don't be so goddamned sensitive, for Christ's sake. I didn't mean anything by it."

"Like hell. You just get off by humiliating me in front of my friends."

Craig stood and chugged down the last of his beer. "We'd better be going, Cindy."

"No, stick around," Adam said. "This will only take a minute."

"No, really. I have some things to do at home. Come on, Cindy. Mr. and Mrs. Rinaldi, good to see you." They left as quickly as Cindy could stuff the baby clothes in a bag and waddle out the door.

Adam closed the door behind them and then turned on Al. "You don't like me, do you?"

"Now what the hell gave you that idea?"

"And you have no respect for me. Why else would you humiliate me in front of Craig?"

"Humiliate you? Are you serious?" Al's expression took on a look of mock innocence.

"This was between you and me, not Craig and not your buddies at work. If you were worried that I was going to stiff you, you should have brought it up in private. Why don't you take out a newspaper ad and tell the whole goddamned world?"

"Come on, you two," Dixie said.

"You know, Adam, you should act a little more appreciative, after all I've done for you." Al took a swig of beer and wrinkled his nose.

"That's it. Carla, what did I tell you? I didn't want to borrow from him in the first place. I knew he'd find a way to rub my nose in it."

"Adam, Daddy, please don't." Carla was ready to cry.

"Tell your father," Adam said. "I'm not the one who started it."

"Bullshit. I just stated a simple fact, and you flew off the handle."

Adam threw up his hands and turned away. "Every Sunday we put up with this crap, and I'm getting tired of it."

"I don't have to take these insults."

"Then why don't you leave?"

Al struggled up from the couch. "Come on, Dixie. Let's go someplace where we're welcome." He headed out the door.

Dixie turned to Carla with a blank expression and shrugged. Then she shuffled off behind him.

The house shook when Al slammed the door. Then his car screeched away.

Adam bounded up the steps with a paper grocery bag under his arm and rang the doorbell. He wanted to get this over as quickly as possible. After a few moments, Dixie came to the door. "Is Al here?"

"Yes, Adam. Come in."

"No, thanks. I can't stay. I just need to see him for a second."

"Al," Dixie yelled from the doorway.

"What?"

"Adam is here."

"Wonderful."

"He wants to see you."

"What for?"

"I don't know. Why don't you come and ask him?"

After a minute or two, Al came to the door in his stocking feet, holding the front section of the newspaper. "Yeah," he scowled.

"Got something for you." Adam handed the bag to Al.

"What's this?"

"A little gift."

Al looked inside. "A case of Bud?"

"Yep." Adam opened his wallet and pulled out a wad of hundreds. "Got something else. Hold out your hand."

Al shifted the bag to his left arm and extended his right palm.

"One, two, three..." Adam counted twenty one-hundred-dollar bills into Al's hand. He peeled off another four bills. "Here's the interest. Thanks for the loan."

"Oh, Adam," Dixie said. "That's too much. We don't want any interest."

Al glanced at her and frowned as he began recounting the money. When he finished he stuffed it in his shirt pocket.

"Take it, and go to Tahoe for the weekend. I insist." If they were in Tahoe on Sunday, they wouldn't be coming to his house. That alone would be worth four hundred dollars.

"Oh, Adam." Dixie hugged him and pecked his cheek. She then rubbed her thumb over the spot she'd kissed.

"Well, I've got to be going." Adam headed for his car. He glanced up at Al and Dixie watching from the front porch as he drove away.

Adam pulled into Craig and Cindy's driveway and honked.

"Oh my God!" Cindy shrieked as she opened the door. "What is it?"

"A BMW," Adam said. "Has twelve miles on the odometer."

"Oh my God! Craig, come here! Hurry up! Look what Adam and Carla bought."

Craig came to the front porch. "Wow! You got your commission check?"

"First thing this morning. Hop in."

Carla got out. "Why don't you take the front seat, Cindy? It'll be more comfortable."

"That's okay. I'll just sit in back with you."

Craig eased Cindy in beside Carla and then got into the passenger seat in front. "How come you got a Beamer? That's a yuppie car."

Adam backed down the driveway. "I'm too young for a Mercedes. Besides, it fits my image." He put the car in drive, and it glided silently down the street. It felt good to be able to show off a little for his friends.

Craig ran his hands over the leather dash. "Nice."

"Thanks. I wanted one that was loaded. We want to take some trips before Carla's too far along, and this will be more comfortable. Besides, it'll impress my clients."

"They see you driving this, and you won't be able to handle all the business. You'll have your own office with nineteen people working for you, and you can take a trip to Hawaii every year."

"I hope." Adam nodded. "How's *your* job?"

"I spent the whole day there. Weatherly's already got the building all staked out. Says we'll have permits in a week. I still think he's dreaming."

"Did you ever find out what he's doing?"

"No. But he's got some strange-looking people coming and going out there, with tattoos and shaved heads and stuff. Most of them look like escaped convicts. I don't know how they're getting in. They don't seem to be driving in, unless they arrive after I'm gone at night. I just look up, and there's two or three new guys."

"Think they're coming in by boat?"

"Could be. There's the landing strip, too. These guys have been pitching tents and running around like a bunch of ants on a hot stove. It's all pretty secretive, almost like it was some kind of military operation. I feel a little bit out of place."

"I still think he's smuggling drugs."

"For the kind of money he's paying me, I don't care if he's an axe murderer. I'm happy just to be the contractor, and he can be the boss. Whatever else he does is none of my business."

"You'd better watch your back, though. I don't trust him."

"Weatherly? He's a pussycat—strange, for sure, but I haven't had any problems."

"How is it, driving out there every day?"

"I got it down to an hour and forty minutes. The thing that bothers me is that if Cindy goes into labor when I'm at work, it could be a problem."

"If that happens, Carla and I can look after her until you get back. You just concentrate on doing a good job."

"Craig, I think I just had a contraction," Cindy said.

"You sure?"

"No, but it was different than anything I've ever felt."

"Oh, jeez. Now what do we do?"

"I think I'd better go home and get my bag."

"Yeah. Let's go home and get your bag. Oh, God."

Adam chuckled. He turned back at the first off-ramp and sped back to Craig and Cindy's house.

7

A dam parked his car in the middle of the block and jaywalked across the street to Cascade Realty. He hadn't spoken to Henry Battles since the close of escrow on the Weatherly property, but this morning Henry had called him out of the blue and asked him to stop by.

The old veteran was at his desk, reading the *San Francisco Chronicle*. He stood and shook Adam's hand. "Glad you could make it, son. Have a seat." He folded the newspaper and tossed it onto the credenza behind him.

Adam sat down in front of an oak desk that looked as old as the man sitting on the other side. Henry folded his hands behind his head and leaned back in his chair. "How is everything at work?"

"Fine. I'm starting to get busy. Have another house in escrow."

"Good for you. That's what happens when word gets out. Right now, you're the boy wonder around this town. And even though I had the other half of that sale, people would much rather do business with a young up-and-comer than an old geezer like me."

"You shouldn't think of yourself as a geezer."

"Well, all right. But I'll be seventy-three on my next birthday, and it won't be too much longer, and they'll be planting me out in the cemetery next to Margaret. That's the reason I wanted to see you."

Henry leaned his chair upright and shifted his weight. "How long have you been in the business?"

"Almost eight months."

"You've got a bright future ahead of you. Are you studying for your broker's license?"

"No. I hadn't even thought about it."

"Start studying. Here's what I'm thinking: I'm getting too old to do this on a full-time basis. I need someone young and energetic to spell me so I can slow down. And the first one I thought of was you. This is what I propose: you come to work here. I'll give you a seventy-thirty split. You can buy in by paying me ten percent from each commission. By the time you pass your broker's in a couple of years, you'll own the business, and I'll switch the license over to you. Interested?"

Adam didn't know what to say. "Uh, sure," he stammered. The offer had caught him completely by surprise. "I'll have to talk it over with my wife and everything."

"Take as much time as you need. And if you decide against it, there are no hard feelings."

"Come in," Dixie said as she opened the front door. At least she was dressed tastefully for a change, and her perfume was hardly noticeable.

Carla followed her in, with Adam a distance behind. The last thing he wanted was for Carla to drag him over here. He'd made several excuses, but she insisted that he was going—said it wasn't open for discussion.

He and Carla followed Dixie into the family room, where Al was sitting back in his recliner, reading the *National Enquirer*.

The TV blared a wrestling match, the crowd worked to a frenzy. Al glanced up and returned to his newspaper.

"Al," Dixie said, "put down your paper." She snapped off the TV.

Al looked up at Dixie, who held a steady gaze. He finally shrugged, folded the newspaper and dropped it in his lap.

"Okay, now sit up straight."

Al mumbled something as he straightened his chair.

Dixie strolled across the room. "Carla and Adam, why don't you sit on the couch." She gestured in that direction.

Adam wanted to go home. He glanced at Al, who appeared to be no more comfortable than he was. Adam sat down and found himself facing Al from across the room. He stared at the floor.

Dixie stood with folded arms and leaned against the wall. "Adam, your father-in-law has something to say." She looked at Al, who acted as if he wanted to hide behind his newspaper. "Al…" she

44

stared.

Al shifted his weight and looked down. "I just wanted to say..." he paused.

"Go on," Dixie prodded, as if trying to pull the words from him.

"I'm sorry for bringing up the money the other day."

Adam glanced at Carla as she squeezed his hand. He knew that she expected him to say something nice in return. He couldn't think of a thing as she stared a hole through him.

Okay, he'd try. "I'm sorry I overreacted." That was a dumb thing to say. He hadn't *really* overreacted. He just wanted to be treated with respect. That's all.

Carla and Dixie breathed a collective sigh as Al continued. "I guess you can tell that Carla means a lot to Dixie and me."

"She means a lot to me, too."

Al nodded. "I know. But you can understand how we want things to be perfect, and sometimes I guess I stick my nose in when I should stay out of it. I shouldn't have brought up the money the way I did."

Adam fidgeted. Now he'd have to say something nice about Al. "I appreciate you giving us the loan when we really needed it, and I shouldn't have gotten angry. But you have to remember that Carla chose me with all my faults, and we come as a package. You have to accept that." That didn't come out the way Adam wanted it to.

Al nodded, staring straight ahead. Had Adam finally gotten through to him?

"And Adam," Dixie said, "we're proud of you, for doing so well in your job, aren't we, Al?"

"Yeah." Al nodded, finally making eye contact with Adam. "Yeah, we are."

"Another ten feet." Craig motioned the U-Haul truck up the driveway.

Adam stared into the side mirror as he backed toward the two-car garage. When Craig raised his hand, Adam set the brakes and shut off the engine.

Carla opened the door from the kitchen. "The pizza will be here in about ten minutes."

"Okay," Adam said. "That will give us just enough time."

"Is this the last load?"

"Yep. The only thing left at the other house is the junk for Goodwill."

Craig pulled out the ramp. Adam climbed up and unlatched the door, then began wheeling boxes into the garage. Their very own home, at last—Adam had wanted to buy one since before he and Carla had gotten married. Now they were not only able to acquire a house, but a nice one in a good neighborhood.

"Well, I'm glad that's done," Adam said as he rolled the dolly into the corner. "After lunch, I'll take the truck back and then start organizing this place."

He followed Craig into the house, where boxes were spread through the kitchen and dining area. The kitchen table hid in the corner, under several cartons of groceries.

The doorbell rang. "Adam, will you get that?" Carla said. "It's the pizza."

Adam went to the door, where a teenage girl stood with two pizza boxes. He took them and handed her three tens. "Keep the change."

"Drinks are in the ice chest," Cindy said.

Carla opened the pizza boxes, and Adam grabbed the closest slice. A baby cried from the living room. "Sounds like Justin is hungry, too," Adam said.

"It figures." Cindy set down the pizza wedge she had just picked up and headed toward Justin, who wailed in his car seat. "Don't forget to save some for me."

Adam found a Sprite at the bottom of the ice chest and handed it to Carla. He grabbed two beers and held one out for Craig. "When you get through at Weatherly's, have you got time to do a little job for us?"

"Sure. What do you need?"

"We want to put in a sliding door off the master bedroom and remodel the kitchen." Adam sat on the floor, next to Carla.

"Sure." Craig took out his notebook and thumbed past several pages. "I should be available in about a month. That soon enough?"

"Yeah. We aren't in any hurry."

Craig scribbled something and returned the notebook to his pocket.

"I want to get a dog," Carla said.

"What kind?"

"I don't know—a golden retriever, or maybe a black Lab like the Kinneys have."

Craig finished his first slice of pizza and grabbed another piece.

Cindy returned with Justin over her shoulder, and handed him to Craig. "It's your turn. He needs to be burped."

"That sounds gross," Adam said.

"Better get used to it, sweetie," Carla said. "Won't be long, and you'll be doing it, too."

"I almost forgot." Adam stood, wiped his hands on his jeans and went into the garage. He picked up a box that stood in front of the others and returned with it to the kitchen. "Sorry about the wrapping. I didn't have time." He set it in front of Carla.

"What's this?"

"A little housewarming gift. Open it."

Carla pulled back the flaps and looked inside. "Oh, Adam, the Tiffany lamp." She blinked back tears. "I didn't think you were even listening when I said I wanted it." She clamped her arms around his neck.

"You deserve it for putting up with me the past few months." Adam couldn't believe how lucky he was, with a wife he adored and two of the best friends anyone could have. Life couldn't be any better than this.

8

If only there were more hours in a day. Since he'd sold the coastal property, Adam had been swamped with new clients. Business gravitates toward success. At least that's what Mr. Battles always said.

He felt bad that he hadn't seen much of Craig and Cindy lately. Craig was as busy as he was. It seemed as if the only way he and Craig would get together was if he drove out to Weatherly's, and he hadn't had time. At least Carla saw Cindy every few days, as well as two-month-old Justin.

Carla was beginning to show. It pleased Adam that she would work just one more month and then take maternity leave. With his success, she could become a full-time mom.

Adam sat reviewing his appointment schedule when his intercom buzzed. He picked up the phone to hear his best friend. "Hey, Craig. What's up?"

"You need to get out here." The background crackled with static.

"You on your cell phone?"

"Yeah. Can you make it?"

"How were you able to get through? I can never get a signal out there."

"I don't know. You really need to get out here."

"Yeah. I've been busy. How's Friday afternoon?"

"I mean right now, man."

"Today?"

"Yeah, now. I just found something."

"What?"

"I'll tell you when you get here. It's important."

"Can't it wait? I've got work stacked up all week."

"Come on, damn it. Don't do this to me. I need you here ASAP."

"What's wrong?"

"Remember what we were talking about?"

"No. Make sense, man."

"I can't talk." Craig's voice dropped to a whisper. "Look, somebody's coming. The gate code's 3472. Just be here."

"What gate code?" Too late — Adam heard a click and then a dial tone. He scribbled the numbers down and flipped open his daily planner. Craig was sure wigged out. He'd better get out there.

The Hogans would be in at eleven to write up an offer, and he couldn't break that appointment. He'd been working with them for over a month. After agonizing over a house for two weeks, they decided this morning to buy it. If he postponed, they could change their minds.

What had set Craig off? He was usually pretty laid-back. Adam had better reschedule his two afternoon appointments and drive out to Weatherly's.

Adam pulled away from McDonald's drive-up window and headed for the freeway. The Hogans were gone, and he'd sold another home — this time, his own listing. By the time he'd written the contract and presented the offer by telephone, it was after one. He stuffed some fries into his mouth and washed them down with Coke as he took the off-ramp and headed west down a two-lane road.

From the open valley floor with large farms and straight rows of crops, the road climbed into the foothills. The fields became smaller, with a smattering of oaks, small plots of vineyard and apple orchards.

Craig spent too much time at work. That's probably why he was so uptight. Since Justin was born, he'd been complaining that he hadn't had enough time with his family. Craig and Cindy were so devoted to Justin, it made Adam long for the day when his and Carla's baby arrived. He did the math in his head and realized they had just four months to go.

Over some distance of miles, redwoods gradually replaced the farms. The open areas became fewer, and the forest soon became so dense it blocked out all but a few laser-like shafts of light. The road seemed darker and gloomier this trip, and Adam couldn't figure out why. He turned on his headlights as the shadows closed in.

He focused on the winding strip of asphalt as it threaded its way through the foothills. This was his first trip to the coast in his BMW, and he should enjoy it. His car was built for this type of road, and he would put it to the test.

The tires protested as he sped around hairpin turns and into the straightaways. If he let his mind wander, it could be all over. He wouldn't dare to drive this way if Carla were along.

Could Weatherly be the cause of Craig going off like that? Adam thought of some of the things — the pistol that time on the beach, for one. And there was all the secrecy. What was he hiding?

That property was a perfect spot to bring in drugs — remote, with a nice cove to unload a boat. Adam had read about boats bringing in bales of marijuana. Could this be what Weatherly was doing? If he got busted, Craig most likely wouldn't get paid. He'd better discuss this with Craig.

Adam shouldn't let his imagination run wild. When he got there, it would probably be something minor — one of those things that Craig got hung up on once in a while.

The road climbed up the mountainside, around several switchbacks. Adam reminded himself to watch for logging trucks that sometimes came around these blind turns. He eased his foot off the accelerator.

The tight curves were replaced by long, sweeping ones as Adam descended from the hills approaching the coast. Soon, the pavement ended, and he found himself on a narrow gravel road. He slowed, not wanting to get any chips in his car's finish, and finally arrived at a gate.

A security fence topped with barbed wire now bordered the property. Adam drove up to a keypad resting on a post at window level. He sifted through his notes on the passenger seat, hoping he'd brought the gate code Craig had given him, finally pulling it out of the pile. Three-four-seven-two — he punched in the number and watched the gate slowly swing open. Continuing another half mile and around a turn, he reached a meadow and the familiar landmarks of the property.

Two vicious-looking dogs barked from an enclosure — Rottweilers. He'd been wary of big dogs ever since one had bitten him when he was a kid. If they'd been running loose, there was no way he'd get out of his car.

A new, good-sized building was almost completed. Another structure took form near the barn, and it appeared that the barn itself had gotten some remodeling. Adam saw that new corrugated metal had replaced the wooden shake roof. The old door had a new deadbolt lock. Several vehicles were parked nearby, and Adam pulled in beside them. There was no sign of Craig's truck.

Weatherly came out of the cabin. "How did you get in here?" His voice had an edge.

"Craig gave me the gate code."

"Oh." Weatherly almost smiled. "Well, good. I'm glad you came." His voice relaxed. "Let me show you around."

"Where's Craig?"

"He took off for town a couple of hours ago. Had to pick up some materials. I'm surprised you didn't run into him on the road. Come on. I'll give you the tour."

Adam looked around, puzzled, as Weatherly practically led him by the arm toward the cabin. Craig would have phoned if he were planning to go back to town.

"You won't recognize this place," Weatherly said as he steered Adam around a stack of drywall. "We've completely remodeled the kitchen and added two bedrooms and another bathroom."

Adam sized up the kitchen. It looked as if Weatherly planned on doing a lot of entertaining. He'd installed a Wolf stove, the kind used in restaurants, and the wall between the dining and living rooms had been knocked out. Several long folding tables, with chairs along each side, sat in place.

Adam followed Weatherly through the cabin and then into the shed as the two Rottweilers gave forth with throaty growls. "Why the guard dogs?"

"We got them to patrol the property at night. You can't be too careful, being as remote as we are out here. As soon as we finish the fence, we'll turn them loose to roam."

Craig's miter saw sat in the middle of the floor, surrounded by scraps of lumber. And his nail gun lay nearby, its hose trailing across the room. A few feet away, his cordless drill rested on a stack of lumber.

"Craig wouldn't leave his tools like that."

"I don't know," Weatherly said. "He just dropped everything and took off. Said he'd be back tomorrow."

Adam had worked with Craig for almost three years, and Craig never left his tools out, even for fifteen minutes. When he finished with one, it would go back to a central location, so he wouldn't have to look for it the next time he needed it.

Weatherly headed back toward the cabin. He opened the cabin door for Adam, and they went inside. "Care for a Coke?" Weatherly went to the refrigerator.

"No thanks." Adam felt the anxiety building in the pit of his stomach. Craig needed him, but he couldn't do anything about it standing here with Weatherly. He looked at his watch and realized he'd been here for over an hour. "I've really got to be going."

"Thanks for coming out. Too bad Craig isn't here."

"Yeah." Adam headed toward his car. He'd never seen Weatherly this outgoing.

"I'll call you after we're finished so you can see everything," Weatherly said.

"Okay." Adam started his car and headed toward the gate. As he rounded the bend in the driveway, he looked in his rearview mirror and saw Weatherly staring. Then a tree came between them.

He pulled up to the keypad and entered the code. The gate opened, and he rolled through. Craig would never have left his tools lying around like that, even if he were just taking a coffee break. And he wouldn't have gone anywhere after insisting that Adam come out here. Weatherly had lied. Adam was convinced of it.

9

Craig was in trouble, and Adam couldn't leave until he found him. He never liked snooping where he wasn't wanted, but this was different. Craig needed him. That's all that mattered.

About a hundred yards from the gate, Adam pulled his car in behind some redwoods, where it couldn't be seen from the road. He trotted back to the gate and punched in the code. The last thing he wanted was to run into Weatherly or one of his stooges. Better to cut through the woods.

The terrain rose steeply, with huge trees standing along the hillside. Adam hiked a zigzag pattern around them, over logs and through open areas with waist-high weeds. He wished that he'd worn jeans, as his slacks were soon covered with dust and burrs.

As he came over a rise, he heard construction sounds to his right and adjusted his trajectory toward them, soon reaching cover in the trees behind the shed.

Two carpenters were nailing a piece of siding into place. Adam was dying to ask them where Craig was, but he couldn't risk talking to any of Weatherly's guys. One carpenter had a shaved head and several tattoos. The other one sported a goatee and a ponytail.

Adam circled the clearing from behind the first line of trees, stopping at each vantage point. The dogs barked. He stopped.

Weatherly came out of the cabin and spoke to a man with a buzz haircut. "What's with the dogs?"

"Probably an animal."

"Don't assume anything. We've got a lot at stake here. Any time they start raising hell, I want you to check it out." Weatherly scanned the area from the porch for a moment and then returned inside. The man wandered around the perimeter, glancing toward the woods now and then. He didn't seem to have his heart in the search. Adam didn't dare move, though, for fear of giving himself away.

Soon the man returned to his work and Adam resumed breathing. He slipped from one tree to the next, stopping behind the redwood closest to the barn. When he finally caught sight of the dogs, he almost lost his nerve. They looked even larger from this closer view. Low rumbles erupted from their throats between barks, and even the guy with the buzz cut seemed to give them a wide berth.

Adam paused, eyeing Buzz-cut, and tried to form some courage. The only other people in view were the two carpenters, and they seemed engrossed in their work. Buzz headed toward the cabin, and Adam slipped to the back of the barn.

He crept toward a window a few feet from the corner and eased his head over far enough to see inside. The barn looked almost empty, and Craig didn't appear to be there. But there was a lot he couldn't see without going inside. Adam continued to a door, halfway down the back, and turned the knob. It held fast.

Looking through the window again, he saw that the door on the opposite side sat partially open. It could be the only way in. He began to have second thoughts as he realized he'd have to pass within sight of the cabin to get there.

But Craig might be around here somewhere. Adam had to check out the barn, no matter what the risk. He stood, leaning against the wall, trying to will his shaking legs to support him. After taking a moment to psyche himself up, he made his way around the end of the building.

Everyone seemed preoccupied, and Adam couldn't see anyone inside the cabin. If he was going in, he had to act now. He dashed down the side of the barn and through the door as the dogs resumed their yelping.

The smells of paint, wallboard and freshly cut lumber surrounded him as he eased the door closed. They'd done a lot of construction inside the barn since he'd last been here, most noticeably, pouring a concrete floor, adding a stairway and putting a wall around the loft.

Adam heard Weatherly's voice. "See what's riling them up, and don't stop until you find it."

This was not a good spot to be if they came searching.

It took a moment for Adam's eyes to adjust to the dim light. He tiptoed up the steps to the loft, stopped at the landing and put his ear against the door. Silence. He cracked it open and looked in.

Lights blinked on a console filled with dials. A computer tower clicked from a corner, and a plush desk chair faced a monitor and keyboard. The screen displayed a moving geometric pattern that was almost hypnotizing. Next to the monitor was a printer/fax machine.

A door in the corner caught Adam's attention. He slowly opened it. All he found was a closet containing a couple of half-filled boxes of office supplies. Still no Craig.

Adam was running out of ideas and didn't know where to turn. Better to go back to his car and think this out. Now to slip away quietly. Just thinking about those dogs made his knees weak.

A telephone rang behind him, and it startled him so, he almost cried out. Then the fax machine clicked into action and began feeding out a printed sheet. He tried to read it as it emerged, but there wasn't enough light.

Several men conversed outside. Adam peeked out the window and saw Buzz giving orders to the two carpenters. He wished the dogs would stop barking so he could hear. The guy with the goatee grabbed a hammer and headed toward the barn.

Adam froze as he heard the door slowly squeak open. He barely breathed, fearing that his thumping heart might give him away. The element of surprise should work in his favor, though. If the carpenter came upstairs, Adam would drop him on the spot and hope the commotion didn't alert the others.

After a moment, the door squeaked and latched.

Adam couldn't tell if the man had come inside or simply glanced in. But he knew if he stayed here, it would be just a matter of time before they found him. It might already be too late.

The fax machine dropped the copy onto the desk and beeped its ending signal. Adam waited and listened for any sign that the carpenter was coming upstairs. It remained quiet in the barn.

He picked up the fax copy and held it to the window. *The Righteous Confederacy* was in logo form across the top. The message was some kind of double talk that Adam couldn't figure out. He finally dropped the fax where he'd picked it up.

He opened the door enough to peek down the stairway, then

eased onto the landing. No one was in sight. He tiptoed down the steps and headed to the back window. The barn was empty, so he slipped out the back door.

Craig might be in the cabin — had to be. Adam would have to wait until dark to get close enough to see. For the time being, he'd eavesdrop from the cover of the woods. The dogs went silent. Now to get to the trees without being discovered.

He glanced around the corner and saw Weatherly speaking to Buzz. As they turned their backs to Adam, he dashed for the closest tree.

The dogs went into a frenzy.

Adam leaned against the back of the tree and listened. "Turn them loose," was all he heard.

He ran, knowing that his commotion would increase the dogs' agitation, but also that their barking would mask the sounds of his escape. Praying that he had enough time, he hurdled limbs and ran through bushes.

The barking grew louder.

He tripped and rolled down the hill, got up and ran toward the gate. It was a hundred yards ahead. Fifty yards.

Adam reached the fence. He could hear the dogs' footfalls and low rumbles erupting from their throats — no time to get to the gate. He grabbed a crosspiece about six feet high as he heard a snarling sound close in.

Three strands of barbed wire were strung over the fence. He lunged for the top of the closest post that held them. With one motion, he swung himself up and over. His trousers snagged on the top wire, and he sprawled across the gravel. The dogs lunged, their throaty snarls resonating through Adam.

He cowered for an instant, half expecting the animals to rip out his windpipe. Then realized that the fence now separated him from them. He climbed to his feet and sprinted to his car. In barely more than a single motion, he clicked his remote, jumped in and fired up the engine. The car sprayed gravel and dust as it bounced down the road.

10

Adam stared at his throbbing palms, shredded from his spill in the gravel, and the bleeding scratches on his arms. A raw knee gaped through a hole in his slacks, and the back of the other pants leg was torn. He couldn't stop shaking.

It was time to call the sheriff. Weatherly would probably be more forthcoming with them than he was with Adam. He tried his cell phone, but couldn't get a signal. Nothing seemed to be going right. Hopefully Jack and Elsa were home, and he could use their phone.

He was still breathing hard when he pulled into the Kinneys' driveway. Bruno barked, and Elsa opened the screen door and looked out. "My God! What happened to you?" She came down the front steps, drying her hands on her apron.

"My friend is missing. I think Weatherly's done something to him." Adam fought to control the panic creeping into his voice.

"How could that be? Mr. Weatherly seems like such a nice man. Come now. We need to get you cleaned and bandaged."

"The man's a whacko. You've got to believe me."

Elsa gave Adam a quizzical look. He could tell she wasn't buying it.

"Come, come. I'll get the first aid kit." She motioned Adam toward the house as she held the door open.

"Could I use your phone?"

"Of course." She led him into the kitchen and showed him to the wall phone at the end of the counter.

Adam felt so grubby he didn't dare sit down. He dialed 9-1-1.

"9-1-1 operator. What is your emergency?" the female voice answered.

"I'd like to report a missing person."

"How long has this person been missing?"

"Since around ten this morning."

"I'll connect you with the sheriff's department."

Adam waited. After what seemed like several minutes, a woman finally answered, and Adam gave her the information.

"Officially, Mr. Knight, a person is not considered missing until they've been out of touch for forty-eight hours."

"Yes, but Craig would never go off without telling someone."

"Someone said he was running an errand?"

"That's what Weatherly told me. He was lying."

Elsa began to busy about near that end of the kitchen, encroaching on Adam's space. "Mr. Weatherly wouldn't lie," she chimed. Adam turned his back to her and stuck a finger in his ear. He wished she'd butt out.

"People reported missing usually turn up," the woman on the telephone said. "The sheriff's department would waste a lot of resources looking for them,"

Adam listened as she went on about department policy. He finally interrupted her in mid-sentence. "Are you going to send someone or not?"

"I'll forward this information to the dispatcher. He'll have a deputy check it out when he's in the area."

"Okay." Adam sighed. Maybe this was the best he could hope for. But what if Craig had left when Weatherly said he did? Adam would feel pretty stupid if Craig were sitting at home right now. He'd better phone to make sure.

Cindy answered on the second ring. "He isn't home yet. You want him to call you?"

"Yeah. Have him call my cell phone." He didn't want to worry Cindy. From his conversation with the sheriff's office, it didn't appear that they would be much help. It was beginning to look like he'd have to find Craig himself.

"Come on," Elsa said. "You need to clean up."

"I should really call Carla first, so she won't worry." He dialed. "Hi, hon, I'm at the Kinneys'."

"I've already started dinner. When will you be home?"

"I don't know. I can't seem to locate Craig so I'm going to stay and look for him. I could be kind of late."

Elsa interrupted. "You need to go home and see a doctor."

Adam put his hand over his ear. "I couldn't hear you, hon."

"He needs to see a doctor," Elsa said in a louder voice.

Adam put his hand over the phone. "Elsa, please."

"You need a doctor? What's wrong?" Carla sounded worried.

"I'm fine, but I'm concerned about Craig." Adam told Carla everything he knew.

"Let the sheriff handle it. You don't know what kind of person you're dealing with."

"I just wasted fifteen minutes talking to the sheriff's office, and they don't believe me."

"Adam, come home."

"I'll only be here for an hour or so."

"You could get hurt. Don't do this."

"I have to."

"Adam, please."

"Why don't you go over to Cindy's? She could probably use some company. I've got to go. Love you. Bye." Adam hung up and turned to leave. It would take some doing to smooth this over with Carla. He turned to Elsa. "Thanks for the use of your phone."

"You're not going anywhere looking like that. We have to get you cleaned up and bandaged."

"I can't stay. My friend's in trouble."

"Adam, you called the authorities. There is nothing more you can do."

"Oh, yes there is. He could be hidden anywhere on that place."

"Now, Adam, I'm telling you, if you insist on going back, I'll report you to the police myself. Now go into the bathroom and clean yourself up!"

Adam sighed. "Okay." He had to do something to get her off his case. He'd stay here just long enough to clean up and let Weatherly put the dogs away. Then he was going back to find Craig. The next place he'd look was in the old bedroom in the cabin. Weatherly hadn't taken Adam in there when he was showing him around. If Craig wasn't there, there might still be other places on the property where he could be.

Elsa handed Adam a towel and washcloth and practically

59

pushed him into the bathroom. He looked in the mirror. His hair was matted with cobwebs and leaves, and he had a diagonal scratch across his cheek. His knee contained a mixture of blood and grit. When he applied soap and water, he could barely touch it. He combed the clumps out of his hair and stripped to his waist. After washing away the dirt and blood, he gingerly patted himself dry.

Elsa quickly hung up the telephone as Adam emerged from the bathroom. "Who were you calling?" She was beginning to act strange.

"Oh, no one," Elsa stammered. "I just called… I just called to see when Jack would be home."

"Oh. I thought you might be calling Weatherly."

"Of course not, Adam. I barely know the man. Now come here and sit down while I look after you. You look terrible." She plopped into the chair at the kitchen table, where a first aid kit lay open. Adam winced as she dabbed disinfectant on his wounds and then bandaged them. When she finished, she carried the medical kit away, and returned with some Levi's and a long-sleeved denim shirt. "I think these will fit you. Jack has put on some weight, and they are too tight on him." She dropped them on the table in front of Adam.

"Where *is* Jack?"

"He's off doing something. I expect him home soon."

"But didn't you just talk to him?"

"Yes. He has the cell phone with him."

Adam changed in the bathroom. The clothes fit as if they'd come from his closet. When he came out, Elsa was standing at the stove. "You'll stay for dinner, won't you?" She'd already set an extra plate on the table.

Adam glanced out the window and saw that it was almost dark. He'd completely lost track of time. "Thanks, but I really have to go."

"Then let me make you a sandwich to eat on the way."

"Okay, thanks." He had to do something to get her to stop bugging him.

Adam got in his car, carrying a wrapped roast beef and cheddar on dark brown bread that was still warm from Elsa's oven. It smelled wonderful.

Elsa walked out to the car with Adam. "Now you go straight to the doctor when you get home, promise?"

"Okay, I will. Thanks." Adam turned right, toward town and pulled off a mile or so down the road to think out his plan. He washed the sandwich down with a warm Coke. Hopefully, the dogs would be back in their kennel by now.

But dogs or not, Adam had to find Craig. He headed toward the Weatherly compound, pulling into a turnout about a quarter-mile from the gate, and parked behind a large tree. His better judgment told him to let the sheriff's office handle it, as Carla and Elsa had insisted. But he was convinced that if he wanted to find his friend, he'd have to do it himself.

A flashlight—he'd been meaning to put one in the car ever since he'd bought it. A lot of good that did him now. He'd have to rely on the penlight attached to his key ring—almost worthless, but it was all he had. Then, remembering he needed the gate code, he rummaged through the papers on the seat until he found it. He stepped out into the coastal chill, wishing he had something warmer to wear than Jack's denim shirt.

The redwood trees closed in, blocking out the light of a half moon. Adam headed down the road and soon made his way to the gate.

He punched the code into the keypad and got no response. He squinted at the number in the dim glow of his penlight – 3472. Once again he tried it without success. Carefully this time he reread the number, pressed 3-4-7-2 and waited. Nothing. Someone must have changed the code.

With his muscles tightening from his fall, the fence would be hard to scale, but Adam had no other choice. The barbed wire across the top was the main obstacle. If only he had something to put over it.

His Raiders' blanket: when he and Carla picnicked at the beach they brought it along in the old Mazda. Hopefully he'd put it in his new car. He trotted back to the BMW and opened the trunk, and there it was, a black and silver blanket with an Oakland Raiders logo. Al had given it to him last Christmas. He knew Adam was a 49ers' fan, and probably did it just for spite.

As he trotted back to the gate, Adam realized that he was no longer cold. He unfolded the blanket and draped it over a fence post and the barbed wire on both sides. Grabbing the top of the post with both hands, he pulled himself over the top, his every joint and muscle throbbing from the strain.

61

Several redwoods loomed nearby. He lifted the blanket from the barbed wire, dropped it behind the closest one and headed off through the meadow.

The dogs barked sporadically. Thoughts of what they could do to him if they were running loose gave him chills. Stay still, he thought as he searched for something to use as a weapon. That's what you were supposed to do when confronted by a dog. They don't like sudden moves. If you ran, it could trigger their attack reflex. If you took it slow and easy and didn't turn your back on them, they might spare you. But just in case, he picked up a good-sized branch that lay on the ground. It had a good feel as he swung it back and forth several times.

Adam was careful to step quietly, and so far, had not alerted the dogs. When he reached the cabin, he saw a sheriff's car parked in front. He slipped into the shadow of the tree closest to the house and crept to a window.

Weatherly and Buzz sat on one side of the room, sipping drinks. Two deputies were on the sofa across the room, each holding a coffee mug. The conversation seemed casual, and Adam heard his name.

"He won't be back." Weatherly said. "My dogs almost got his gonads this afternoon — scared the living shit out of him." Everyone laughed.

"You might want to be careful," one of the deputies said. "Even though he was trespassing, you could still have some liability." Soon they got up to leave, and Adam eased back into the shadows.

"Sorry to bother you," the taller one said as they stepped onto the porch, "but we have to check these things out."

"No problem. I'm sure Craig will be back to work tomorrow," Weatherly said. "Nice meeting you." They shook hands. "Give my regards to Sheriff O'Donnell." Weatherly gave a nod and closed the door.

Adam watched the black-and-white as it rounded a curve and disappeared behind a stand of trees. Judging from the conversation, this could have been a social call.

When the porch light went dark, Adam tiptoed around to the bedroom window. The dogs had been barking continuously since the deputies came out, making it hard for him to concentrate. But it would at least mask the sounds of his movements. He had no idea what he would he do if he found Craig inside. It might be hard to get him out without alerting everyone.

The curtains were drawn, and the bedroom was dark. Adam checked the window. It was unlocked. He slowly lifted it, being as quiet as possible. He listened. Not a sound came from the room.

He pulled the curtain aside. "Craig, you in there?" he whispered. He lifted the window higher and leaned in, pointing a weak penlight beam around the room. All he could see were faint shadows. It seemed quiet in there, but with the dogs still barking, it was hard to tell for sure. Adam hefted himself higher, resting his elbows on the windowsill as the dogs finally went silent.

Two voices spoke quietly from the next room. He'd trained for stuff like this in the army—no problem. They wouldn't hear a thing. He pushed through the window and slid into the room headfirst.

11

Ow!" Adam cracked his elbow on a wooden chair arm on the way in. The resulting sound must have carried into the next room. "Damn it!" he muttered. He slid across the wood floor on hands and knees, not daring to stop and rub his elbow, and praying that the sounds he made wouldn't be his downfall. The bed was straight ahead. He rolled onto his back and slid underneath.

The window—Adam had left it open. Then there were footsteps. He held his breath as the door swung in. An overhead light came on. Weatherly eased his way into the room. He cracked the closet door open for a moment and then closed it. Then, after what seemed like minutes, the light went off, and he was gone. "I guess I'm getting jumpy," he said as he closed the door.

From under the bed Adam started breathing again. He slid out and swung a weak beam from his penlight around the room. Hopefully he'd find Craig in the closet. If he wasn't, then Adam was out of ideas. He tiptoed toward the closet door and turned the knob.

A faint click came from the latch. As he slowly drew the door open, the hinges groaned softly. He clicked his penlight on and shined it into the opening. Except for a few clothes on hangers, it was empty.

The beam of light found its way to a military cap resting on the shelf above. He pulled the door further open. On the inside of the closet door hung a neatly pressed uniform on a wooden hanger. Two brass stars reflected from each side of the collar.

This wasn't a standard-issue US military uniform. What was it? Adam studied it under the dim light. A stylized pin of an eagle was affixed to the front of the jacket. Below it were a dozen or so ribbons, none of which looked familiar. A reflection flashed off one of the brass buttons, and his breath caught as he instantly recognized the emblem — the swastika of Nazi Germany. This might be the proof he needed — something he could take to the sheriff.

Adam crept to the window and listened. It was quiet outside so he climbed back through, landing on a brushy plant that crackled when he hit it. One of the dogs growled, and soon both had worked themselves into a rage. The porch light came on, and Adam had no choice but to head for the cover of the forest. As for finding Craig, he didn't know where else to look. Time to go home and call the authorities again. He trotted toward the gate.

The barking finally stopped, and the night became still. Adam slowed to a walk to catch his breath.

That sound in the distance: what was it? Adam stopped. The muted roar of the surf was there, but there was something else, like a tractor. And it seemed to be coming from the beach. Adam reversed direction and headed down the trail.

The sound grew louder as he broke through the forest and reached the shore. Through the fog, he saw a glow of lights from a boat anchored in the cove.

Adam continued toward the sound, staying close to the tree line, as far away from the boat as he could. He hurried past the cove, over the rocks and to the beach on the other side, where the resonance of a diesel engine engulfed him. The activity was to his left, possibly a hundred yards from shore. With the fog completely blocking out the moonlight, he could see nothing. But he heard a tractor moving about in the dark.

Adam tried to make out the movements as he crouched behind a rock, but with no light, it was impossible. How could they work in the dark? The only thing he could come up with was night-vision goggles.

For a few seconds, moonlight filtered through a break in the fog, and Adam glimpsed the silhouette of a skip loader. Just as quickly, before he could tell what it was doing, the fog took it back into the night.

Maybe if he got closer he could make it out. He crept along the rocks and made his way toward the sound of the engine. Suddenly it stopped.

Voices carried down from somewhere in the trees. Then Adam heard the sounds of a small gasoline engine and power tools.

He didn't know how long he'd been lying motionless on a large, damp rock, but he finally realized the uncomfortable coldness it gave off had gone right through him. And he sensed that he had done all he could for now to find Craig. It was better to go to Cindy's and give her support, and take this new information to the sheriff. Adam headed back to the trail leading to the barn. The fog ended as he reached the trees, allowing the moon to illuminate his path.

When he reached the parking area near the barn, he saw a reflection flash from the ground momentarily. He went for a closer look. Lying in the gravel was a framing hammer—a Vaughan twenty-ounce framing hammer. Moonlight reflected from its head, and Adam could see the initials, *CH*, engraved on it. Adam picked it up. Craig would not have allowed his framing hammer to end up on the ground.

That boat in the cove: they could have taken Craig out a few miles, tied a weight around his ankles and dropped him overboard. No one would ever find him. Adam couldn't dwell on stuff like that. It was already messing up his mind.

A damp breeze came out of nowhere and blew through Adam's shirt. He shivered and picked up the pace, feeling his muscles tighten even more. He draped the blanket over the fence and tossed the hammer over the top. Then, using the last of his strength, he struggled up and over once more, landing hard on the other side.

He wrapped himself in the Raiders blanket on the way to the car, and by the time he arrived, his shivering had subsided. After starting the engine, he cranked the heater up to high, and soon it blasted warm air. He rubbed the chill from his arms and then checked his voice mail.

The static was pretty bad, but he was able to hear a message from Carla. "Craig still isn't home, and Cindy is frantic. We called the sheriff. I'm going to spend the night with her. I'm worried about *you*, too. Come home." She'd left the message at around ten.

Adam dialed Craig and Cindy's number as he started down the road, but couldn't get through. He'd keep trying.

The dashboard clock flashed to midnight. He drove on, his

headlights cutting through the blackness as he corkscrewed around a turn, heading onto a bridge. That's when he noticed that a long section of railing was missing. He braked to a stop.

His heart pounded against his chest as he grabbed the penlight and shined it over the edge. The maw beneath him sucked up the light. He strained to see. The sound of rushing water filled in the silence. It was no use. He'd have to go down the embankment.

It was almost too steep to descend. He grabbed a bush to keep from sliding, and his penlight slipped out of his hand. "Damn!" He inched downhill toward the pinpoint of light as it rolled to a stop against a rock. As he grabbed it, he saw Craig's truck, lying on its side against a redwood.

"Craig!" Adam skidded and half-rolled down the slope, feeling nothing from the brush and rocks that scraped and tore at his skin. "Oh, no! Craig!" he shouted.

No answer.

"Craig! Can you hear me?" Adam reached the truck and pulled on the door. It wouldn't budge. His dim penlight found Craig's crumpled form lying in a corner of the cab. "Craig!" He pounded his fist on the door.

He climbed onto the side of the truck and pulled as hard as he could, but the door was jammed. God, he had to get in there.

He kicked the windshield, but his shoe was no match for the safety glass. "Can't panic," he muttered, feeling his heart in his throat. "Stay calm." He swept his dim light around. What could he use to break in?

There—a rock—half buried. "If I can just get it out..." Adam scratched at the dirt with his fingers, but it was like scraping them against concrete. A dead branch lay nearby. He broke off a piece and dug at the hardpan. Pieces broke from the end of the stick, and he made little headway. It seemed that it would take forever, but finally, he pried the softball-sized rock loose. He grabbed it with a raw hand and pounded it on the windshield. The safety glass crackled into little pieces. It didn't give.

What could he do? He clambered around the truck. There was no other way in. "Got to get help," he hissed through his breath. "Got to get help." His shoes searched for traction. He grabbed a bush and pulled himself up the embankment. When he reached the road, he was panting and bleeding. He couldn't stop now.

He shook so much he could hardly grab hold of his cell phone. Would it even work? He dialed 9-1-1 and breathed a silent prayer.

12

ir, please slow down. I can't understand you," the emergency
operator said. "Where are you calling from?" Her voice
fragmented away.

"Bear Creek Road, about ten miles past the big red barn. The truck
went off the bridge. It's bad."

"Where? Sir, I can barely hear you."

"Bear Creek Road."

"Bear Creek Road? How far up?"

"About ten miles past the red barn. Can you hear me?"

"Yes. Are there any injuries?" The static all but drowned out her
voice.

"Yes! He may already be dead! Hurry, please!"

"I'm dispatching—" The line went silent.

Adam tried dialing again. The signal was gone. Hopefully they'd
heard enough. He tossed the phone on the seat and slid back down
the hill. Still no movement from Craig, and he smelled gas. If a fire
started, it would be over. He picked up the rock he'd used earlier and
bashed it against the shattered windshield. It was like pounding on
a stretched piece of canvas. He felt so helpless.

Then his overworked penlight flickered and died.

He groped his way uphill, lost his footing and slid backward on
his stomach. He started upward again, grabbing a bush for support.
He was losing precious time.

"Got to find a flashlight." Adam rummaged through his trunk—
nothing. There had to be something he could do. His headlights—if
he positioned his car just right... it might work. He started the engine
and turned on the headlights. How close could he get? Would it be

enough? He pulled the car as far as he dared toward edge of the bridge.

The headlights aimed straight ahead at a clump of redwoods. It was way too high, but some light reflected off the trees. When Adam looked down he saw Craig's truck, deep in the shadows. It was better than working in complete darkness.

Then as he climbed out of the car, he saw it: Craig's hammer, lying on the seat. He grabbed it and took it back downhill with him. He swung the hammer full-force at the windshield. It was easier to use than the rock, but the safety glass still held.

He turned the hammer and bashed the windshield with the claw end—a small hole. One more swing—the opening got bigger.

Adam continued one blow at a time around the edge. It was slow, but at least it would get him inside the cab. Finally, the windshield folded down and away. Adam crawled inside.

The smell of gas fumes filled the air. It was insane to move Craig, but moving him with all its risks was better than letting him burn to death. "Craig, can you hear me?" Adam could hardly see inside the cab.

Craig's eyes fluttered. At least he was still alive, but barely. With each breath, Adam could hear a faint gurgling sound. He'd heard this once during his hitch in Afghanistan. If help didn't come soon, Craig could drown in his own blood.

It was almost impossible to maneuver around inside the truck's cab. Adam pulled on Craig's legs, the only things he could get a hold of. Craig was wedged into a corner under the dash, and Adam couldn't get any leverage. He finally pulled Craig far enough to grab his arms. Straining with every ounce of will, he lifted and finally got Craig through the windshield opening and onto the ground.

On this steep slope, it was hard to maintain his balance. He heard the creek rushing below him, and it was all he could do to resist gravity's pulling them toward it.

By the time he had Craig clear of the cab, Adam was out of breath. He rested briefly and then pulled Craig to a fairly level spot behind the closest tree—not much protection if the gas ignited, but still better than being out in the open.

Blood oozed from Craig's mouth, and his eyes stared into nothingness. "Hang in there, buddy. Help is coming." He had to remain calm for Craig.

Craig's breath came in shallow gasps. He opened his mouth, as if to form words. Nothing came out. Even in the dim light, Adam could see he was losing the battle.

"What? Say it, Craig." Adam put his ear close to Craig's mouth. "Bridge ... bridge..."

Adam could barely hear the whisper. "Bridge? Yeah, you drove off the bridge."

There was no further sound from Craig, and Adam thought he might be drifting into unconsciousness. He couldn't let that happen. "Hey, Craig, don't forget Cindy and Justin. They need you." An involuntary sob came from Adam. No, he couldn't let Craig see him like that.

If the emergency crew came from the CDF Fire Station, it would take about an hour and a half to get here. Adam checked his watch and saw that he would be waiting close to an hour more before it arrived. If his message hadn't gotten through, they were in trouble.

Craig stared blankly. Adam couldn't tell if he was still breathing. He put his ear next to Craig's mouth. What was taking the ambulance so long? He should have taken that first aid class last year.

Adam covered Craig with the Raiders blanket and tried to make him comfortable, an impossible task. Craig's breathing became more labored, and Adam could do nothing but watch as his life slowly drained away.

A siren—was that what he heard in the distance? He listened as the sound grew louder. The rescuers were here. Craig's body tensed slightly and went limp.

Adam clawed his way up to the road as the glare of headlights and flashing red lights appeared from around a curve. "Here!" He jumped onto the roadway, waving his arms. An ambulance pulled alongside, and a man emerged from each door.

"Down here!" Adam headed downhill as one of the men went to the back of the emergency vehicle. God, they were slow.

The two paramedics stood on the shoulder, each shining a flashlight downward. One of them stepped gingerly off the edge. The other followed.

"Hurry up!" Adam screamed. "He's dying!"

The two paramedics slid gingerly downward with their bags held high, acting as if they were afraid to get their uniforms dirty.

"Come on, hurry up!"

The medics reached Craig. One of them felt his pulse. The other opened his medical kit and pulled out a stethoscope. Adam could only watch.

More sirens screamed to the scene, and red and blue lights reflected off the trees. Within moments, two firemen rappelled down with a stretcher, and two floodlights focused on the area from above. A medic covered Craig's colorless face with an oxygen mask while the firemen readied the stretcher. Two other men began bathing Craig's truck in fire-retardant foam.

"No heartbeat," one of the medics said.

"Do something!" Adam screamed. Why were they moving so slowly?

"Sir, you'll have to leave," a fireman said.

"I'm not going to abandon my friend."

"Sir, please go up to the road. You're just in the way here."

Adam looked up toward the flashing lights as the truck's radio squawked. "You can't let him die," he said, his voice cracking. "He's got a wife and a new baby."

"We'll do our best." The fireman wrapped a harness around Adam and snapped it onto the end of a rope. Unseen persons on the roadway pulled him upward. When Adam got to the top, a uniformed deputy reached out to help him. He turned to see Craig's body jerk as the paramedics tried to restart his heart.

This can't be happening. Adam started downhill, but the deputy held him tightly. Craig was dying. He watched his friend's body stiffen again as another jolt of electricity surged through him. One of the medics put a stethoscope to Craig's chest and nodded. Adam resumed breathing when Craig did.

The firemen immobilized Craig's spine and helped the paramedics load him onto the stretcher. Adam watched helplessly as they attached lines to the stretcher. Then two firemen pulled it up the embankment. The back door of the ambulance opened, and Craig was secured inside. They slammed the door, and the ambulance started toward town.

Adam followed it over the twisting road, tailgating most of the way. If this was the fastest the driver could go, he should find a different job.

It seemed that they would never reach the hospital, but they finally arrived at the edge of town, and the ambulance raced, screaming, through a red light. Adam reluctantly stopped at the signal as the flashing emergency lights shrunk in the distance.

Then he remembered Cindy. It was almost morning, and she still didn't know where Craig was. He picked up his cell phone and dialed her number.

13

He can't be dead." Adam didn't believe the ER doctor. He'd barely looked at Craig—didn't even try any emergency procedures. The television blaring from the waiting room wall grated on Adam's nerves.

"I'm sorry. There was nothing I could do."

"That's not possible. He's got a new baby. He's got plans."

"I'm sorry." The doctor patted his shoulder. "Has his wife been notified?"

Adam nodded and stared straight ahead as numbness consumed him.

Cindy ran in. "How is he?" Adam shook his head, then held Cindy as she collapsed, sobbing, into his arms. Carla soon followed, carrying Justin. They all stood huddled in the center of the waiting room.

The deputies who had been at the accident came in and spoke to the receptionist. One deputy was buzzed through a locked door. The other approached Adam.

"Thanks for coming," Adam said. He motioned the deputy toward an unoccupied corner of the room, not wanting Cindy to hear. "Are you investigating this as a crime?" he said.

"A crime? No. We came to see the emergency room doctor so we can complete our report."

"I know for a fact that it wasn't an accident."

"What do you mean? You think somebody caused it? Unlikely."

"Craig phoned me from his job that something was wrong. He wouldn't say what, just that I needed to get out there fast. When I arrived, he was gone. He didn't turn up until I found him at the bridge."

"The CHP says he was going too fast for the road."

"Maybe he was. But he wouldn't have unless someone else caused him to. Has anyone checked into that? He drove that road every day and knew it as well as anyone."

"Okay, what do *you* think happened?"

"Craig discovered something, and Weatherly wanted to shut him up. What better way to do that than to stage an accident?"

"Weatherly?"

"Yes, the man Craig was working for. You were out at his place last night."

"The coastal property at the end of Bear Creek Road? I think that was Delgado and Young. But tell me about Mr. Weatherly."

"Strange guy. He's been acting real weird since the day I met him, is real secretive about everything."

"Why do you think he caused the accident?"

"The guy's weird." Adam's mind went blank. "He just acts strange," Adam stammered, "and he carries a pistol in a leg holster. Oh, and he's a Nazi."

"A Nazi?" The deputy gave Adam a strange look.

"Yeah. I saw the uniform in his closet." Adam wished he could think of more, but his brain wasn't working. Cindy's tearful conversation with Carla across the room wasn't helping his concentration. "He's just weird," was all Adam could think of.

"How do you know all this stuff?"

"I just know." Why wasn't the deputy taking notes? "And he's doing something out there on the beach. I don't know what, but I'm sure it's illegal."

"Can you give me any specifics?"

"Well, there's a skip loader at night, working in the dark. Tell me who would do that unless it was something illegal. And there's always a boat anchored in the cove."

The deputy glanced at his clipboard. "Well, according to the CHP, Mr. Hubbard was simply going too fast and failed to negotiate the curve."

"That's BS. Craig drove that road every day. He wasn't *that* stupid."

The deputy sighed. "Look, I know you're trying to find a more rational explanation, but the CHP knows what it's doing. They just don't make mistakes about these things. Why don't you give them a call?" The deputy tried to ease past, but Adam stood in his way.

"Someone could have tampered with the brakes."

"I suppose. Give the CHP a call."

Suddenly Adam realized he was wasting his time. He looked at Cindy across the room. "You seem to have more important things to do. Just forget about it." He returned to Cindy's side as Justin cried for a moment and drifted back into sleep. Adam put an arm around her and held her close.

"I'll phone Cindy's parents," Carla said. She handed Justin to Adam and went to the pay phone on the far wall.

Adam cradled Justin in his arm. The infant barely stirred. The deep loss that Justin was unable to comprehend fell on Adam. He would make certain that Justin knew about his father.

Telling Craig's parents was another matter, a job he dreaded. It tore him up to think of the grief that this would cause them.

The deputy had just brushed off the stuff about Weatherly. Weatherly couldn't be allowed to get away with it.

Carla returned. "Cindy's mom and dad are coming right down."

Adam transferred Justin into Carla's arms. "Stay here with Cindy. I've got some things to do."

"What?"

"They're trying to sweep this under the rug, and I can't let it happen."

14

This was too nice a day for the mood he was in — climbing toward seventy-five degrees with just a few clouds in an all-blue sky — too nice a day to drive to the site of Craig's accident. Adam headed up the winding road and into the shadows of the redwood forest.

Time seemed to be in a holding pattern, in a dream. Adam hadn't seen his bed since he awoke the previous day. But with all that had happened and all the responsibilities ahead of him, he was too keyed up for the luxury of sleep.

As he approached the bridge he slowed to a crawl, almost afraid to look, unsure of how his emotions would handle it. He stopped, but did not want to get out of his car and gaze over the edge, as if seeing it closely would make it real.

Craig had been dead just a few hours. Though he'd been there to try and comfort his friend, Adam could still not accept that Craig's truck had gone off the bridge last night, and that he was never coming home. Maybe when he arrived back in town he'd find that it was just a horrible nightmare, and that he and Carla were expected at Craig and Cindy's for Scrabble. No, that wouldn't happen.

Judging by the amount of missing railing, Craig *was* driving too fast, just as the deputy had said. But as well as Craig knew the road, he'd have been cautious here. Something — or someone — caused him to go off the bridge.

Adam continued past the bridge. There might be something farther up the road that would foretell the accident. He drove slowly, checking the pavement and both shoulders. Strangely, there were no skid marks at the turn approaching the bridge.

After crawling along for about a mile and seeing nothing more, Adam made a U-turn and returned to the bridge, parking on the shoulder. He sat behind the wheel, not wanting to relive the previous night's tragedy, but knowing he had a responsibility to follow through. He pulled two cardboard boxes from the back seat.

Tools were scattered downhill toward the creek, some coming to rest against the solid stand of trees. Adam made a mental note that he also had to get the tools Craig left at Weatherly's—maybe next week. He couldn't deal with it now.

The ground was gouged and scraped, with the dirt mounded in several places. Craig's mahogany level lay half buried in a dirt pile. He'd freak if he could see the tools he took such pride in resting like litter tossed from a moving car.

Adam lobbed the boxes down and sidestepped and slipped his way toward them. After the beating his body had taken the previous day and night, he could barely move.

Around him were many of the familiar tools Craig had used to earn his living—tools he would no longer need. Adam felt numb as he surveyed the area.

His thoughts drifted back fifteen years, to a day in the fourth grade. Adam's mother had just left his father, and they had moved here to start a new life alone. Besides missing his father, he had to deal with being the new kid in a strange school.

On the first day, several boys began to taunt him on the way home. He'd tried to ignore them, but they cornered him against a fence. One of the boys reached for his backpack, and Adam pushed him away. Another boy shoved Adam, and he sprawled backward over a rock.

"Leave him alone," a voice ordered from behind. "He's not bothering you."

Adam looked up and saw Craig for the first time. The bullies dispersed. "Come on," Craig said. I've got this cool spot under the bridge where we can catch some blue-bellies."

"What's that?"

"Lizards. Come on, let's go."

They checked under the bridge, where Craig soon had a wiggling lizard in his hands. After a few misses, Adam finally caught one. They played with them for a while, released them and caught some more.

Later the boys scaled a large boulder and sat and talked until the sun dropped behind a nearby oak tree. Then they climbed over a barbed-wire fence, jumped an irrigation ditch and skirted a pasture on the way to Craig's house.

Craig's mother always had a bottomless cookie jar, and his dad normally had an old car he was tinkering with in the garage. It made Adam long for the times when his parents were happily married, before his dad returned from Vietnam with a drug problem. He began hanging out at Craig's after school, and soon the two boys became best friends.

He remembered their first double date with Carla and Cindy, and their becoming an inseparable foursome soon after. The memory was a heavy weight in the center of his chest.

"I figured I'd find you here."

Jack Kinney's voice startled Adam.

"Too bad about your friend. Heard it on the radio this morning." Jack looked down from the road. "Saw your car and figured this must be where it happened. What a dirty shame."

Adam squinted up. "Yeah. I just came to get his things."

"Well maybe I can help. This stuff sure got scattered." Jack stepped off the shoulder and inched his way toward Adam.

"There's not much to do." Adam wanted some solitude right now, to be alone with his thoughts—and Craig—as he gathered everything. Jack didn't look like he could be easily dissuaded, though, and Adam didn't know how to stop him from coming down.

It was surprising that Jack was so agile. He reached Adam and patted his shoulder. "Too bad," he said, and shook his head. He picked up a small metal toolbox. It rattled as he turned it upright, opened it and rummaged through to the bottom. Then he closed it and set it in one of the cardboard boxes.

"I'll take care of it." Adam didn't want Jack messing with Craig's stuff.

"No, I insist. It's hard enough on you without having to do it all alone. I'll help you, and you can get it over with that much sooner." He picked up a pipe wrench, then went downhill to retrieve a package of sandpaper.

It angered Adam that Jack had just come and taken over, but Adam felt so down that he knew if he said anything, he'd regret it later. Just tough it out and get it over with. That was probably the best course of action. Friends were too hard to come by right now.

Jack fanned the sandpaper, glancing between the sheets. Then he stepped past some wrenches scattered together to pick up some drill bits in a plastic case. He quickly opened and closed the case. God, he was nosy.

"This must be hard on you," Jack said, dropping a double handful into a half-filled box. "Why don't you take this stuff on up? I'll get the last few things."

"That's okay. I can handle it." Adam caught a reflection from the creek bed. Looking closely, he saw that it was the small handsaw Craig kept in his toolbox. Water washed slowly over it, and a thin film of rust covered the portion of the blade that was exposed to air.

Adam skidded his way down to retrieve the saw and wiped the wet blade on his jeans. As he turned he saw a green pocket-sized spiral notebook—Craig's notebook—that had been hidden from view. He picked it up and thumbed through it.

"Whatcha got there?" Jack sidestepped down from behind a redwood.

Adam stuck the notebook in his hip pocket. "Nothing. I just spotted this saw here."

"What was that you put in your pocket?"

"Nothing. Just his notebook."

Adam and Jack headed uphill. Finding nothing else, they each grabbed a cardboard box and carried it to the road.

Jack nodded toward his Corvette, parked on the shoulder. "You haven't seen my old '56 yet, have you?"

Adam shifted his weight back and forth and adjusted the cardboard box he held. "I'm late. Maybe I can check it out next time." He backed toward his car.

"Aren't you going to see what's in the notebook?"

"It's just construction notes."

"Well, keep your chin up, and if there's anything I can do for you, just holler."

"Thanks." Adam watched Jack drive off. He felt a little guilty cutting him off, but Jack was a pain in the butt right now. It was good to have a friend like him, though, someone he could count on.

As he climbed in the car he pulled Craig's notebook from his hip pocket. One word scribbled on the last page in bold block letters gave him chills. It was as if Craig had had a premonition. It read simply, *BRIDGE.*

15

Adam was running on coffee and adrenaline, with sleep the last thing on his mind. And when he finally had time, he'd probably be too wound up to doze off. As he followed a man carrying a six-foot-long crowbar, he went over his mental list. He still had much to do before his day ended.

The teal-blue GMC rested next to a wooden fence, totaled. Craig had been so proud of this truck he'd bought just four months earlier. Every weekend he'd detail it, as if he were a sixteen-year-old caring for his first car.

"Your friend's dad stopped by this morning to pick up his stuff, but they hadn't brought the truck in yet," the man carrying the crowbar said.

"That's strange." Adam had just told Craig's dad about the accident this morning, and he'd taken it so hard, Adam didn't think he'd be going anywhere. "You sure it was his father?"

"I don't know. He said he was."

"What did he look like?"

"Let me think. Tall, around fifty, short hair, on the gray side."

"Did you see what he was driving?"

"A silver Hummer. Nice rig." The man dug the crowbar into the edge of the door. He pulled on the latch and pried. The door snapped open. He pulled it until it creaked around enough for Adam to climb inside. The shattered windshield folded along the passenger side of the opening and drooped toward the ground. It didn't seem possible that Adam could have pulled Craig through that opening.

"Let me know if you need anything," the man said.

"Okay." Adam began pulling things from the jumble on the floor and putting them in a cardboard box—Craig's guitar, scratched, but intact. There was also his coffee-stained mug, surprisingly unbroken, and a clipboard filled with notes, some of which had come loose and spread across the floor. Adam picked up a set of blueprints with changes scribbled over the sheets, Craig's cell phone and his boom box. He couldn't see what Weatherly would want with any of them.

Adam opened the glove compartment, finding only the truck's registration, a bottle opener and a piece of paper with a note scribbled on it that he couldn't make out. He stuck the paper in his pocket.

The truck-bed toolbox sat open and almost empty, most of the stuff having been scattered down the hillside. Adam put the few remaining items in the box and carried them to his car. He wanted to stay longer and look the truck over, but he had an appointment at the sheriff's office.

He trotted up the steps and into the reception area, not yet sure what he would say. It was four p.m., and the deputies who'd gone to Weatherly's the previous night were just coming on duty.

The receptionist showed him into a conference room, and soon, two uniformed men arrived. "Mr. Knight, I'm Sergeant Delgado," the taller man said. "This is Deputy Young." They shook hands with Adam and sat down.

"Some things just don't add up," Adam said. "When you drove to Weatherly's, did you see the missing railing on the bridge?"

The sergeant answered. "It wasn't missing when we went by."

"I don't see how that's possible. Craig had already left. He had to have been there before you went past."

"Don't think so. We'd have seen it."

"Couldn't you have just overlooked it?"

"Not likely. We're trained to be observant."

"That would mean Craig stayed at Weatherly's for several hours after he left the job and before he wrecked."

"Maybe he did."

"Where was he all that time?"

The sergeant fidgeted in his chair. "Look, I don't know, but I guess he had to have been somewhere else."

"Is anyone looking into where?"

"Not that I'm aware of."

"Don't you think Weatherly could be responsible?"

"For what?"

"Craig's accident."

"No, I don't."

"What makes you so sure?"

"For one thing, Mr. Weatherly was home when we talked to him, and he didn't look like he was going anywhere."

"He could have gone out and come back before you arrived."

"We saw him before the accident. Remember, the railing was intact when we went past." The sergeant shifted his weight.

"Then he went out after you left. Or he could have had one of his skinhead goons do it for him."

"Wouldn't you have seen it then?"

"Not necessarily." Adam couldn't believe this attitude. "Craig's death wasn't an accident, and I want something done about it."

Delgado squirmed in his chair. "Okay, what do you want us to do?"

"Question Weatherly, and if you don't get the answers you're looking for, throw his ass in jail."

The sergeant smirked. "We can't just start arresting people on your say-so."

Adam was wasting his time with Sergeant Delgado. "I'd like to talk to your supervisor."

The deputies exchanged glances and suppressed smiles. "Okay. Let me set it up with the sheriff," Delgado said. He left the room for a time, then returned and pointed Adam to an office at the end of the hall.

Sheriff Clancy O'Donnell looked up from his desk as Adam marched in. He had a receding red hairline turning gray around the ears, matching bushy eyebrows and a paunch pressing tightly against his khaki-colored shirt. Judging by the stack of paper in front of him, he didn't appreciate the interruption.

But that was too bad. Adam had to change the sheriff's mind-set, and it appeared that the only way to do it was to get pushy. "My best friend was killed last night," Adam said, "and I hear you're sweeping the investigation under the rug."

The sheriff removed his glasses and gestured toward a chair. "Sit down, son." He laid his pen on the desk and folded his hands. "Now tell me what we've swept under the rug."

Where did this guy get off, talking down to him like that? Adam felt like telling him off, but that wouldn't serve his purpose. "For one thing, it wasn't an accident."

"The CHP said it was. They said he'd been driving too fast and just ran off the bridge. And not only that, he wasn't wearing his seat belt."

"That's a crock. Craig had been driving that road for two months. He knew it too well to just drive off the bridge. Even when we were in high school, he was a careful driver. And he always buckled up — always. Look, I was just up there and looked around a hell of a lot more than the CHP and your so-called investigators did. There weren't even any skid marks on the curves leading to the bridge."

"Was your friend an epileptic? Could he have had a seizure?"

"No. He was in perfect health."

The sheriff shook his head. "Well, the CHP always does a thorough investigation. I'm sure they checked out everything."

"Did they check if someone tampered with the truck?"

"Probably. I'll have to review the written report to tell you for sure."

"Why bother? You've already made up your mind."

"Okay, what do you think happened?"

"I think someone messed with the steering or brakes or something."

"Who?"

"Weatherly."

"That's impossible. I've known Mr. Weatherly for over twenty-five years. We were in the Marines together. He's one of the most law-abiding men I know."

"Did you know he's a Nazi?"

The sheriff laughed. "A Nazi? What in God's name gave you that idea?"

"He has the uniform in his closet."

"Who told you that?"

"I just know."

"Doesn't mean a damn thing, son. His father served in Germany. He probably brought it home."

"Why was Weatherly down at the auto wrecker's first thing this morning, looking for Craig's truck? Did he think Craig had something on him?"

"At the auto wrecker's? What makes you think he was there?"

"The guy who runs the place told me."

"How did he know it was Mr. Weatherly?"

"Just from the description, it had to be. And he was driving a silver Hummer. Not many of them around. Look, when Craig called me yesterday morning, he was scared. And why did he leave the job without putting his tools away?"

"I don't know."

"Did you know Weatherly carries a concealed five millimeter pistol?"

"Yes. He had to get a permit for it."

"Why does he carry it? And why are there always boats anchored off his property or in the cove? And why did divers come ashore to talk to him?"

The sheriff sighed. "I don't know, son, but as far as my office is concerned, this investigation is closed." He looked down at his stack of paper.

Adam started to say something, but decided it wouldn't do any good. If the sheriff had already closed this case, Adam would reopen it himself.

16

I t was horrible the way Craig had died, and Adam was furious about the whitewash the cops had given it. Even the CHP, whom he'd always thought to be professional, wouldn't help him. He pulled out Craig's notebook, trying to figure out what he meant on the next-to-last page: *BARN: ALMOST DUE WEST 457 STEPS. CALL COPS.*

How could anyone take even twenty steps due west from the barn, without running into a redwood tree? Craig must have meant something else. And if he was planning to call the cops, what did he know? But when Adam mentioned it to Sheriff O'Donnell, he'd been promptly dismissed. No surprise there, since he and Weatherly were Marine buddies.

The slip of paper Adam had found in the glove compartment was just as confusing. It looked like a map, but of where, he couldn't tell. The only word on it was *cove*, with an arrow from there to an X in the middle of the page. But if it were Weatherly's cove, Craig didn't know how to draw a map, because it didn't look at all accurate to Adam.

Henry Battles—maybe he'd know something. Adam dialed the number to Cascade Realty.

"Battles here," the voice in the receiver said.

"Hi, Mr. Battles. It's Adam. Got a minute?"

"When are you going to start calling me Henry?"

"Sorry, Henry."

"What's on your mind?"

"You know quite a bit about the Weatherly place, don't you?"

"Reckon I do. Been going out there for years."

"What can you tell me about it?"

"Well, I'm not sure what you mean, but let me think. It's got about a mile of coastline..."

Adam already knew that. "Anything unusual?"

"Unusual, no, not that I can recollect. There's a spring back up the hill from the cabin. It's usually running 'til late summer, and the pond's stocked with catfish." Henry paused for a moment. "Oh, and there's an old rundown shack up over the next hill. No, wait a minute. The shack's on Wilbur Maxwell's place, I think."

Adam listened as Henry rambled on. He finally wound down and stopped. "You going to be there for a while?"

"Afraid so."

"Be right over." Five minutes later he pulled into a parking space in front of Henry's office.

Henry looked up from the newspaper. "Just going through the obituaries. You know, when you get to be my age, all you ever do is go to your friends' funerals. Kind of a depressing thought, don't you think?"

Craig's smiling image flashed into Adam's head, and a lump formed in his throat. "Yeah, I know what you mean." It reminded him of the eulogy he had to give at Craig's memorial service in a couple of hours. If he didn't put it out of his mind for now, he'd never make it through this conversation. He unfolded Craig's drawing and placed it in front of Henry. "Can you make anything of this?"

"Let me see." Henry rubbed his chin. "It does kind of look like a map." He ran his index finger along the sketch. "Doesn't look like anything I've ever seen."

Adam pointed to the only word on the drawing. "Do you think he meant the cove on Weatherly's property?"

Henry studied the paper. "I don't know." He scrutinized it for a time and then looked up at Adam. "You sure it doesn't say cave? I'll bet that's what it is. Sure. I remember now. It's the cave just around the point from the cove."

"I never heard anything about a cave."

"You sold the place and you didn't know?"

"I was only out there twice."

"Not many people know about it, but it's there. I was in it a couple of times when I was a little tyke. Not much to it, as I recollect."

Adam scribbled as he listened. "Why wasn't that in the listing?"

"You know, if something like that gets out, you'd have the county and the Coastal Commission and every environmental do-gooder in the country snooping around to see if it was some sacred Indian site or something."

"Is it?"

"The cave? No. Hell no. It's just a little place so the critters can get out of the rain."

"Thanks, Mr. Battles." Adam pumped his hand.

"Henry."

"Yeah. Thanks, Henry."

"We still on for breakfast next Tuesday?"

"Sure thing. And I think Carla and I might be interested in your buyout offer."

"Good. Good. We'll talk about it Tuesday. As far as I'm concerned, we can just write a little agreement on the back of an envelope and take it from there."

"Okay. See you Tuesday."

Adam could barely think as people with somber faces filed in and took their seats. There were friends he'd gone to high school with, and their parents, guys that he and Craig used to work with, and dozens of people he didn't recognize, all here for the memorial service. He didn't know if he could stand in front of them and give the eulogy without breaking down, but Cindy had asked him to do it, and he couldn't very well refuse.

Cindy came in on her father's arm. Adam couldn't look at her. As he sat, trying not to listen to the pastor's words, he reflected: the time they'd cut school and gone deep-sea fishing; the band they'd formed in high school, which lasted but a few months; the evenings and weekends they had spent coaxing new life into old cars. It was all he could do to maintain his composure as these thoughts passed through his mind.

The pastor finished and nodded to Adam. He rose and slowly walked to the podium on unsteady legs, looking over the crowd as he tried to gain control over his emotions.

"Craig was my friend," he finally said in a shaky voice, "my very best friend. He stood up for me when I was the new kid in school, and he stood up for me at my wedding." Adam's voice cracked and then became stronger as his confidence built. "I'd like to tell you what it's like to have a best friend like Craig. The most important things to him were his family and his friends. The last time I saw him…"

Adam's gaze carried to the back of the room, where a somber-faced Weatherly sat. He looked back at his notes. "The last time I saw him…" His hands began shaking, and he couldn't find his place.

Weatherly had no right to be here. He shouldn't have been allowed into a service for Craig's friends. Adam stammered and faltered for a moment until he found where he'd left off. He continued reading, but all he could think about was the man who'd murdered his best friend.

The wake ended and one by one, people filed by to speak to Cindy and Craig's parents. Weatherly brought up the rear, and spoke to them as if he were completely innocent. Adam wanted to knock him on his ass.

As Weatherly turned, he spotted Adam and walked over, extending his hand. "Too bad about your friend."

Adam willed his hand forward. "Yeah." It was all he could do to be civil. Weatherly patted his shoulder. "I've got to go. Come out sometime."

"Sure." Adam felt like a wimp, but it was better not to tip his hand just yet. Better to catch Weatherly by surprise.

The BMW's tires crunched on the gravel, and Bruno barked nonstop as Adam and Carla pulled into the Kinneys' driveway.

Jack came out of the garage dressed in coveralls, wiping his hands on a faded blue grease rag. "Hello there, you two. This is a nice surprise."

"Just in the neighborhood and thought we'd stop in," Adam said. "I hope it's okay."

"Gosh, yes. We live so far out we hardly see anyone except the UPS man once in a blue moon. Let me take this outfit off, and we'll go in the house. Your timing couldn't be any better. The missus just put the frosting on a German chocolate cake."

Jack went into the garage and emerged in a couple of minutes wearing his trademark jeans and long-sleeved denim shirt. "So what brings you out here?"

"Just wanted to go for a drive."

"You know, more people ought to do that on Sunday afternoons. With all the television and football games and the like, all the old-time pleasures are disappearing." He headed toward the house with Adam and Carla close behind.

Elsa, dressed as Jack's twin, served cake and coffee. "I was so sorry to hear about your friend."

"Thanks," Adam said. "That's one of the reasons we drove out. Carla hadn't seen where it happened."

"How is his wife doing?"

"She's tough. Right now, she's spending some time at her brother's up in Grants Pass. It'll take a while to get over it, but she'll make it."

"Tell her that Jack and I pray for her every night."

Jack nodded.

Adam sipped his lemonade. "Did you ever hear about a cave on the Weatherly property?"

Jack seemed surprised. "Where did you hear that?" He and Elsa exchanged glances.

"Henry Battles. You know him?"

"I know *of* him. I've been all over that property, and there's no cave there."

"You sure?"

"Positive. If there was a cave, I'd know about it."

"Henry said that not many people are aware it."

"Must be thinking of someplace else."

17

Adam fidgeted as the phone rang for the eleventh and twelfth times. Where was Henry? It was almost eight o'clock, and he'd never been late for their Tuesday breakfast before.

Adam dialed Henry's office, but got the answering machine on the second ring. He waited until Henry's recorded voice stopped. "Hi, Henry. Just wondering where you are. I'm at Denny's. Call me on my cell phone."

He checked his appointment book. His day was so full he couldn't wait any longer. As it was, he'd probably be working until seven this evening. He ordered oatmeal, wheat toast and orange juice, then put cream and sugar in his third cup of coffee.

If Henry was going to be a no-show, Adam could get an earlier start on his day. He wolfed down his breakfast and headed for the office.

After checking on his escrows to make sure they were going smoothly and then planning his day, he realized that it was almost ten, and Henry still hadn't called back. He phoned Cascade Realty and got the answering machine again. Then he tried Henry's house. The phone rang for well over a minute before Adam hung up.

Since he was running ahead of schedule, Adam decided to take a quick trip to Henry's place. "Rosalie, I'll be back in a few minutes," he said into his intercom.

Henry lived in a nice older neighborhood that Adam had gotten acquainted with when he sold a home here the previous month. His house was probably built in the twenties or thirties, but Henry had kept the yard up nicely, and the shake siding had a fresh coat of gray paint. The lawn had been recently mowed, and beds of well-tended flowers encircled the house.

Henry's car sat in the driveway. As Adam passed it, he felt the hood. It was cold. He trotted up the front-porch steps and rang the doorbell. Henry might be getting a little senile. Adam felt that he wasn't as sharp lately as he had been.

Adam rang the bell again and knocked on the door. The sound of a television came from inside. He waited and then banged on the door again. The TV could be drowning out the doorbell.

He went to the side of the house and peered through the only window with an open curtain, but could see nothing. "Henry, you in there?" He banged on the pane and squinted through the glass again.

Adam's stomach tightened. Henry wouldn't have gone anywhere without turning off the TV or taking his car. At his age, he could have had a heart attack or stroke. Adam pulled out his cell phone and dialed Henry's number. He heard the phone ring a dozen times before he hung up. Something felt wrong.

Adam pulled the screen door open and tried the doorknob. That's when he saw that the door was unlatched. He pushed it open and went inside. The television blared from the back of the house. "Henry, are you here?"

There was no answer.

"Henry..." Adam followed the sound to the television in the bedroom. The room looked meticulous, as if his late wife had dusted and straightened the previous day. The bed had been slept in, but felt cold to Adam's touch. He snapped the TV off as he left the room.

"Henry..." Adam knocked on the bathroom door.

Silence.

He turned the knob, slowly pushing the door open, and his breath caught in his throat. Blood and brain matter were sprayed across the tile of the tub enclosure and up toward the ceiling. Henry, wearing pajamas, slumped in the tub, his eyes staring blankly, his mouth partially open. A portion of his skull just above his right ear was missing. His right hand dangled over the side of the tub and a pistol lay on the floor about three feet away.

Adam quickly closed the door as he began to gasp. His stomach churned, its contents working their way upward. He dashed to the front porch and heaved over the railing.

18

He couldn't get it out of his mind. Now, almost two weeks later, he still shivered, thinking about the way Henry Battles had ended his life. Even in Afghanistan, Adam had never seen anything like it.

There had been nothing in Henry's makeup indicating a tendency toward suicide. But according to the police, he'd gotten up about two in the morning, gone into the bathroom and blown his brains out. The entire community was in a state of shock.

Between Craig's death and now Henry's, Adam needed time off to regain his sanity. His boss had loaned him his cabin cruiser, the *Lindsay Marie*, for several days, and Adam hoped that a trip with Carla along the coast would settle him down.

The seas were calm under a hazy morning sky as he steered the *Lindsay Marie* out the harbor entrance and headed south. Carla sat beside him in the wheelhouse, scanning the shoreline. This was their first fun activity since before Craig had died, and Adam could see from her mood that she looked forward to their time alone as much as he did.

They planned to make the most of it, checking out spots of interest along the way, even doing some detective work if the opportunity presented itself. When they saw something they wanted to investigate, they could go ashore in the skiff that rested on the rear deck. Adam also wanted to do some halibut fishing, and if he got lucky, he could barbecue their catch right on the boat.

Redwoods, some over two hundred feet tall, stood tightly packed from the shoreline to the top of the hill, where they faded into the mist. Some familiar coastline came up on the port side. Adam eased back the throttle, grabbed the binoculars and scanned left to right, from the beach to the ridge.

Through the haze, the suspension footbridge emerged from behind a stand of redwoods and soon, Weatherly's cove came into view with a boat anchored inside, a gangplank connecting it to the shore. No one appeared to be on board.

Carla gazed over Adam's shoulder. "What are you looking for?"

"I don't know." Adam handed the binoculars to her and steered closer as the shoreline curved inward around the outcropping of rocks, and the beach widened to about fifty yards. This is where the skip loader had been working in the dark, but now there didn't seem to be a trace of it—no tracks or anything. He sighted up a ravine. "Is that something?"

"Where?"

He pointed toward a dark area behind a gap in the first line of trees. "Could that be a cave?"

"I don't know." Carla looked for a time and then handed the binoculars back.

With so many trees, Adam couldn't tell what secrets the shadows between them held. He eased closer to shore, maneuvering the *Lindsay Marie* as near as he dared, staying just outside the surf line. Then he ran parallel to the coast, eased a little farther offshore, dropped anchor and cut the engine.

"Let's see if the halibut are biting. We can look around while we fish." He dipped a net into the bait tank, bringing out several anchovies. Then he placed one on each hook, cast out away from the boat and eased his bait along the bottom.

Adam might be making too much of this, but Craig had been so freaked out the last time they had spoken that Adam had to find out what had scared him.

There had to be something up there for sure. Otherwise, why would those guys have been working there in the middle of the night? He wished that Henry could be here to counsel him, but since he couldn't, Adam would check things out for himself.

He placed his fishing pole in its cradle and picked up the binoculars. His gaze held on the area deep in the shadows for several minutes, but he didn't see anything. Suddenly he felt the hair on the back of his neck stand up. He swung his binoculars around to the boat in the cove. Someone stared back at him through *his* binoculars.

Adam cranked in his fishing line. "We've got an audience. Let's get out of here."

"You look like someone in a spy movie," Carla said, laughing nervously.

"I guess." Adam was in no mood for levity. He looked at Carla in the dim light of the boat's cabin, dressed as he was, in all black sweats, shoes, gloves and stocking cap. The only thing missing was something dark to rub on their faces.

He eased back on the throttle and checked the depth gauge. When he found the spot he wanted, he brought the *Lindsay Marie* to a stop and dropped anchor. He shivered, in spite of being warmly dressed, and could see that Carla did, too. "I want you to stay here," he said.

"I'm not letting you go alone."

The cover of darkness was no guarantee that someone didn't have eyes on them, although in the moonless sky, their arrival would be less conspicuous. "I still don't feel right about your going."

"Too bad."

"You're pregnant."

"Like I didn't know? I won't slow you down."

"You're five months along."

"I barely show."

"Could be dangerous."

"Then you're not going."

When Carla made up her mind, no one could stop her. She had a streak of stubbornness, just like her mother. "Okay." Adam swung the boom around and lowered the skiff into the water on the side away from shore. As near as he could tell, the boat anchored in the cove had pulled out. But just in case, he didn't want to alert anyone who might be nearby.

"Adam, you forgot the barbecue."

A measured sound of metal tapping against metal came from the stern. He'd forgotten to secure the barbecue, and it matched cadence to the rock of the *Lindsay Marie*. "It'll be okay. I'll take care of it when we get back."

Carla climbed over the railing and down the ladder to the skiff, with Adam right behind her. "Got your flashlight?"

"Right here."

"Make sure it's working." He watched as Carla clicked the light on and off. He did the same with his and stuck it in his backpack. Then he disconnected the skiff from the boom while Carla held onto the ladder to steady them.

"Aren't you going to turn on the anchor light?" Carla asked.

"I think I'll leave it off. No need to advertise." Adam squeezed Carla's hand. "You sure you want to come?"

"I wouldn't miss it." Her voice belied the show of confidence.

"Okay, let go."

Carla pushed off, and the electric motor began to whir as they headed off through the darkness. The sea barely rippled, so they should have little trouble getting ashore.

A breeze cut through Adam's sweatshirt, and he shivered. He snapped open his compass and looked at the luminescent dial. They seemed to be going in the right direction. He steered the craft to the starboard, so they wouldn't come up on the rocks, and clicked his flashlight on and off. Hopefully, there were no witnesses to their arrival. Within minutes their small boat bobbed in the surf and skidded to a stop in the sand.

Adam tilted the motor out of the water and then jumped off the bow. Carla followed as an incoming wave engulfed them to the knees. He pulled the boat partly out of the water, realizing that he hadn't checked the tide table—stupid. Better drop the anchor, just in case. He pulled it as far away from the water as he could.

"I can't see, Adam."

"Shh. Don't turn on your light," he whispered. "If you concentrate, you can make out a few things." He turned Carla slightly and pointed. "Look up there, and you can just see the tops of the trees."

It appeared that no one was around, although the surf would have drowned out any noise. At least he didn't hear a diesel engine running.

Carla squeezed Adam's hand. "This gives me the creeps," she whispered.

"Yeah. I want you to stay here." He imagined countless eyes watching them in the darkness.

"I'm going with you."

"I need you to keep an eye on the boat for me. I'll be back in less than an hour." Adam wished he hadn't let Carla come ashore. His confidence faded as he walked slowly toward the tree line. Then he collided with something knee high. "Ouch!" He clicked on his light without thinking and saw a log he'd stumbled into, part of a long row of driftwood. He immediately snapped the light off. This was hardly the way to arrive unnoticed.

Everything seemed different from here. Adam hiked along the solid line of trees until he reached a bluff where it ended. Then he turned and walked back in the opposite direction.

It was pointless to stay here on the beach. The secrets behind the cover of the forest were what he really came for. If he didn't check them out, the trip would be wasted.

He headed inland. As he reached the trees a black void engulfed him. He stopped and listened as he waited for his eyes to adjust to the darkness. A breeze barely stirred the trees. Other than that, he heard no sound.

If Adam wanted to see anything, he would need some light. No one was here—of that he was certain. He clicked his flashlight on and shined it along the path in front of him. If there really was a cave, it was well hidden, and it would probably involve a lot of time in finding it. Maybe Henry had gotten it wrong. He sure missed Henry.

Someone moved behind a large redwood, and Adam almost cried out. He stopped and shined his flashlight in that direction as a possum trotted into the open. He took a deep breath and slowly exhaled.

As Adam neared the rock outcropping that separated this beach from the cove he came to some large tire tracks in the sand. He ran a flashlight beam along them as they headed uphill and disappeared behind some trees.

He started up the tracks, being careful to step softly. Soon he got to an open, almost level area mounded with dirt. It took up an area about fifty feet square, with the top of the pile reaching eight or ten feet. This had to be where the loader was working. He followed the tracks toward the hillside, where they faded into the landscape.

He turned and shined the light behind him, hoping to see where the tracks might have veered off. But they just kind of vaporized for no apparent reason as they neared a large boulder jutting from the hillside.

They couldn't just vanish like that. Adam directed a beam toward the rock that protruded from the hillside, then to the ground. On closer inspection he saw that someone had camouflaged the tracks, scattering leaves and dirt over them. He scraped the covering away with his hands and could see that the tracks appeared to run right through the boulder.

Grabbing it with both hands, he tried to dislodge it. It wiggled, as if it had recently been placed there. He directed a beam of light around the edge, where the boulder met the hillside. A crack sucked the beam in.

Laughter came from somewhere close by. Unable to determine its source, Adam clicked off his flashlight, pressed his body against the boulder and froze.

The voices seemed to surround him, and he didn't dare move. He had no idea where they came from, and could only listen and hope he was in a safe spot.

Then he heard the voices again. Their apparent source was the boulder. He pressed his ear against it, but the sounds seemed to fade away.

He ran his fingers along its surface and found a gap where it met the hillside. The voices disappeared, and Adam clicked on his flashlight, wondering after it was too late if it was safe to do so. There, on the right side of the boulder, two hinges lay hidden behind a pile of brush. He checked the opposite side and found a barely perceptible latch. Then he pulled it, and a camouflaged door cracked open.

19

Adam stopped breathing and listened. Not a sound came from inside. Why did it get so quiet in there? He was dying to find out.

Then there was Carla, waiting for him by the boat. He checked his watch and realized that he was more than a half-hour late getting back to her. The best thing he could do now was to take her away from this possible danger. He hurried back to the beach.

Where was Carla? Adam's heart skipped a beat as he realized she wasn't with the dinghy. He swept a flashlight beam around, but she was not in sight. "Carla!" he shouted. His heart pounded. "Carla!"

A form emerged from the darkness. "I'm right here. Where have *you* been?"

"God, you scared me." Adam wrapped his wife in his arms. "Where were you?"

"I just had to pee. I was worried about *you*, too. You're late."

Good thing he'd dropped the anchor, as the tide had risen, and the skiff bobbed in the surf. He pulled the line attached to the anchor, until the small boat ran aground. Carla climbed in, and he lifted the anchor aboard and pushed off.

Fog had appeared offshore, making it impossible to see the *Lindsay Marie*. Adam checked his compass and headed into the night, his only reference point the roar of the surf behind him. As the dinghy entered a fog bank, the sound at their backs seemed to encircle them. Adam had heard that in fog, it was impossible to tell the source of sounds. He'd just never experienced it before.

He checked his compass, lest he become more disoriented. A flashlight would be useless in this total whiteout.

He checked his watch — 10:24 p.m. He shined his light toward Carla and saw her shivering, her arms folded. Why had he let her come along? He wrapped a blanket around her and pulled the hood of his sweatshirt over his head.

When they reached a point where Adam thought the *Lindsay Marie* should be, there was nothing but water around them. The waves slapping against the dinghy's aluminum hull and the distant surf were the only sounds.

What if they couldn't find their boat? They might have to spend the night on the beach. But with Carla's condition, that was the last thing he wanted to do. He headed off in another direction.

As they got further from shore, a large swell lifted the skiff and dropped it back down. They must have gone out too far. Adam was completely confused now and had to fight to control the spark of panic he felt. He rechecked the compass, but it was useless from this perspective.

Soon they found themselves riding over another large wave. "Sea's getting heavier." He didn't want to worry Carla, but it really wasn't safe being in such a small craft in these conditions.

Going aimlessly back and forth did not help. He had no idea how long the motor's battery would last. If they were adrift out here, they could end up miles offshore and could conceivably be adrift for days — not the best scenario for a pregnant woman.

Adam stopped the motor. It would be better to do this systematically — return to the shore and gradually work their way out — easier said than done.

"Listen," Carla said. "Do you hear it?"

"What?"

"A clanging sound."

"Where?"

"I'm not sure."

Adam listened. "I don't hear anything." Then as their dinghy rose to the top of a crest, he caught the sound. "The barbecue!" It was barely perceptible — a metallic tone, in measured beats. "Where is it coming from?"

The skiff pitched over the ever-larger swells. Adam stopped and listened, but could no longer hear the clanging. He reversed direction. As the dinghy reached each crest, he heard the sound again. It became increasingly louder, only to fade after a time.

Adam turned back to where the clanging was loudest and then turned ninety degrees to port. The volume of the metallic sound increased. "Turn on your flashlight," Adam said. "I think we're getting close."

Carla snapped her light on and gave a startled yell as script letters reading *Lindsay Marie* emerged from the fog. She grabbed the ladder and steadied the skiff as Adam attached it to the boom. Then they each climbed aboard, and he quickly winched the small boat onto the deck. He'd put it away in the morning. Right now all he wanted to do was get out of here. Had anyone seen them? He'd never know for sure.

"God, what a mess," Carla called from below. "Adam, come here."

Adam went below to see.

"Our stuff's all over. Look at this."

Adam hurried to Carla. Clothes were strewn over the bed and the floor, and their provisions were scattered everywhere.

20

don't believe it. Someone comes on our boat, and there's nothing you can do about it?"

Sergeant Delgado shook his head. "It's not that we *wouldn't* do anything, but there's nothing to go on. If they broke into your house, we might have footprints or tire tracks to start with. Out on the water, you don't have those kinds of clues."

"What about fingerprints?"

"We'd find yours and everyone else's who'd been on that boat."

"Well someone invaded my privacy, and I don't like it."

"I know how you feel, but you said they didn't take anything."

"That's not the point. I tried to talk my wife into staying on the boat when I went ashore. She could have been killed. Besides, I don't like people digging through my stuff."

"I understand, but if nothing's missing, I wouldn't worry about it." He handed Adam a business card. "If you think of anything else, give me a call."

"Right." Adam watched as Sergeant Delgado and Deputy Young got in the patrol car and drove away.

What a bunch of incompetents. They just shined Adam on every time he reported something. That's the last time he would ever call them.

The digital readout of the dashboard clock flashed 9:52 p.m. when Adam pulled in behind the row of redwoods near Weatherly's gate. He walked along the chain-link fence separating Weatherly's property from Kinney's, shining his flashlight ahead. The fence stopped where the trees met the sand, turned and ran parallel to the shore. Adam clicked off his light as he hiked along the beach under a quarter moon.

A Rottweiler barked in the distance, giving him goose bumps. He took a deep breath and exhaled, glad for the recently completed fence around Weatherly's property. Just in case, though, he placed his hand on the pepper spray in his pocket.

He and Carla had argued before he left, and he felt terrible about it. She didn't want him to come out here, and he'd tried to convince her that it was his obligation to Craig. She broke into tears as he left. He said he'd call her on his cell phone later, but that didn't pacify her. He'd have to make it up to her when this was over.

The cove was empty when he passed. He clicked on his flashlight to see his way over the rocks just past the small inlet, and shut it off as he came to the beach on the other side. He veered left, along the upper edge of the beach, and continued until he reached the tire tracks he'd seen on his earlier visit. As he entered the forest, he snapped his light on again.

Adam had a gut feeling that something was back here, and it might shed some light on Craig's death. This time he could check without worrying about Carla's safety. He listened. Other than the muffled roar of the surf, there wasn't a sound.

Adam crept along, his senses honed for signs of people. Soon he passed the dirt mound and reached the door camouflaged as a boulder.

He pulled on it and saw the crack grow wider. He braced himself against the hill and put his weight against that immense rock. It swung out, exposing a gaping hole in the hillside. What appeared to be a rock from the outside was just a facing, the rest having been cut away. He studied it closely as he shined the beam over each part of the mechanism that held it. The facing was attached to a metal frame and was hinged and counterbalanced. Adam moved it back and forth with ease — pretty clever.

He stepped slowly through the opening, shining his light around. This had to be Henry's cave.

There wasn't much to it. It was barely six feet high and ten feet across, and narrowed to a dark opening in the shadows, about twenty feet into the mountain. He pulled the boulder back over the entrance and headed toward the rear of the cave.

From there, parallel steel tracks led into a tunnel. It had been widened in the narrow spots to accommodate the tracks. Adam stepped slowly in, directing his light all around. The ceiling had been excavated where it was too low, and he could walk fully erect. The cavern branched off a short distance in, but there was little sign of activity in the side tunnel.

He continued along the tracks, down the main channel. In some places the walls, floor and ceiling had been scraped smooth. It gave Adam a kind of creepy feeling, passing through here. Water dripped in steady plinks into unseen puddles, and it made him feel damp and clammy. This was the type of thing that he and Craig always did together. Adam got a lump in his throat. At least Craig was with him in spirit.

As he followed the tracks through a long passage he entered another natural chamber. Low-wattage lamps glowed just bright enough to light the path.

Muffled voices came from farther inside the tunnel. They were getting closer. Adam pressed himself into a crevice and clicked off his flashlight. The glow of approaching light brightened the chamber.

The voices got louder, the light brighter. In a moment, two men appeared, wearing miners' lamps on hard hats. One talked nonstop as they ambled past, close enough for Adam to touch. They disappeared toward the exit. Adam took a deep breath and exhaled slowly. Had they looked his way, it would have been over.

The tunnel from this point on was entirely excavated. It seemed to go on forever. Adam headed farther in, through a passage that seemed almost precision-cut.

He walked around a bend and into a lighted chamber before he realized it, too late to backtrack. Luckily, it was empty. A flatcar with steel wheels rested on the rails, which ended next to a primitive-looking lift, about a foot from the wall.

The cavern was about twenty feet square. A ladder embedded into concrete in the floor disappeared through a four- or five-foot-square opening in the ceiling. Two sodium vapor lights glared from opposite sides of the chamber.

Adam listened for a moment, then grabbed hold of the ladder and slowly pulled himself upward. It was a good thirty or forty feet up, and he could feel a touch of vertigo as he neared the top.

Barely audible voices drifted downward as he reached the opening and peeked out. A hatch cover hinged to the opening leaned back against the wall. The surroundings in this large room, even in the dim glow of several night lights, were familiar — frighteningly familiar. On one end, a stairway led upward to a landing and a closed door with the sounds of a printer coming from the other side. He was in Weatherly's barn.

21

A hushed conversation drifted through an outside window across the room. Adam climbed into the barn and crept toward the voices.

Gravel crunched underfoot as two men walked slowly together, collars pulled up and shoulders hunched against the dampness. Each had what looked like an M-16 rifle hanging from a strap over his shoulder. One took a drag from a cigarette, dropped it and ground it out under his foot as he exhaled. The men disappeared into the darkness.

The barn was empty except for a skip loader and a pickup truck with a crew cab and camper shell. Adam noticed a wooden crate against one wall and went to check it out.

He ran his fingers over the smooth wooden surface. It was of cabinetmaker quality, precision-cut and assembled with screws. He shined his light around the outside of the box, his beam finding its way to some stenciled lettering — strange foreign-looking print he'd never seen before. On the opposite side, *CCCP* was stenciled in bold letters.

It sounded familiar, but Adam couldn't remember what it stood for. He was curious to know what was inside the box, but couldn't chance finding out now.

The telephone rang in the room upstairs, and Adam ducked behind the loader. It rang once more and then stopped. Then the upstairs room went silent.

He tiptoed up the steps and listened, then slowly turned the knob, eased the door open and stepped inside. By the time he'd closed the door, the fax machine had dropped a sheet into a box on the desk and began pushing out a second one.

Several printed sheets sat in the box. Adam pulled the top one out and tried to read it by the glow of a nightlight. Unable to see, he put the message on the floor under the desk and clicked on his flashlight, covering the lens with his fingers, letting just a sliver of light shine through. He doubted anyone on the outside could see his light through the window this way, although he couldn't be sure.

To Alpha, the message began. *SCREWED AGAIN BY THE EGG-SUCKING LIBERALS: Now they want to put in a job-training center for the wetbacks. Why should lazy Mexicans get everything handed to them? The white race is what made this country great. We can't let the coons and wetbacks ruin our country.*

Adam leafed through other messages in the box. *To Alpha*, read the next one. *Armored truck: Hwy 1, north of Ft. Bragg: May 9th. Details to follow.*

A postscript read, *Mission accomplished re: Battles.*

Battles was spelled with a capital B. A chill went through Adam.

He was still trying to understand the meaning of that statement when he read the next message: *To Alpha: Knight knows. Should we target?*

He crumpled that fax into a tight ball and stuffed it in his pocket. What did they think he knew? Had they really killed Henry? He began to tremble.

Laughter came from below, too close to be from the guards. Someone had come in from the tunnel. He clicked his flashlight off and crouched in a corner. An adrenaline rush made his shaking stop.

The voices got louder, and soon he heard two men talking inside the barn. "Check the faxes," a man's voice said.

Adam tiptoed to behind the door. He wrapped his hand around the pepper spray. Footsteps slowly started up the stairs.

Spray first. Then hit him with the flashlight. Adam figured his chances weren't good. If he stopped the first man, the commotion would alert the second one—and the guards. A light came on in the barn, its glow washing under the door, barely an inch from Adam's feet. He held his breath as the footsteps reached the landing, casting a shadow into the office.

"What the hell are you doing?" a third voice yelled from below.

"I'm just going to check the fax machine," the man on the landing said.

"Turn off the goddamned light and get your ass out of here. The general don't want nobody in that room. You know that. I got a notion to write you up."

The sound of footsteps went back down the stairs and the light went off. Adam heard the door close, then silence. He finally exhaled.

Someone would likely be back before long. Adam unlatched the door and eased it open just enough to slip through. The barn was quiet, so he tiptoed down to the trap door and pulled the latch. It wouldn't open. He pulled it several times, hoping that somehow it would release. Then he noticed the lock.

The voices outside faded into the distance. One of the guards scolded the men from the barn. If Adam was going to escape, this might be his best chance—his only chance. He slipped out the back door. It clicked closed, and a dog growled. Adam moved quickly away from the barn, his footsteps crunching in the gravel. Soon, both Rottweilers were barking continuously. Adam's skin crawled as he heard the dogs lunging against the chain link fence.

He dashed toward the beach trail in the dark, hoping their agitation would mask his footfalls. As he glanced over his shoulder, a flashlight beam swung his direction, and he dropped to all fours and crawled behind a bush. All he could think of was getting over the fence.

"See anything?" a security guard asked.

"You kidding? Those dogs go ballistic if a raccoon farts."

Adam's heart pounded as he looked toward the barn, his breath coming in short bursts. He couldn't hear anyone approaching. He got back on the trail and continued along its path, glancing over his shoulder from time to time. When he got into the redwoods, he turned his flashlight on, and quickly made his way to the fence and over the top. Then he ran alongside it, and by the time he got to his car, he was out of breath.

When he reached for his keys, he felt the crumbled fax in his pocket and remembered its message, sending chills through his body: *Knight knows. Should we target?* Were there other faxes such as this? Even if this were the only one, Weatherly would eventually get the message. The faxes would surely keep coming. Adam couldn't intercept them all.

22

The fax messages spun through his head as he drove home. Were Weatherly's men planning to kill him? Were they really responsible for Henry's demise? He should tell the cops about Battles. Henry's death was in the city's jurisdiction so at least he wouldn't have to deal with the sheriff on this one.

If only Adam could have foreseen the events after Craig's death, he would never have gotten involved. But now it was too late to turn back. He had to protect Carla, and was terrified of the danger he'd put her and their baby in.

Adam hated this road — too many hairpin turns — too many ghosts. As he drove toward town he wondered what it was like for Craig the night of his death. What had he seen or heard? Would Weatherly come after Adam the same way he'd gotten Craig?

His goons could be waiting around the next curve, waiting to force him off the road. What would Adam do if that happened? What if they came up behind him and bumped him and he lost control? He knew his way pretty well, though, and his car took the curves better than most. He touched the pepper spray in his coat pocket. A lot of good it would do if they started shooting at him.

Craig's GMC wasn't designed for this type of driving and would have been easy to outmaneuver. Adam's BMW would be an entirely different matter. He felt he could hold his own in that type of situation.

The railing Craig had knocked down when he ran off the bridge had been replaced. Adam slowed as he drove past. Before long, all trace of the accident would be gone.

Accident? No way. The cops could have seen that if they hadn't already made up their minds. Being a friend of the sheriff worked in Weatherly's favor, big-time.

The headlights cut through the blackness, moving the shadows through the redwoods, as if legions of evil ghosts were passing through.

A man jumped out from the shadows, aiming a rifle at Adam. He slammed on his brakes. The man became a deer and bounded across the road. Was he losing his mind? For Carla's sake, he had to maintain his composure. He needed a clear head now, more than ever.

Carla — right now her life could be in danger as much as his was. If Weatherly's thugs were out to get him, they might also harm her. He leaned on the gas pedal and the tires whined around the curves.

The clock flashed 3:25 as he turned the corner onto his cul-de-sac. He pulled into his driveway, hit the door control and drove into the garage. As the garage door groaned to a stop, he heard a noise in the back yard. Something just banged into his wheelbarrow. Adam snapped on the patio light in time to see a man vaulting the back fence.

"Hey, what are you doing?" Adam yelled, dashing out the back door.

The man cursed as he landed on one of Harry Ridgeway's rosebushes. Adam heard him run down the side of Ridgeway's house, to the next street.

Carla — was she okay? Adam rushed inside to find her asleep.

"Oh, you're home. I was so worried, I didn't think I'd ever doze off."

"Are you all right?"

"Yes. Why?"

"I think we had a prowler." He didn't want to alarm her, but couldn't just let it slide by. He dialed 9-1-1.

A police car arrived within minutes. Adam was glad to see that one of the cops was Rick Alvarez, a former classmate. Carla slumped on the sofa in her pink terrycloth robe, arms folded, almost motionless, as Adam took Rick aside and described what had happened.

Rick and the other officer looked around the outside of the house and checked the back yard, shining their flashlights into all the corners, behind bushes and over the fence. Rick's partner went over the back fence to the neighbors' yard. "No sign of forced entry," Rick said. "Nothing seems out of place."

Just the same, Adam felt violated that a stranger had been here. Adam motioned Alvarez onto the porch, away from Carla. "I'd like some police protection for Carla and me."

"He won't be back. He's just a two-bit burglar."

"Like hell. He came to kill me."

Rick laughed. "Get real. Why would anyone want to kill you?"

Adam pulled the crumbled fax from his pocket and opened it, smoothing it on his thigh. "See this?" He pointed to the now barely visible message.

Rick stared at the fax for a moment. "This could mean anything. It doesn't mean anyone is going to murder you. Where did you get it?"

"From their fax machine."

"You broke in?"

"No. Actually, the trap door was open, and I just went in. I didn't take anything."

"You took this fax. Jesus, Knight, you can get your ass in trouble for stuff like this. If I were you I wouldn't mention it to anyone."

"These are the guys that killed Craig. They might have murdered Henry Battles, too. I can't just let them get away with it."

"Give it a rest, Knight. Craig died in a car wreck. Old man Battles shot himself."

"Craig was forced off the bridge."

"I read the report. He was driving too fast."

"That's what they want you to think. It was a big cover-up. Can't you see? If they call Craig's death an accident and Henry's a suicide, no one has to answer for it."

"The reports were accurate. And even if they weren't, you can't just go breaking into peoples' places like that."

Adam burned inside. "Okay, so I'm the criminal. They kill my best friend and a harmless old man, and put a contract out on me, and I'm the bad guy."

"I didn't say that, but you can't just go out and do your own detective work. There are laws you have to follow."

"Yeah. And while I follow all those laws, I get my head blown off.

112

Why are the criminals the only ones with rights?"

"Come on, Knight, chill out. I'll ask the chief about protection, but I know what he's going to say."

"But how the hell am I going to look after Carla?"

"We can send a car by a few times every night, but you're really freaking out over nothing."

Adam was wasting his time arguing with Rick. "Thanks for coming out." He watched the patrol car leave. It was no longer safe to stay here.

He went back into the house and looked around. Nothing seemed out of place, but it probably wouldn't if all the prowler did was bug the house. Adam unscrewed the mouthpiece of the kitchen telephone, having no idea what to look for, but he had to try something.

Carla came in. "What are you doing?"

Adam returned the phone to its cradle and put an index finger to his lips. He grabbed Carla's hand and led her into the bedroom, where he switched on the TV and turned up the volume. "Get packed," he whispered. "We're going on a trip."

"It's five minutes to five," she said loud enough to make Adam wince.

Adam brought his index finger back to his lips and whispered, "It's not safe here. I think they're after me."

"Weatherly?" Carla mouthed.

Adam nodded. He saw the fear in her eyes.

When the suitcases were ready, Adam put them in the car. He wanted to get out of there quickly, before something else happened. They headed down the street, got onto the freeway and took the airport exit. The sun peeked above the eastern mountains, and Adam squinted as he headed toward it.

He pulled into the parking lot at Stenner Aviation and trotted into the office. A man sat at his desk, leaning back in a swivel chair and sipping coffee from a stained mug. "Hi, Ed."

"Adam, what are you doing here?" Ed came to the counter and shook Adam's hand.

"I have to rent a plane."

"When do you need it?"

"Right now."

"I wish you'd told me yesterday. They all need to be serviced, and Clyde doesn't get here 'til eight."

Adam looked over his shoulder, half expecting to see one of Weatherly's men behind him. "I don't care about that. Just gas it up, and I'm out of here."

"No way. You know I don't do business like that. There's liability to think about, for one thing. I can probably have one ready by nine if it's that important."

"That's too late." Adam glanced at Carla in the car. She looked so vulnerable, sitting there alone. He should have had her come inside with him. "Can't you make an exception just once? I'm not going to sue you. It's real important."

"Sorry."

"Then is there anyone who can fly us out on short notice?"

"Where you going?"

"Anywhere but here."

"Let me check." Ed got on the two-way radio, glancing toward a plane warming up on the tarmac. Adam couldn't hear the conversation, but the pilot shut down the engine and came into the office.

"If you can use a lift to Sacramento, you're welcome to tag along," the pilot said.

"Thanks." Adam returned to the car, where Carla waited. "I got a guy to fly us out."

"I hope you know what you're doing. I'm scared." Carla gave Adam a worried look.

"I'll explain everything when I'm sure we're alone. Too many ears around here."

The plane bounced over the coastal mountains and was soon flying above the expanse of flat Central Valley farmland. Adam gazed down through the morning haze as the Sacramento River meandered toward the delta. They passed over several small towns, and before long, the city of Sacramento came into view. After circling in a holding pattern for a time, they glided in for a landing.

The plane taxied to a stop amid other small aircraft. Soon a golf cart arrived. Adam tossed his and Carla's luggage in back, and they climbed aboard. The cart took them to the main terminal and then sped away.

Now that they were finally alone, Adam felt he could explain things to Carla. "We need to stay away for a while. I figure we'll be safe at your sister's for now. They won't think of looking for us in Seattle."

23

Adam swung the rock aside and went into the cave. He reminded himself to be on guard, and had worked out a plan to hide in the maze of tunnels. This time he'd remembered to bring his three-cell Mag flashlight. It felt a little cumbersome, but was especially dependable.

As he made his way through the cavern lit only by his flashlight, he thought about Carla, whom he'd left with her sister the previous day. She wanted to come back with him, but he'd convinced her that she had to think of the baby's and her own safety. Her pleading voice as he left made him feel guilty for leaving her.

Water plinked into unseen puddles. It gave Adam the creeps to go through here, and his skin felt damp and clammy. He was relieved when he finally arrived at the ladder below Weatherly's barn.

Adam pulled himself up to the trap door as the first light of dawn came through the window. He crept over and looked out and saw that everything was quiet.

This might have been a dumb move. Now that he was here, he realized that he had given no thought to the risk of someone finding him. But he had to learn how Craig died, no matter how dangerous it might be.

The best place to start was the fax machine. When he got up to the office, the tray in front of the machine sat empty.

The sound of an airplane caught Adam's attention. Through the window he saw a small single-engine plane land and taxi to the open area near the barn. One of the guards came over and shook hands with the pilot and his passenger when they stepped down.

As the sun came up, more men appeared in the open area, and the surroundings took on a bustle of activity. Then Adam recognized Weatherly's voice. He peeked out again and saw him speaking to the pilot.

Over the next hour, four more planes landed, with everyone congregating in the open area between the cabin and the barn. One by one and in pairs, people straggled out of the dorm. Adam guessed that there must be at least fifty men there. He didn't see any women.

His second floor window offered a perfect vantage point. He felt a little panicky, knowing that he should probably leave. But he couldn't move. This might be the opportunity he needed to learn more about Craig.

"All right, gentlemen, gather around." The familiar voice silenced the crowd. Weatherly stepped to the podium, wearing the Nazi uniform. He scanned the crowd, seeming to delight in the impression he made with his audience. "Secure the perimeter," he finally said.

Several men with M-16s emerged from the group and went off in different directions.

"This meeting of the Righteous Confederacy will come to order." Weatherly paused until he had everyone's attention. "I'd like to thank everyone for coming. This is an important cause, and we have to be well-trained and organized to succeed."

"All right," someone yelled as a smattering of applause rippled through the crowd.

"We'll have orientation for you newer members at the end of this meeting. There will be training on guerilla warfare, bomb making, recruitment, fund-raising and public relations. And anyone not certified with firearms must be before the weekend is over. Ready for the challenge?"

"Yeah," several men shouted. The crowd applauded, punctuated with a few whoops and whistles. Someone on the far side waved a Confederate flag.

"The Alpha Committee will meet in the barn to finalize plans. This will be the single most important step toward legitimizing the Confederacy."

Weatherly continued. "Our objective just got a financial boost with the donation of three and a half million dollars." This brought a loud cheer and a long ovation. Adam wondered who would be stupid enough to donate money to this group of whackos.

"Our thanks to Brinks for their generosity," Weatherly said.

The Brinks robbery: Adam recalled hearing about an armored truck heist not far from here while he was in Seattle. Then he remembered the fax: *Armored truck: Hwy 1, north of Fort Bragg: May 9th.* Is that how Weatherly raised the money for this place?

"Our battle to right injustice continues," Weatherly said. "But with all the press about 9-11, our message has been lost. We are still here. Our cause still lives. And we *must* get the nation's attention again."

"Yeah," someone shouted as the crowd applauded.

"Say what you want about Al Qaida, but they got their message across. Now it's *our* turn to send the country a message it won't forget."

The crowd cheered.

"A message about affirmative action, for instance. Bobby Huff here can tell you all about that. Come up here, Bobby."

"All right, Bobby," someone shouted as a young man stepped forward to an ovation.

Weatherly put an arm around the young man as he continued. "Bobby is a fireman. He started as a volunteer at his local fire department, just out of high school and spent two years at the fire academy. How long have you been trying to find a job, Bobby?"

"Two years."

"Two years." Weatherly paused as he slowly scanned the crowd. "Two years, after spending all that time and money training, and still no job. Last spring the CDF had twenty openings for their summer crew in Bobby's hometown. Bobby tells me that not one white male was hired."

The crowd booed.

"They chose twenty people—coloreds, Mexicans, women who weren't built for this type of work and should have been home, caring for their babies. Most had no firefighting experience at all. And here's a man, all trained, and still looking for a job."

Everyone spoke at once, as the crowd became more agitated. "The coons and beaners are taking all our jobs," someone shouted.

"Yes, they are out to take our livelihoods away. They are trying to take this country away from us. Now Bobby's family has been in this country since the mid 1800's. He's earned the right to get a job. Why should he or any white man have to take a back seat to someone who can barely speak English?"

"Yeah," someone shouted over the applause.

Weatherly held up a hand, and his audience went silent. "We will do whatever is necessary to insure the future of the white race. But we can't win by direct action alone. There are too many of them, not enough of us."

Weatherly had the crowd worked up and seemed to revel in the frenzy he'd created. He continued. "The Jews spread lies about us, just as they did about the Nazis. Jews like Morrie Rosenthal, who turn the public against us, have got to be silenced. Every time Rosenthal opens his mouth he creates hatred — hatred for our cause, hatred for the very things we believe in. Morrie Rosenthal must be stopped." He spoke the last three words in staccato, tapping his index finger on the podium as he emphasized each one.

Adam heard footsteps at the top of the stairs, and then before he could react, a man appeared in the doorway. "Who the hell are you?" the man said.

Adam pulled the can of pepper spray from his pocket and blasted the man in the face. He cried out and put his hands over his eyes as Adam came down with his flashlight to the top of his head. The man slumped to the floor.

He had to find a place to hide, but where? He slipped out the back door and glanced at the crowd from around the corner. It surprised him to see Sheriff O'Donnell, wearing a colonel's uniform, step up to the podium and begin to speak. No wonder the sheriff wouldn't cooperate with him.

Adam had to get out of here, but he couldn't go back through the tunnel. The guys with the M-16s would be waiting for him at the other end. He felt vulnerable out here in the open, especially since the man who'd discovered him would be coming to at any moment. There seemed to be no way out.

The airplanes — if he could get to one of them he might be able to fly out before anyone else discovered him. Since the planes had recently arrived, they were all warmed up. He could probably start one and take off immediately.

The sheriff stopped in mid-sentence, and the audience shifted its attention to the man Adam had hit as he staggered from the barn. He mumbled something to the sheriff.

"There's a spy on the loose in the compound," the sheriff shouted. "Fan out and find him." The crowd began to disperse.

The planes rested side by side, facing the runway. The closest one, an old Piper Cub, stood at least fifty feet away, across an open area. It was also the slowest plane there. He preferred to take the Stearman biplane sitting nearby. It had broad wings and an oversized engine — probably put in for stunt flying — and sported a bright red finish.

"Get the dogs," someone shouted.

The dogs — just the thought gave him chills. Adam could wait no longer. As near as he could tell, he had a better than even chance of getting away in the first plane. Even if they saw him, he'd have a good head start. It might be close. But as long as the plane started right away, he knew he could do it. He dashed toward the Piper from behind a shed.

"There he is!" someone shouted. Three men sprinted toward Adam. From the corner of his eye he saw the two Rottweilers bound from behind the barn and head his way. Adam stopped. There was no way he could beat the dogs to the plane. But if he didn't make any abrupt moves, hopefully they wouldn't maul him.

When the Rottweilers reached the lead man running toward Adam, one dog grabbed an arm, and the man went down. The other dog sunk his teeth into a leg. The two other men turned to assist their friend. This might buy Adam just enough time.

He swung open the Piper's door and jumped into the cockpit. He flipped a switch. The prop slowly turned. If the plane sputtered, he was screwed. The engine fired and immediately roared to life. No time for the checklist. Adam released the brakes. A man with a shaved head and a goatee closed in. The tail swung around. The man tried to grab hold, stumbled and fell. The plane barely missed him.

On the runway now, Adam went to full throttle. The plane roared. It vibrated as it picked up speed. Several men ran alongside, but he soon left them behind. A line of redwoods stood directly in front of him. He prayed that he had enough runway to clear them.

The speed increased to takeoff velocity. Adam pulled back on the stick, and the small plane eased up and off the dirt strip. He immediately turned the plane and guided it into a gap in the solid stand of trees, picked up some altitude and cleared the closest one by several feet. He was safe.

Ping, ping. Two bullets ripped through the fuselage to the right of Adam's leg. He held his breath, waiting for another round to connect, but none came.

The plane gained altitude, and Adam circled back. Six hundred feet below, people ran back and forth. Then he saw two men jump into the Stearman and head down the runway. One of them appeared to have a rifle.

Adam had maybe a three-minute head start, hardly enough time to escape before they overtook him. If he could reach the gap between the trees just ahead, maybe he could sneak away before they located him. He wished he could have taken the other plane.

Another round tore through the door less than an inch above Adam's leg. The Stearman crossed in front of him. It had an open cockpit with tandem seating. The man in the front seat held a rifle. The plane moved faster than Adam had anticipated.

He banked left and headed toward the offshore fog. If he could get there in time, he could fly north without being seen, then quickly cut in toward the airport. With the right timing, hopefully he could get away. The airfield was about fifteen miles from the coast at its closest point. If he hugged the ground, he might be able to blend in. This would also be risky, but seemed to be his only chance.

How could that plane turn on such a short radius? The other aircraft headed back at Adam, the rifle aimed straight at him. A flash came from the end of the barrel as it fired when the plane crossed in front of him. Adam sideslipped downward. He had no idea how close they came to hitting him.

The fog appeared to top out at about 700 feet. Adam plunged into it at 420 feet and was enveloped in white. Another round shattered a side window, inches from his head.

He continued to fly west over the ocean, then turned north, and began a slow climb. The fuel gauge showed about a quarter tank, and he guessed that he had an hour of airtime left, at most.

At 675 feet Adam unexpectedly emerged from the fog and immediately headed back toward it. He banked left just as the Stearman popped into view and quickly closed the distance.

Adam slipped back into the cloud. He'd hug the ocean for now, where he knew there would be cover, and then head straight for the airport as soon as he could. A small mistake here and it would be over. He wished he'd gone for his instrument rating when he had the chance.

Flying at 100 feet, he emerged from the fog again to see only clear skies ahead of him. The other plane had to be close. He turned left and caught sight of it flying just above the water, heading toward him. No time to react. He had to get back into the fog and hope he got there before they shot him down.

The fog clung to the shore, and Adam made a straight line toward it, feeling as if he might never get there. As he plunged in, he knew that redwoods stood dead ahead. He pulled back on the stick. The branches of the first trees reached almost close enough for him to touch as he passed over. He climbed higher. Hopefully, there were no taller trees ahead. The Piper immediately emerged into clear skies.

This couldn't go on. The fog bank continued to shrink. His hiding place would soon be gone. As he headed back into its diminishing cover, he noticed a plume of black smoke reaching toward the sky. Through the mist, he saw the burning remains of the plane that had been chasing him, stopped by the first row of redwoods.

24

TALK SHOW HOST KILLED: the headline jumped out at Adam as he passed the newspaper stand in front of the 7-Eleven. He bought a paper and began reading that activist and radio personality Morrie Rosenthal had been gunned down in his driveway the previous night. The article said the assailants were unknown.

It didn't take a genius to figure out who was responsible, after hearing Weatherly's ranting at the rally. Rosenthal favored everything Weatherly was against, including gun control and affirmative action. And the fact that he was outspoken and Jewish seemed to give Weatherly all the justification he needed.

Adam had kept out of sight for the two days since his encounter with the Stearman. He'd left town in a rented car and headed south on Highway 101, staying in out-of-the-way motels and getting his meals through fast food drive-up windows. He didn't know if anyone had recognized him at the rally, but by now, they had to have found his car near Weatherly's gate.

Adam would drive to Santa Rosa this morning and inform the FBI about Rosenthal's killers. After they were arrested, maybe he and Carla could get back to a normal life.

Adam glanced in his rearview mirror again. The only car he could see was a good quarter-mile behind and had maintained that distance for ten or fifteen minutes. He took the next off-ramp, went down a country road and made a U-turn. It appeared that no one was pursuing him, but just to make sure, he'd wait here for a few minutes.

Was he being too paranoid? Maybe, but with all that had happened, he couldn't take any chances. He'd even put the FBI's number in his cell phone memory the day before.

Since he'd abandoned his car, he had to rent one at the airport. Now there was no way these low-life characters could find him—or was there? They could have gotten the plate number from the rental desk.

When he got back on the freeway, Adam punched the FBI's number into his cell phone and was connected with the agent in charge.

"This is Agent Botelli," said a baritone voice.

"Hello, my name is Adam Knight. I have information on the men who killed Morrie Rosenthal."

"How do you know?"

"I heard the killers discussing it."

"When can I meet you?"

"I'm on 101 just south of Healdsburg. I'll be in Santa Rosa in less than an hour. "

"Do you know where our office is?"

"No."

"How about the Red Lion Inn?"

"Yes. In Rohnert Park?"

"That's the one. I'll meet you in the lobby there when you arrive."

The Red Lion Inn—Adam drove through the parking lot and spotted an empty space near the entrance. Two men in business suits and dark glasses got out of a car and headed his way. He slowed and rolled down his window just as they drew automatic pistols from shoulder holsters and aimed them at him.

Adam hit the gas pedal and squealed away. As he rounded the corner, a shot shattered his rear window. Either those guys were imposters or the FBI was in Weatherly's pocket.

He skidded onto the frontage road and jammed the accelerator to the floor. When he looked in his rearview mirror, he saw a car pull out and begin closing the gap. It appeared to be a Pontiac or maybe an Oldsmobile—no match for the Mustang he'd rented. They might hold their own on the straightaways, but he'd smoke them in the turns.

At the first intersection, Adam slid right and stomped on the gas, glad that no pedestrians stood in his path. As he turned right at the next intersection he checked his rearview mirror and saw the chase car reach the first corner. A couple of more blocks like this and hopefully, he'd be rid of them.

His tires screamed in protest as he made a left at the next intersection. An elderly man jaywalked in the middle of the block, and Adam headed straight toward him. He slammed on his brakes and slid broadside toward the man, who reacted in slow motion.

Adam released his foot from the brakes and tapped the accelerator. The tires grabbed the asphalt, pulling him from the slide, missing the terror-stricken man by inches. At the next intersection, Adam turned right and slowed down. He began to shake as he realized how close he'd come to killing the old guy.

A glance in his rearview mirror showed the chase car rounding the corner. Adam stomped on the gas and squealed into the next turn. The street was clear, and he picked up speed. When he turned at the next cross street, his pursuers were gone.

A shopping center, its lot nearly full, came into view. It might be possible to blend in if he parked in the middle somewhere, although his shattered rear window would stand out. He pulled into a space surrounded by twenty or thirty other cars. No one seemed to notice the window, and he slipped out of his car inconspicuously.

As Adam turned around, he saw the hit men pull into the parking lot a couple of rows over, and he ducked between two cars until they drove past. He watched as they slowly drove up and down each row. Then they turned down the row where he'd parked, and he knew that in a minute, they would find his car. This was not the time to hang around.

Adam moved quickly between the cars. As the hit men passed, he ducked behind an old wreck that looked familiar. A Mazda, just like the clunker he'd owned until recently, sat in the space. If this were his old car, he could hot-wire it.

This car was unlocked. He opened the door and slid behind the wheel. The interior looked the same. In his Mazda, he'd always kept a short piece of wire for such emergencies, but he didn't have any here.

He checked the glove compartment, pulling everything from the car registration to hamburger wrappers out onto the floor. At the back was a small zip-lock bag of alligator clips—roach clips, no doubt. He might be able to make them work if he could fasten them together.

He connected the two clips and ducked under the dash, grabbing a screw terminal with one. Then he fastened them to another terminal with a third clip. He checked the dashboard gauges—nothing.

Adam breathed deeply and exhaled. He peeked over the dash to see the two goons walking between cars a couple of rows over. He began to formulate an escape plan in case the car wouldn't start. Nothing came to him. He felt like a sitting duck.

Sweat dripped into his eyes as he continued to work with the ignition terminals. He picked up a Burger King napkin on the floorboard and wiped his forehead and eyes. He checked the gauges again—still no luck. The thugs had split up and moved diagonally in opposite directions. It might buy him a minute or two. Then one of them spotted Adam's Mustang and yelled to the other.

Adam had to find some wire—anything to help him get this car started. He pulled down the sun visor. A set of keys fell into his lap. He stuck one in the ignition. The starter slowly turned over and groaned to silence. Adam pounded the steering wheel.

The thugs seemed to get a shot of adrenaline from finding the Mustang. They separated and began half walking, half trotting, searching between the rows. Adam could see that each of them had a hand ready to draw his pistol. He grabbed the door handle, ready to run.

A woman got into the car directly in front of him. She released the brake, and her car rolled forward and tapped the Mazda's fender. "Sorry," she said, leaning toward the window.

Adam waved. Then he realized that the Mazda rested on a slight incline. Adam checked for the goons. One walked toward the mall, looking down each diagonal row, but the other headed his way and appeared to look straight at him. Adam released the parking brake and depressed the clutch. The car slowly rolled backward.

He stuck the gearshift into reverse. When the car picked up some speed, he popped the clutch, and the Mazda coughed to life. This engine had a rough idle just like his old car did, and the muffler was a ticket in the making.

As Adam pressed gingerly on the gas pedal, the decibel level picked up. It wasn't as loud as he'd feared, though, and he hoped he'd be able to slip past. A blue baseball cap sat in the passenger seat with a white LA logo on the front. He normally wouldn't be caught dead wearing a Dodgers' cap, but this was an emergency. Adam put it on and drove toward the exit. The goon closest to him headed his way. Adam rubbed his nose as he drove by, and the goon barely glanced his way.

Adam held his breath, hoping that now he'd be able to put some distance between him and the thugs, yet knowing that they could recognize him in an instant. And if they found him in this car, he wouldn't have a chance.

He didn't begin to relax until he reached Highway 12, several miles away. It wasn't far to Napa, and he could rent a car there.

He couldn't figure out how the FBI fit into this. It didn't seem possible that Weatherly had Agent Botelli in his hip pocket. Could the FBI's phone line be tapped? Unlikely, but he could never chance going back to them now. It seemed that he could count on no one.

As he drove through the Sonoma Valley toward Napa, Adam remembered how he and Carla had always talked about taking a winery tour here. He thought of Carla and how much he missed her, and made up his mind to bring her here after this ended — if it ever did. He wanted to call her, but if he did, they might be able to locate her.

When Adam reached Highway 128, he turned left. The city of Napa was coming up, and he wanted to ditch this car fast.

There would be car rentals at the airport, but he couldn't just drive up, park the car and give the rental agent his name and address, since they could easily trace him to this car. He stopped in front of a motel, went to the pay phone and called a taxi company.

Adam wanted do something for the car's owner. He'd gotten the name and address from the registration, and would send him a hundred bucks for the inconvenience. It would at least pay for a new battery and maybe buy him some gas. And it would ease Adam's guilty conscience.

He'd barely had time to scribble down the name and address when his cab arrived. He climbed into the back seat. "To the airport."

Adam had been driving around the San Francisco Bay area since he'd rented this car, wondering if he was being followed and not knowing when or where the next shot would come from. It was almost nine p.m., and he felt hungry and exhausted.

A motel sign loomed about a quarter-mile ahead, and he decided that he could go no farther. He took the next off-ramp and pulled into the parking lot.

Judging by what happened in Santa Rosa, he couldn't go to the authorities. There weren't many people he could trust right now, but he could sure use some help.

He checked in, picked up dinner to go from the motel's restaurant and went to his room. After washing down a Reuben sandwich with a beer he'd bought at the liquor store next door, he called his in-laws, using the motel's phone. "Mom? Hi. It's Adam."

"Oh, Adam. Where are you?"

"Carla and I had to leave town for a few days. Can I speak to Al?"

"Wait. You can't just go away without saying anything. Where are you? Is Carla okay?"

"Carla's fine. Will you get Al for me?"

"Can I speak to Carla?"

"Damn it, Mom, get Al."

Dixie grumbled and called her husband.

"Adam. Where are you?"

"Say, I need some information. How easy is it to tap a phone line?"

"Why?"

"I just need to know."

"It's easy. Why do you want to tap a phone line?"

"I don't."

"You're not making sense. What's wrong?"

"Nothing. Some guys found out something about me, and the only thing I can figure is that they tapped my phone."

"What's wrong, Adam?"

"Nothing."

"Adam, don't bullshit me. You take off in the middle of the night and don't tell anyone. Dixie's been worried to death, not knowing where Carla is or whether she's alive or dead. Now what the goddamn hell is going on?"

"Carla's fine. I can't tell you where she is, though." Adam told Al what had happened the past few days, about the intruder at home, being chased and shot at and now hiding out.

"This is the guy you sold the coast property to?" Al's calm reaction surprised him.

"Yeah. A real weirdo, but I never dreamed he was a killer."

"I can probably help. Where are you?"

"What can *you* do?"

"You'd be surprised. I have a friend in security at the phone company. He can hide you out."

"You sure?"

"Yes, I'm sure. You worry too much. Now tell me where you are."

"How long before he gets here? I've got a feeling that someone could bust through the door at any minute."

"Shouldn't be more than a half hour or so. He'll hide you out so even the CIA won't be able to find you."

Adam gave the name of the motel and his room number. He felt better about Al than he ever had. It was nice to have his father-in-law in his corner for a change. He hung up. For the first time in several days he felt safe.

25

Adam couldn't sleep. He felt so keyed up that he paced about his small room. A *Friends* rerun blared from the TV, its laugh track grating on his nerves. He clicked off the switch. Then there was a knock on the door. "Who is it?"

"Al sent me."

Adam opened the door to a large, scowling middle-aged man. He had dark hair with a buzz cut, and wore a silver skull ring on one of his sausage-like fingers. His left forearm sported the faded tattoo of a heart with a flowing banner inscribed, *Shirley*.

Adam extended his hand. "I'm Adam Knight."

"I'm Frank. The car's right outside. We need to go." Frank left Adam's hand hanging in midair.

"What about my rental car?"

"We'll have somebody return it for you. Don't worry about it."

"Can we stop at a drugstore so I can buy a toothbrush? I feel really grubby."

"We have all of that where we're going."

"Where's that?"

"The Santa Cruz Mountains."

Adam couldn't imagine this guy being Al's friend. Al had few social graces, but this guy was a Neanderthal.

They climbed into an older Plymouth that smelled of dust, dog and grease. Even though Adam hadn't had a shower in two days, it made him feel dirty when he sat in the passenger seat. When Frank fired the car up, it had a rough idle.

As they reached the freeway, Adam finally began to relax. The hum of the road had a soothing effect on his tired body, and he soon drifted into a scene flying the Cessna 152 in which he'd gotten his pilot's training. The sun shone bright overhead and a carpet of fog lay beneath him.

Suddenly the familiar red biplane flew in front of him, a rifle blazing from an open cockpit. Adam sideslipped downward and skimmed the ground between some redwoods.

Then he was no longer in the plane, but walking, a flashlight illuminating his way. His path stopped abruptly at a drop-off, and he shined a beam of light down. There was Craig's overturned truck.

"Craig!" Adam tried to go to the truck, but was frozen in place. "Craig!" He tried move, but couldn't budge.

"Don't bother," said a familiar voice. "He's dead."

Adam turned and saw Weatherly grinning broadly.

Frank's voice cut into the dream. "What the fuck's wrong with you?"

It was so real. Adam realized he was hyperventilating. "Just a bad dream."

"You scared the living shit out of me, yelling like that."

They headed up a narrow, winding road with trees on either side. Soon, they arrived at a gate, and Frank came to a stop. He pressed a remote control, and the heavy steel gate rolled slowly open. They continued for about a quarter mile, past a cabin, until they reached an opening in the side of a hill.

"Okay, we're here," Frank said as he set the brake and climbed out of the car. Two men stepped out of the darkness, and one of them opened Adam's door. Even in the dim light, they looked like a couple of toughs.

They appeared to be about Adam's age. One, a longhaired hippie type, wore a tank top, tattoos covering each arm and a Fu Manchu mustache. The other appeared more refined, with close-cropped blond hair and the physique of a man who pumped iron. His eyes showed a hardness that told Adam not to cross him.

Adam wanted to run as he stepped out of the car. "What is this?"

"An abandoned mercury mine," Frank said. "We've got it fixed up real nice inside."

"I'm not going in there." What had he gotten himself into?

"It'll be fine. Come on. Don't be a pussy."

"No way." Who were these guys? They couldn't be Al's friends.

Frank stopped and faced Adam. "Now what do you think Al's going to say when I tell him you're not cooperating? He could have left you back there to get your ass blown away, and I could have been home watching the ball game." He grabbed Adam's arm.

Adam jerked away, but the guy with the muscles grabbed him from behind, pinning his arms to his sides. Adam felt those massive arms tighten around his chest and could barely breathe. Then the guy with the Fu Manchu buried a fist in his stomach, and Adam went limp.

"What the hell did you do that for?" Frank said.

Fu Manchu rubbed his fist on his palm. "Just helping him get the right attitude."

"I ought to knock you on your ass. You know what our orders are."

"What orders?" Adam could barely get the words out.

"Just shut up," Frank said.

They took Adam over some parallel tracks inside the dark tunnel. Frank led the way, shining his flashlight. The other two men held Adam, one on each side. He felt wobbly from the fist to his gut and they had to half-carry him. Otherwise he'd have been fighting to get away.

It appeared that the mine had been out of use for years, with nothing here but dirt walls reinforced with timber. A strong, musty odor, combined with that of animal droppings permeated the air. Adam tried to think of a way to escape, but being outnumbered three to one, it hardly seemed possible.

They continued, their footsteps crunching in the gravel between the tracks, and then they stopped in front of a dark hole – what looked like a mineshaft to Adam. Frank shined his light into the void for a moment, and then turned away. "Okay, do it." The two toughs brought Adam to the edge.

"Hey, wait!" Adam wouldn't go without a fight. He grabbed the guy with muscles as he felt himself being shoved toward the hole. Muscles tried to pry his hands off as he backtracked, but it was too late. The momentum carried them both over the edge. Muscles screamed as they plummeted headfirst into the abyss.

"Oof!" They hit something hard, with Adam landing on top of Muscles, whose body went limp. The two of them teetered for a moment. Then Adam felt them sliding off. He found a handhold and jerked to a stop as Muscles resumed his freefall, no longer screaming.

Adam dangled from a piece of timber, his arm wrapped over the top and his hand gripping the edge. His body swung in midair. An instant later he heard a thud, as Muscles hit bottom. It sounded far away.

A burning feeling engulfed Adam's rib cage and left arm, and he realized that the hand that held him in place was quickly losing sensation. He swung his right arm up and over the timber and grabbed the far edge. Then he tried to catch his breath. Each gasp brought on another wave of pain, and he thought he might pass out.

Finally, he wheezed a few gulps of air, and his head began to clear. There didn't seem to be any way of getting out of this mess. He hung from this timber, his body dangling in space. Other than that, he had no idea what it was around him.

A beam of light swung back and forth just above him. It appeared to be coming from about thirty feet up. If they spotted him, it wouldn't take much effort from them to knock him off the timber and send him to the bottom. He hung motionless for what seemed like minutes. His left arm felt completely numb and useless. His right arm began to tingle.

"Let's go," Frank finally said, his voice drifting down.

"What about Chad?"

"You dumb shit. He's dead." Then the light was gone, and the footsteps crunching in gravel faded away.

26

Where was he? Suspended like this, there didn't seem to be any way out. His right hand and arm were tiring fast, and his left arm had almost no feeling in it.

He tried pulling himself up with his good arm. It was kind of like doing a one-armed chin-up. On his second try, he decided that it was impossible. Somehow, he had to get a leg over the beam.

The timber rocked momentarily, and Adam's muscles tensed, sending another flash of agony through his ribs and shoulder. He swung his body slowly from side to side, trying to put the pain out of his mind, swinging higher with each pass. Soon he caught the beam with his right foot, giving him another balance point. Then using his good arm for leverage, he got his knee, and finally his upper body on top. He lay there face down, catching his breath. If he weren't in such good shape, he couldn't have done it.

Adam had never experienced complete darkness and silence like this and had never felt so alone. The terror he'd experienced as a preschooler, when his older cousins locked him in a closet, came over him and he began to shake. His mother was not here to save him, as she had been then.

The chance that he could die, right here on this piece of timber, sent a wave of panic through him. Carla would wonder where he was, and it would kill her not to know. Their baby would be born and grow up without him. His body would never be found.

Stop! This wouldn't work. If he expected to live through this, he'd have to show some mental discipline, take control of his fear. No one was going to call the rescue squad. Even if someone reported him missing, no one would know where to look. If he just lay here, feeling sorry for himself, this is where he would die, for certain.

Could he sit up? He dropped a leg over each side of the beam and slowly forced himself up. Working through the agony of this exertion caused him to feel lightheaded, and he felt his center of gravity out of kilter. He rested for a moment and tried again, finally willing himself into an upright position.

His key ring had a penlight attached to it, but with almost no feeling on that side of his body, he didn't know if he could get it out. Pain shot through his shoulder as he forced his hand into his pocket.

He slid his hand down and heard the keys jingle. He could barely feel his numb index finger going through the key ring, and worried that he didn't have enough sensation in his hand to bring them out. He curled his finger around the ring and pulled. This was his only chance, and it had to work.

As the keys reached his pocket opening, he reached over with his right hand and held it under the opening to his left pants pocket. He whimpered as a shard of pain shot through his ribs and shoulder. Then the ring of keys, with penlight attached, was out of his pocket, dropping into his good hand.

Please let the battery be good, Adam prayed as he fumbled with the switch. It snapped on, bathing the area in a faint glow, enough to help ease his feeling of panic.

A tunnel intersected the shaft, and the beam on which he sat spanned the gap. The timber rested not more than a few inches on the opposite side of the tunnel. Above and below him was nothing but blackness. Had this piece of wood not broken his fall, he'd be at the bottom with Chad, however far down that was.

Adam tried rising to his knees and one good hand, but a wave of dizziness hit him and he dropped to his stomach. He stopped to catch his breath for a moment and then scooted forward, pulling with his good hand and pushing with his toes, until he rested on solid ground.

A wave of nausea welled up inside him, and he collapsed. He wanted to take some deep breaths, but even small ones hurt. He lay there, exhausted, and soon drifted into unconsciousness.

Adam awoke to a throbbing in his rib cage. It took a moment or two before he realized where he was. He felt so stiff and sore he could hardly move.

The tunnel was only about four feet high, not nearly enough to stand. He began crawling, using his right hand, and dragging his left behind him. In the darkness, Adam had no way of knowing what lay ahead or how far he'd come. And he'd lost complete track of time. Though he could read his watch's luminescent dial, he had no idea whether it was day or night.

His knees hurt from crawling over the rocks and pebbles. Were it not for Carla and the baby, he might have just thrown in the towel.

As he placed his good hand forward, it fell into nothingness, and he cried out, hearing his voice echo throughout the labyrinth. His injuries tensed as his momentum almost sent him over the edge. That was close.

He clicked on his light to find himself at another shaft. On one side was a ladder. With so much pain, he wasn't sure he could climb it, but he had to try. He extended his arm toward the ladder, his center of gravity reaching precariously close to the edge. He couldn't quite reach it. But he had to.

Adam shifted to a sitting position and rubbed his tender knees as he tried to come up with a plan. If he were healthy, he could just lean out and grab a rung. In his present condition, it would be risky. But there seemed to be no other choice.

He struggled to his knees and stood up as far as the low ceiling would allow. In the dim light it was hard to get good depth perception. He studied the ladder, leaning back and forth to better judge the distance. He had to do it.

But how could he see to grab hold of the ladder? With his injury, he had to figure a way to hold the penlight and grab the ladder, with the same hand at the same time. Otherwise he could easily miss the rung.

He shifted the penlight to his injured hand, but could barely grasp it. He didn't want to chance dropping his only source of light down the shaft.

Could he use his handkerchief to make it work? He pulled it out of his hip pocket with his good hand. Next he ran the end of the handkerchief through the key ring holding the penlight, using his teeth and his good hand to tie it around his injured wrist. He could barely hold the light with his injured hand, but as long as it was tied on, he wouldn't drop it down the shaft.

Now that he had found a way to hold the light, could he psych himself up for the task? He stared, not wanting to commit himself to the risk of jumping for the ladder, but knowing if he didn't, he could die right here in this spot. He waited. If he had just done it without thinking, he'd already be on the ladder, and the worst of the pain would be behind him. He dropped to his knees.

Adam could think of no other choice. So the longer he put it off, the weaker he would become and the less likely he would be in good enough shape to do it. He took a small breath and rose from his knees. He grabbed the penlight and pressed the switch with his good hand. The ladder on the opposite side of the shaft faintly emerged from the darkness.

He studied it for a moment. From a partial crouch, he lunged and caught the nearest rung. It hurt like hell as his muscles jerked him to a stop, and he felt his grip slipping. But he was able to will his hand to grasp the rung.

Now he hung over the edge, his feet on solid ground, his good hand holding the ladder. He wished that he hadn't gotten himself in this position because he didn't know if he had the strength to continue. And from where he hung, there was no turning back.

He cried out from the pain as he shifted his weight and swung his feet onto the ladder. Another wave of dizziness hit him, and he wrapped his arm around a rung. If he passed out now, he would go straight to the bottom. He took several shallow breaths, his ribs throbbing at each gasp. Then he began pulling himself up.

One rung at a time—all he had to do was go up one rung at a time. He pulled himself higher, and then stopped, bracing himself with his injured arm to keep from falling. Then he forced himself up another step. He finally reached the next level and crawled onto solid ground.

This tunnel had more headroom, and Adam could stand up. He shined his penlight down the passage, knowing that by walking upright in the dark, he could fall down another mineshaft before he knew he was there. Still, with so little life left in his batteries, they wouldn't hold out for long. He decided to quickly keep going and use the light as long as it lasted.

A cool breeze blew through Adam, and he shivered. Its freshness meant the air had to be coming from outside. Was he close to the exit? He picked up the pace.

The penlight got dimmer and soon flickered to just a faint orange glow. Adam leaned against the wall and slumped to the ground. He pulled his knees up and rested his arm across them. Sleep was a pleasant diversion.

27

A agh!" Something ran across Adam's chest — a rat? He dusted his body with his hand and tried to go back to sleep. Then tiny legs — thousands of them — swarmed over him. Were they ants? Spiders? He struggled to his feet and rubbed himself all over. The crawling stopped.

Which way — which way should he go? He couldn't remember. He stumbled off into the darkness...dizzy. Adam leaned his good arm against the wall as he continued through the tunnel.

Specks of light danced several feet in front of him like a swarm of fireflies. He trudged ahead, stumbled and broke his fall with his good hand. His muscles tightened, a steel clamp of pain crushing his rib cage.

He rolled onto his back and lay gasping shallow breaths for a time, until the pain subsided. Then he tried to pull himself to his feet, but he could barely move. If he didn't get up, he doubted that he would last much longer.

A faint glow of light shone in front of him. With all the strength he could gather, Adam struggled to his feet and stumbled toward the glow. As he continued, the light got brighter, and for the first time since he'd been in the mine, he could see without a flashlight.

The glare intensified with each forward step and soon glowed so brightly he could barely keep his eyes open. Adam squinted into it to see the silhouette of a man standing against the background of light. "Hey bud, glad to see you."

"Craig?"

"Come on. Let's go." He held out a hand.

Adam reached for it, but it remained just beyond his grasp. Craig turned and walked just ahead of Adam, without looking back. The brilliance was so intense Adam had to shield his eyes.

The light soon muted, and Adam looked around. Craig was gone. "Don't go, Craig."

A rush of air answered his plea. The wind stirred up the aroma of the redwoods that loomed over him. He was out — out in the open with trees and the sounds of life.

Adam staggered down a trail overgrown with weeds. Branches reached out for him, and he had to ward them off with his good hand. He came over a rise and saw a pond in the distance. Water — he was so thirsty his tongue felt as if it had swollen to twice its size.

He picked up the pace, tripped and sprawled across the trail. Then struggling to his feet, he zeroed in on the pond once again. The water shimmered, reflecting the blue sky, and Adam could almost taste its coolness. As he closed the distance, the pond began to lose its luster. With each step forward it began to look more gray and opaque. Then it slowly faded into the background and disappeared. Adam sagged against a tree.

Waves of lightheadedness swept through him like gusts of wind. He staggered forward, scraping against bushes and running head-on into branches.

As he rounded a bend, a cabin came into view — help at last. He stumbled to the front door and knocked. "Hello." He knocked again and waited.

He tried the doorknob, but it wouldn't budge. He shook the knob and kicked at the door. Someone had to be home. He staggered around to the back door and found it also bolted. "Help me," Adam pleaded as he pounded the wall. No one came.

"Break a window," a voice whispered.

"Craig?" Adam looked around, but no one was there. He grabbed a piece of firewood from the porch and swung it through the glass in the back door. Then he reached inside and turned the latch.

Though the curtains were drawn, allowing almost no light in, he saw spiders lurking the corners. A shadow at the far end of the room looked like the grim reaper for a moment, and Adam almost bolted out the door.

The kitchen — water! Adam went to the sink and turned the handle. Water gushed down and through his outstretched fingers, and he cupped his hands under the spout, gulping the lukewarm liquid until his lungs almost exploded for lack of air. Then he stopped and inhaled several deep breaths, whimpering as unbearable spasms tightened around his rib cage with each gasp. He gripped the counter as he felt his legs buckle. Soon his breathing returned to normal and the pain lessened. He drank some more.

"Food." Adam tried to ignore the pain as he opened cupboards. He found canned goods, cereals and pasta stacked floor-to-ceiling in a pantry and grabbed a can of beef stew and a box of crackers.

He pulled the lid off and scooped out some stew, using his fingers as a spoon, barely chewing as he shoved the food into his mouth. Returning to the kitchen faucet, he drank his fill.

A block of cheese rested on a shelf in the fridge. Adam ripped it open and took a large bite. He grabbed a small can of V-8 juice and pulled off the tab. The juice went down smoothly, much better than the water did. He grabbed everything and carried it to the coffee table in the living room.

He noticed his strength returning and his head beginning to clear as he eased onto the couch. The juice went down in two large gulps, and Adam returned for another can.

Now he could taste the food. The cheese had a unique flavor. Adam glanced at the label to see that it was imported. The crackers tasted bland by comparison, and softened the sharpness of the cheese.

For the first time, Adam thought about the owners of the cabin. What would they do when they returned? He'd explain what had happened and pay for any damage. Hopefully that would satisfy them. He sure made a mess here — broken glass from the back door, food packages scattered around, and dirt. He was filthy, and his grime came off on everything he'd touched.

His memory of how he'd gotten here was fuzzy, but in bits, it slowly came to him. Al — oh, God! Was Al one of them? Frank had been sent by his father-in-law to pick him up and kill him.

Was there no one he could trust? The sheriff was as much a crook as Weatherly. Adam couldn't rely on the FBI, either, judging by the reception he'd received at the Red Lion Inn. And even Al Rinaldi, his own father-in-law, had sold him out.

No, that couldn't be. As much as Al disliked Adam, he wouldn't resort to that. Someone had probably tapped Al's phone. Yes. That had to be it.

The sound of gravel crunching under tires came from outside. Then Adam heard car doors slam and the barely audible voices of two men. He went to the window and glanced past the edge of a pulled-back curtain. The men turned toward the cabin for a moment, and Adam saw their faces—Frank and Fu Manchu.

28

Adam remembered it all, now — the ride with Frank, and passing a cabin on the way to the mine — this cabin. His mind raced. He needed a plan.

Rummaging through the kitchen for a weapon, he found only a few flimsy steak knives. He grabbed one and slipped out the back door.

The closest large tree stood about fifty feet away. He stumbled toward it as quickly as his injuries would allow, gasping from the pain brought by each jarring step. Finally behind it, he went from tree to tree, continuing uphill and over a ridge.

Adam hobbled as fast as he could into a dense growth of trees. Then he heard Frank yell. He'd discovered the break-in. "Start looking," Frank said. "I'll phone for help." Adam quickened his pace, wishing he had something better than a useless knife for protection.

As he crossed a footbridge, he noticed several pieces of pipe in the streambed below and sidestepped down the bank to check them out. He found one about a foot and a half long that had a good feel when he hefted it. Then climbing up the bank, he slipped behind a large trunk and waited.

What would they do if they found him? Would they shoot him on the spot or take him back into the mine? They might even do both. He knew he'd have to get the drop on them if he hoped to survive. And if they approached together, he wouldn't have much of a chance.

It seemed like several minutes before Adam heard heavy footsteps. He peeked around the trunk and caught a glimpse of Fu Manchu, alone. The idiot made no effort at stealth, cracking twigs and rustling bushes in his path.

As the longhaired thug tramped by, carrying a revolver like some tenderfoot in a Western movie, Adam brought the pipe down across his arm and heard bones crack.

"Frank!" Fu Manchu cried out and dropped his weapon. He brought his other hand to the broken arm.

Adam swung the pipe again and caught Fu Manchu just above the ear. He crumpled to the ground.

Adam doubled over in pain. Each time he made an abrupt move, he felt as if he might black out. He knelt, using his good arm for support, head down, taking shallow breaths. He needed to stop for a moment, but he couldn't afford that luxury. Frank would be here soon.

Then he saw the pistol on the ground and picked it up—a Smith and Wesson .38 Special. And it had a full cylinder. He found several more cartridges in Fu Manchu's jacket and stuck them in his pocket.

Adam headed downhill to a large madrone tree, moving gingerly to lessen the pain. As he neared the tree, two rounds buried themselves in the trunk, peppering the side of his face with wood chips. He scurried behind the trunk and cocked the pistol. Frank ducked behind a rock.

Adam stood hunched over, wanting the throbbing in his body to ease. His brain told him to stop, but he couldn't. He tried to brace the pistol against the tree, waiting for Frank to make his move. With only one good arm it would be hard to steady it to get an accurate shot.

There was no sign of Frank, and the only sound Adam heard was that of his heart pounding in his head. He was almost afraid to breathe, for fear of giving away his location.

A twig cracked nearby. Adam glanced around the trunk and saw Frank not more than six feet away. As Adam stepped from behind the tree, Frank turned and aimed. It was as if Adam were back in the army, his reflexes instantly resurfacing. He fired a single shot, hitting Frank in the center of the chest, knocking him backward.

Stepping carefully to ease his pain, he slowly advanced toward the motionless body, his pistol cocked and ready to fire. Blood gushed from Frank's chest and puddled on the ground. There was no doubt that he was dead.

Adam looked at his arms and shirt, seeing specs of Frank's blood spattered over him. A wave of nausea washed through him, and he leaned against a tree and retched.

At least now, he had a car. He made his way to Frank's lifeless body and saw a set of keys dangling from a belt clip. Blood had dripped over them, and Adam got some on his hand when he took them.

He returned to the cabin and rinsed off the keys. There was no way he could leave wearing the clothes he'd crawled through the mine in. He checked the closet and drawers and found a shirt in his size and some jeans with a slightly larger waist. He could hold them up with his belt.

He went into the bathroom, turned on the shower and stripped off his clothes. Surprisingly, his wallet was still in the back pocket. He checked and saw that he still had his credit cards, plus a fifty-dollar bill and two twenties.

The shower felt good. He closed his eyes, letting the steaming water pour over him. He soon found injuries he didn't know he had: a raw right elbow that he'd noticed at the first contact of water; a thigh muscle he could hardly touch. He stretched each aching fiber and soaked in the warmth until he remembered that Frank had probably called for help. It was time to leave. He quickly dressed, climbed into Frank's car and headed downhill.

The narrow road wended its way downward. The turns were so tight that Adam had to keep a foot on the brake pedal. And the car was in such need of a tune-up it paused before accelerating when he stepped on the gas.

As he rounded a blind curve, he almost ran head-on into a red Camaro. He swung the wheel to the right, just barely missing the other vehicle. The driver stopped and leaned his head out the window as if wanting to talk. "Hey," the driver shouted as he saw Adam. These had to be Frank's buddies.

29

Maybe he could bluff his way past these guys. They didn't look very bright. Adam rolled down the window.

"Who the hell are you?" the driver asked.

"My name's Jeff," Adam said. "Who are you?"

"I don't know about any Jeff. What are you doing with Frank's car?"

"Uh, I just started yesterday. Frank sent me for help. The other guy's hurt."

"Who?"

"I don't know his name—the guy with long hair and the Fu Manchu."

"Oh." The man seemed satisfied. "What's wrong with him?"

"He got shot. You'd better get up there and help."

"Wait a minute," the driver said. "Frank could have phoned for help. Why the hell would he send you?"

"I don't know. I think his phone battery was dead."

The man on the passenger side got out. Adam watched in the rearview mirror as he went around the back of his car, reaching in his jacket as he started around to the passenger side.

Adam stomped on the gas pedal. The car sputtered, and he thought it was going to die. The engine finally caught, and the car surged forward, peeling rubber as it fishtailed down the road.

He glanced in his rearview mirror as he rounded a sharp curve and saw the Camaro turning around. By the time he spotted it again on the next straightaway, it had narrowed the gap. There appeared to be no way he could escape them.

As he neared the valley floor, the curves opened up a little, and he pressed the pedal to the floorboard. The car coughed and hesitated for a moment, and gradually gained speed. Adam watched helplessly as the Camaro got ever closer, filling his rearview mirror.

He felt a bump from behind and stepped on the gas. By the time his car finally accelerated, he was at the next turn and pressed hard on the brake pedal, as it skidding around. It was all Adam could do to slow down.

Another jolt sent him into a brief skid, and he almost lost control. He grabbed the steering wheel with his bad arm. His shoulder felt as if it was clamped in a bear trap. He had to stay focused. If he gave in to the pain he'd crash for sure. He didn't dare drive any faster, but he couldn't slow down either.

A straightaway came up. He jammed the accelerator to the floor and opened up a small gap. Then he watched helplessly, mesmerized, as the Camaro quickly filled in the space between them.

Almost too late to react, he looked at the road to see a sharp curve ahead. He slammed on the brakes and felt a hard impact as the front of the chase car buried its grill in his trunk.

Adam went into a slide, corrected with the help of his bad arm, and coasted, tires squealing, around the turn. He bounced along the shoulder and skidded through a barbed-wire fence and up the side of a hill. Regaining control, he plowed through the fence again and back onto the road. When he rechecked the mirror, the Camaro was gone. Then he saw the chase car limp around the corner, its grill mashed through its radiator. Water gushed onto the ground. He hit the accelerator, and the Camaro receded away.

It took several minutes for Adam to stop shaking and for his heart rate to return to normal. When he felt he was a safe distance away he stopped to check over the car. The driver's side door wouldn't open, so he slid out on the passenger side. The car looked as if it had been in a demolition derby. The trunk and rear bumper were caved in, as was the door on the driver's side. The rear fender well on the right side came fractions of an inch from touching the tire. It was time to ditch this heap.

Adam coaxed the wreck to the San Jose Airport. As he prepared to enter the long-term parking lot he saw two security guards at the gate. He quickly changed lanes and drove past. With all the airport security these days, he'd have to think of some other place to get rid of the car.

He saw a phone booth while driving through a strip-mall parking lot, and stopped. Checking the Yellow Pages, he saw that an Avis office was on this very street.

Frank's car stood out like a mangy dog in a kennel full of poodles, and the last thing Adam wanted was to look conspicuous. He drove past the car-rental office and parked around the corner.

As he slid across the front seat to exit the car, his foot touched something on the floor—the pistol he'd taken from Fu Manchu. Better take it along just in case. He stashed it into an overnight bag he retrieved from the back seat and headed down the block.

As soon as he got to the car-rental area Adam saw a pay phone. Now he could phone Carla without the call being traced. With the pain in his ribs, it was hard to concentrate, and he was having trouble breathing. He leaned against the wall, gritting his teeth against a spasm that engulfed his chest.

Where was the phone number? Adam emptied his wallet and discovered he no longer had Dave and Lisa's unlisted number. Al and Dixie had it, but their phone had to be tapped, for sure.

Maybe he would remember it if he thought about it. Right now, though, he couldn't concentrate. His chest ached, and he was hyperventilating. A quick trip to a doctor might be in order. He picked up the bag and headed for the car rental counter on unsteady legs.

"You okay?" the matronly desk clerk asked.

"I'm coming down with a bug, I think," Adam said.

"You need to see a doctor."

"As soon as I get my car."

"Take a deep breath." The slightly built emergency room doctor placed a stethoscope just below Adam's collarbone.

"I can't." A sharp pain went through his chest each time he inhaled.

"Do the best you can, then." The doctor moved the stethoscope around Adam's chest and back, and Adam followed orders as best he could.

"Your lungs sound congested. Let's get everything x-rayed. Then we'll determine the best treatment."

"How long is this going to take?"

"Maybe a couple of hours."

"Sorry. I can't spare the time."

"Your body has suffered some serious trauma, and we need to address it. I think you have some broken ribs, and it's affecting your breathing. You ignore it, and you'll get pneumonia, at the very least."

"Okay. Just do it as fast as you can."

"You feeling better?"

"Yeah. The pain pills really did the job."

"I could have given you something even better if you weren't driving." The doctor helped Adam into his shirt, then placed his arm in a sling and adjusted the straps. "There. That should do it. You're lucky. You only have a couple of cracked ribs and some strained shoulder ligaments, but you need to see an orthopedist right away."

"Okay."

"I want you to use this, too." The doctor pulled out a clear plastic contraption and handed it to Adam. It had a clear flexible hose connected to a mouthpiece.

"What's this?"

"It's called an incentive spirometer. It will help you to take deeper breaths so you don't get pneumonia." He showed Adam how to use it.

"Thanks, doc." Adam gingerly stepped down to the floor. "Now how do I get to the freeway?"

Rush hour traffic began to bog down as Adam eased into the center lane. According to the date on his car rental form he'd lost three days in the mine. That meant he was a day overdue in phoning Al, not to mention that he hadn't contacted Carla yet.

As traffic crawled ever slower, he decided that it might be a good time to find a pay phone. He took the next off-ramp and pulled into a Chevron station, parking next to a phone booth.

The phone rang several times. Just as Adam was ready to hang up, he heard Dixie's voice. "Hello."

"Hi, Mom. It's Adam."

"Adam! Oh, my goodness. Al, it's Adam."

Adam heard an extension pick up and then Al's voice. "You all right? Christ, we've been worried sick. Where are you?"

"It's too risky to tell you. I'll be okay. What happened?"

"All I know is that when my friend, Charles went to pick you up, you weren't there. He looked for you for over an hour, he said — checked at the front office and at all the other motels in the area. He said you just more or less vanished. God, we were scared."

"I was damn near killed. You sure he's on the up-and-up?"

"Oh, Mother of God. Adam, you've got to believe me. He's not like that. Someone tried to kill you?"

"If I hadn't gotten lucky, I'd be dead." Adam noticed a green van pull alongside his car.

"What happened?" Al asked.

The two men in the van seemed to be staring at Adam. He didn't like the feeling he was getting. "I can't talk anymore. I'll call you later."

The guys in the van reminded Adam a little of the Blues brothers. Maybe he was paranoid after all that had happened to him, but it made him a little uneasy that he couldn't see their eyes behind their dark glasses. He was certain they were observing him. Did they want to use the phone or were they waiting for him? He wasn't going to hang around to find out.

As Adam got into his car, the Dan Akroyd guy came around and tapped his window with a knuckle. His buddy, the John Belushi look-alike, was visible in the rearview mirror. Adam started the car and jammed it into reverse. Belushi jumped out of the way as Adam squealed backwards, put the gearshift into drive and streaked toward the freeway.

He hit the on ramp at about sixty and immediately jammed on the brakes, almost rear-ending the car ahead. Traffic was practically stalled. From his rearview mirror Adam saw the Blues brothers several cars behind. Construction barriers on both sides of the ramp blocked his escape. Neither he nor the Blues brothers could do more than follow the vehicle ahead.

Belushi jumped out of the van and trotted toward Adam. Damn! The bag with the pistol lay on the floor of the back seat, and in Adam's condition, there was no way he could reach it. This guy was going to shoot him, and there didn't seem to be a thing he could do about it. Under other circumstances it would have been comical to watch this goon, about fifty pounds overweight, holding his hat on as he puffed ever closer.

The car ahead barely moved. Just then Adam saw what he was looking for. As he passed a concrete barrier, the right shoulder opened up, with nothing but traffic cones in the way. He whipped the car to the right and stepped on the gas, zipping past the cars, scattering cones and leaving the Blues brothers behind.

He took the first off-ramp. As he reached the intersection, the light turned red, and he powered through to the sounds of horns and screeching brakes. The green van was nowhere in sight. Maybe he could let up a little. No use getting a ticket.

He made a right turn at the next corner, went down one block and turned left. He seemed to be safe.

Adam found himself in an industrial area. A chain-link fence encircled a yard stacked high with empty pallets. He pulled in behind them and under a metal awning to wait. How had those goons found him? From now on, he'd have to keep his guard up. Time to get the pistol. He'd keep it in his sling, just in case.

No cars came along while Adam waited, and he began to relax a little. Roughly thirty minutes had passed since he'd ditched the van. He would come out now, but he'd watch his back from now on.

Daytime gave way to dusk and streetlights began blinking on as Adam drove to a main part of town and stopped at a service station to get his bearings.

An "X" on the station's map indicated that he was in Cupertino—suburban San Jose. He studied the map a while longer and planned his route. He'd take the 605 Freeway to I-80, get on the 505 to I-5 and go north. Then he'd head for Seattle to pick up Carla, and try to disappear for a while.

Fairfield on I-80: a motel sign loomed ahead, and Adam was dead tired. He hadn't slept in a bed in several days. His shoulder ached, and his ribs throbbed, a constant reminder of what he'd been through.

When he got to his room he dumped the contents of the overnight bag onto the bed and sorted through. It would be too much to hope that there was a brand new toothbrush in here.

What was this? Adam picked up a metal and plastic electronic-looking gadget about the size of a deck of cards. It looked interesting, but he had no idea what it was. Maybe he could figure it out tomorrow. Right now, he could barely keep his eyes open. He shoved it into his pocket, pulled off his clothes and immediately fell asleep.

Adam's eyes snapped open. What was that? He listened to the muffled buzz of freeway traffic. Then he heard the sound of a metal object digging into the door.

30

Wood fibers tore apart as someone tried to force open the door. Adam jumped into his pants and shoes, fumbling with his good hand to pull up the zipper. He grabbed his shirt. No time to put it on or to lace his shoes.

The only way out would be through the bathroom window — if it opened. He prayed that it would. The sound of breaking glass came from the next room as he slid the window open. He climbed onto the toilet and squeezed through the small opening, landing hard on the ground.

The pain felt as if someone twisted a knife in his ribs, and it practically paralyzed him. It took all his willpower to get moving. His ribs and shoulder throbbed as he ran behind the motel to the shopping center next door, glad that he still had the pistol in his sling. His shoelaces clicked on the pavement as he trotted along.

Keeping in the shadows, he made his way along the back of a Safeway store and down a loading ramp, hiding behind a trash bin. He removed his arm from the sling and gingerly slipped into his shirt. As he tied his shoes he realized that if these guys found him here, pistol or not, he wouldn't have much of a chance.

A hedge bordered the fence — Adam trotted toward it, trying to step lightly while bent over from the pain. He squeezed through the bushes. The branches pressed against his rib cage, and he wanted to scream.

Something big and square pressed into his injured thigh from inside his pocket. He pulled out the electronic-looking thing he'd found in Frank's bag. Then it dawned on him — could this be the reason they always found him? How could he have been so stupid?

A tracking device? It had to be.

He held it over a steel post, ready to bash it apart. Then as cars moved slowly past on the other side of the fence, he thought better of it. He held the gadget ready until he saw what he wanted.

A black pickup truck seeming to skim the pavement came along with the bass sounds of hip-hop booming from its speakers. Two teens, caps turned backward, nodded to the beat. As traffic waited for the signal to change, Adam lobbed the electronic box into the truck bed.

The kids seemed oblivious to everything but the music. They turned left at the signal, took the freeway on-ramp a half block down, and disappeared.

Adam grabbed hold of the pistol and ducked back into the hedge as the van soon pulled into sight and stopped. Through the shrubbery he saw that the Blues brothers appeared to be arguing, although they were too far away to tell for sure. After several minutes, they drove off. Adam breathed a deep sigh and sagged against the fence as they headed for the freeway.

Though he wanted desperately to sleep, he knew that he wouldn't be able to until he put some distance between him and these creeps. He'd head east to Sacramento. It would be easier to disappear in a big city.

The dashboard clock had just passed midnight as Adam reached Sacramento, glad that his drive was almost over. For the past half-hour or so, he'd had trouble staying awake and wanted nothing more than to find a bed.

He took an off-ramp to I-5 and headed toward the airport to turn in the rental car. As he glanced at a map, a car pulled in behind him, its headlights almost blinding him. Then flashing red and blue lights filled his mirror. He pulled onto the shoulder.

Minutes went by, it seemed, and no one stepped out of the police car. Finally a CHP officer appeared on the passenger side. Adam rolled down the window.

"Could I see your driver's license, please?" the patrolman said.

"What did I do?" Adam fumbled for the license with his good hand.

"You were weaving a little back there."

"I haven't been drinking." The muscles in Adam's throat tightened as he realized he still had the pistol in his sling. And he sure as hell couldn't ditch it in front of a cop. He waited for what seemed like an eternity, as the officer scrutinized his license. He couldn't let him find the gun. He couldn't.

Cars whizzed by as the officer walked back to the patrol car. Adam adjusted the rearview mirror and saw him hand the license to a second patrolman who got into the car with it. He reached to remove the pistol from his sling, but saw the officer returning.

"Will you step out of the car, please?"

"Why?"

"Sir, please step out of the car."

Adam reached over with his right hand and unlatched the door. All he could think of was the pistol—Fu Manchu's pistol. And now there was no way to get rid of it. He stepped out onto the shoulder, turning awkwardly so the patrolman wouldn't see the gun. After doing it, he realized that it probably made him appear drunk.

"Please step over to the other side of the car," the officer said, directing Adam to the passenger side.

He shined his flashlight in Adam's face, and Adam couldn't see a thing. "What happened to your arm?"

"Got injured in a fall." He tried to act casual, but figured he wasn't pulling it off.

"All right, we're going to do this little test. Close your eyes, lean your head back and touch your nose with your index finger." The officer demonstrated.

Why were they putting him through this? He hadn't been drinking. He closed his eyes and leaned his head back and felt his equilibrium shifting. He took a step backward. This wasn't fair. After all he'd been through he just felt weak and tired.

The officer stepped up and grabbed Adam as he lost his balance. He glanced down into Adam's sling and quickly backed up several steps and drew his revolver. "Put your right hand behind your head and don't move." He pointed the barrel at Adam's chest as the second officer approached, also with drawn pistol.

The first patrolman slowly sidestepped toward Adam's left. When he got close enough, he reached in with his left hand and took the pistol from Adam's sling. The second officer came up, swung

Adam around and leaned him against the car.

"It's not mine." Adam yelled as his arm, and then his ribs made contact with the hard metal surface. He collapsed onto the pavement.

The cops rolled him onto his stomach, patted him down and pulled him to his feet. It felt as if someone pounded his ribs and shoulder with a sledgehammer. His legs buckled. He felt a wave of lightheadedness, then darkness.

31

You awake, Adam?"

Adam's eyes fluttered open to see his father-in-law standing over him. He lay in bed in a dimly lit room. "Al," he mumbled.

"Man, you gave us a scare. When we heard, we drove right over. Carla's on her way from Seattle."

"Carla." Adam didn't want her in the middle of this, but he sure missed her. Dixie stood beside Al, with a nurse a few feet away. An invisible weight held him down as he tried to sit up. It was hard to put his thoughts together.

"Don't worry," Al said. "We got you a good lawyer."

"What? Why?" Then he remembered. "This is crazy." Why had he been so stupid? He should have gotten rid of that gun right away. But the cops should have realized that he wasn't a criminal. They probably didn't even check him out.

Al fidgeted and cleared his throat. "Adam, what's going on?"

"I already told you." He tried to turn his back on Al, but it sent spasms through his body.

"Don't con me. I want to hear the whole story. If you're in trouble we want to help."

He glanced at Dixie, who appeared ready to cry. "When will Carla be here?"

"Her plane lands in about an hour."

The door opened, and two men entered, one a large black man, the other, Hispanic. "Mr. Knight, I'm Lieutenant Duncan with the San Francisco Police Department," the black man said, flashing his ID. He towered over the others. "This is Detective Caldaron. We're the chief investigators in the Morrie Rosenthal case, and we'd like to ask you a few questions." He turned to Al and Dixie. "I'm sorry, folks. We have to talk in private."

"I don't want him saying anything until his lawyer arrives."

"I haven't done anything wrong."

"Doesn't make any difference. You need to have your lawyer present."

Adam was exhausted, and he hurt all over. He just wanted to get this over with so he could go home. "What do you want to know?"

"Adam, don't do it," Al said.

Duncan turned to Al. "Sir, you and the lady will have to leave."

"Adam, if you say anything, you're an idiot."

"Sir, if you don't leave, I'll have the officer outside the door physically remove you."

"Don't talk to him like that." Adam couldn't believe the lieutenant's rudeness.

Al faced the lieutenant and took a step forward. "Go ahead. You guys think you can push people around just because you have a badge."

"Al, just go," Adam said, wanting to quickly get it over with.

"You're going to hear from my lawyer," Al said as Dixie pulled him toward the door.

Duncan gave Al a side-glance and then turned his attention to Adam. The other agent stood a few feet away. Duncan cleared his throat. "I want you to know that you have the right to remain silent."

Adam barely listened as the detective read him his rights. He hadn't done anything wrong and had nothing to fear. Once he set them straight, they'd drop this stupid gun charge.

"Where were you last Thursday night?" Duncan asked.

"Thursday night?" Adam couldn't think. "I don't know." He felt so confused. How many days was he in the mine?

"The day Morrie Rosenthal was murdered. You don't know where you were?"

Adam tried to remember. "I think that was the night I slept in my car near Ukiah."

The detective acted as if he hadn't heard. "The ballistics report from your pistol showed that it's the one that killed Rosenthal."

"What?" Adam tried to sit up, but it hurt too much. He hadn't expected this. "I keep telling you. It's not my gun. You think I did it?"

"Well, what are we supposed to think? Rosenthal's dead. You've got the murder weapon."

"I'm not a murderer. Didn't you check me out? I took it from a guy that tried to kill *me*."

Caldaron took a step closer. "Look, Leon, maybe he's telling the truth."

The lieutenant ignored his partner as he slid a plastic chair up, rested his foot on the seat, and loomed over Adam. "Now we know you weren't in on it alone. This was a hate crime—a death penalty case. Tell us who your accomplices are, and it might go easier on you."

"I don't have any accomplices."

"Come on, son, I know you couldn't have pulled this off by yourself."

"I didn't do it at all. I didn't have anything to do with it. Why won't you believe me?"

Duncan pulled out a spiral notebook. "Don't bullshit me. Why are you protecting them? We're going to find out anyway, so just tell us."

The door burst open, and a middle-aged man wearing a tweed jacket and rimless glasses barged in. He carried a scuffed leather briefcase that could have been rescued from a Salvation Army trash bin. "Don't say another word, kid." He handed Adam a business card and another to Lieutenant Duncan.

"Who are you?" Adam stammered.

"Herk Bigbee here. I'm the guy that's gonna get you out of this mess."

Adam glanced at the card, up at Bigbee and then back at the card: *H. W. Bigbee, Attorney at Law.* Was this guy for real? His unbuttoned jacket highlighted a bay-window midsection, and from his rumpled appearance, he might have slept in his clothes.

"Okay gents, if you'll excuse us, me and my client have got a lot of catching up to do."

Caldaron sidestepped toward the door. Duncan didn't move.

Bigbee removed his glasses and glared up at the lieutenant. "Look, mister, I'm a busy man. Haven't got time to dance with you."

Duncan glanced at the card. "Mr. Bigbee, your client is giving us a voluntary statement."

"*Was* giving you a statement. Now he's gonna give one to me.

Don't let the door hit you in the ass on the way out." He glared at Duncan, who eased toward the exit.

"We'll be waiting outside," Duncan said over his shoulder.

Bigbee turned toward Adam. "Okay, kid, now what the hell's going on around here?"

"They think I killed Morrie Rosenthal."

"Did you?"

"No. How can you even think that if you're my lawyer?"

"I've represented murderers before. Now tell me what happened."

Adam couldn't concentrate looking at Mr. Bigbee. He had a pudgy face with jowls that shook when he spoke. His glasses rested halfway down his nose and his thick lips looked as if a tire pump had filled them.

Adam tried to figure a good starting point for his story as Bigbee removed his jacket, tossed it over a chair, then pulled a legal pad from his briefcase. "Okay, kid, I'm listening."

"The first I knew about Morrie Rosenthal being killed was in the paper the morning after it happened." He went through events of recent days: eavesdropping on the rally at Weatherly's; the meeting with the FBI that didn't take place; Frank and Fu Manchu and being chased, shot at and pushed down a mineshaft.

Bigbee lifted his arm and scratched his ribs. "You call the cops about any of this?"

"I tried. But then when I went to meet the FBI in Santa Rosa, someone almost killed me."

"You let me take care of everything. I'll go and fill in those two clowns out there. Then we gotta get you a place to hide until the real crooks are behind bars."

The door swung open, and Carla dashed in. "Oh, Adam." She threw her arms around his neck and sobbed into his shoulder.

"Aagh, that hurts!" Adam felt almost smothered as a spasm shot through his ribs and shoulder.

"Sorry." She wiped her tears with the heel of her hand. "Look at you. You're all cut up and bruised. What have they done to you?"

"I'll be fine." He glanced at his attorney. "This is Mr. Bigbee. My wife, Carla."

Bigbee nodded. "Ma'am, a pleasure. You two lovebirds go ahead and catch up. I'll go out here and explain the facts of life to Laurel and Hardy."

Adam put his hand on Carla's stomach. "You're beginning to show."

"A little. I was worried sick, with you not calling and all. Look at you. You're all bruised and cut. And you have a broken arm..." She began to cry again.

"It's not broken, just some strained ligaments. Come on. Don't do that." Adam brushed a tear from her cheek.

Carla grabbed a tissue from the stand next to Adam and blew her nose. "You're the kindest, sweetest guy I know. Why would anyone want to hurt you?"

"I don't know." He didn't feel like telling her, and hoped she wouldn't press him too much. "The CHP stopped me and found a gun. Then they hauled me in."

"What were you doing with a gun?"

"I just had it for protection."

"Adam, you're beginning to worry me. Why do you need protection?"

He was getting in deeper than he'd planned. "Weatherly and his group know I'm onto them. I just wanted to be ready if they tried anything."

"This scares me. Could you go to jail?"

"I haven't done anything. And now I have a lawyer."

"Well, why is there an officer outside?"

"Just for protection."

"That's what scares me. Can't they just arrest whoever it is?"

"They're working on it. Don't worry." Adam felt weak, and he was tired of being on the spot. "Let's just be together and not talk." He clutched Carla's hand. He was caught in the middle, with both the police and Weatherly's group after him. It would kill Carla to know what he was really going through.

Bigbee pushed through the door. "Well, the Bobbsey twins want to hold you for now. They have a real weak case, but since they found you with the murder weapon, they think they have cause."

"What murder weapon? Adam..." Carla seemed stunned.

Bigbee looked down at Adam and scratched the back of his head. "You didn't tell her, huh? Well, honey, your hubby here's stuck in a

SILVIO CADENASSO

big pile of doo, and until we can get him out of it, they're charging him with murder one."

Carla looked at Bigbee, then at Adam. "That's ridiculous. Who are you supposed to have killed?"

"Morrie Rosenthal."

"I heard about that on the news. You weren't anywhere near there. Didn't you tell them?" Her eyes welled with tears.

"Yeah, I told them." Adam watched her reaction, wishing she'd never been told and that somehow this whole thing would go away. This was not the reunion he'd hoped for.

162

32

Bigbee burst into the room and put his briefcase at the foot of Adam's bed. "How you doing, kiddo?"

"Get me out of here."

"I'm working on Duncan right now, but reasoning with him is like reasoning with that damn bedpan over there. Look at it this way. If you weren't here you'd just be in the slam. At least in here the bed's comfortable."

"Can't you get me out on bail?"

"Be pretty hard. I spoke to the judge, but the SFPD has trumped up a case that doesn't make you look very good. Might be a few more days."

"A few more days? I'm already a basket case."

The door slowly opened, and Lieutenant Duncan stuck his head inside. "Mind if we come in?"

Bigbee glared. "I don't recall sending you an invitation, Duncan. You need to call me first."

Duncan entered the room, with Caldaron taking up the doorway. "We just want to ask a couple of questions. It will only take a minute."

"Do I have to draw you a picture? You're not talking to my client."

"Wait," Adam said. "What do you want to know?"

"You're not talking to him," Bigbee said.

"I don't have anything to hide."

Bigbee looked at Duncan. "Will you excuse us for a second?" He waited until the door closed behind the detectives. "Are you nuts? The guy's devious. Can't you see that? He came in because he thought I wasn't here, hoping like hell you'd incriminate yourself.

Before he gets through with you, he'll have you admitting you're the hillside strangler, for Christ's sake."

"You won't let that happen. Get him back in here."

Bigbee rolled his eyes and shook his head as he shuffled to the door. He motioned the detectives in. "Just for the record, Duncan, my client insisted on this over my objections, so here's the ground rules: he answers your questions if I say so, and you don't ask anything incriminating."

Duncan glanced at Bigbee and smirked. "Why don't you just *give* me a list of questions?"

"Don't be a smart ass. You heard what I said."

Duncan scooted a chair to the side of Adam's bed and dropped his huge frame into the seat. He scanned his notes and then zeroed in on Adam. "Tell me how you got the murder weapon?"

Adam looked at Bigbee, who nodded. "This guy came after me with it."

"Who?"

"I don't know — some long-haired guy with tattoos all over his body — one of the guys who pushed me down the mineshaft. I hit him with a piece of pipe and took the gun away. I didn't know it was a murder weapon. I just took it for protection."

"This guy came at you with a .38 Special, and you just took it away from him? Quite an accomplishment." The lieutenant got up and sauntered to the foot of the bed. "How did you learn the skills that allowed you to overpower this assailant?"

"I was in the army, but it didn't take any skill. I took him by surprise and just hit him."

"Oh. You were in the army. Ever belong to a militia group?"

"No. Of course not."

"I wouldn't blame you if you did. The minorities are taking over, and the government isn't doing anything about it."

"Cut the crap, Duncan. He wasn't in a militia group."

"Okay, so you used your army skills to surprise this guy and take his weapon."

"I guess."

"Whoa — hold it right there," Bigbee said. "He didn't say that. You're putting words in his mouth."

Duncan didn't react to Bigbee, but zeroed in on Adam. "You expect me to believe that you just took the sidearm away from some guy we can't find?"

"Yes. Why would I lie?"

"Plenty of reasons. To save your ass, for one thing."

"Okay," Bigbee said. "You're through."

"Wait," Adam said. He tried to sit up, but a pain shot through his ribcage. "I don't want you to leave here thinking I did it."

Bigbee shook his head. "Why are you paying me good money if you're not going to take my advice?"

"I'm not guilty. The sooner I get everything out in the open, the sooner I can get this behind me."

Bigbee sighed and buried his head in his hands.

Duncan ambled back toward Adam. "This abandoned mercury mine – where did you say it was?"

"In the mountains out of San Jose. I'm not exactly sure where."

"We've had our people check all the mines in the area and haven't found one like you described."

"Come on," Bigbee said. "He'd just been shoved down a mineshaft and was running for his life. You think he had time to draw you a map?"

Duncan unwrapped a piece of Juicy Fruit and stuck it in his mouth. "What do you think of African Americans?" he said as he chewed. "Think I'm pretty uppity, don't you?"

"We're not going there, Duncan."

Calderon stepped forward. "Why don't you take a break, Leon? I can handle it for awhile."

Duncan stared straight ahead for a moment, then looked over at Caldaron. "I'm going to go take a leak."

Adam turned to Caldaron as the door closed behind Duncan. "What's his problem? I'm not making this up."

"It's not that we don't believe you," Caldaron said. "We just have to cover all bases." He opened his pad. "Okay. Why don't we go over what you found at Mr. Weatherly's compound?"

Adam sighed and told the story again.

Nighttime was the worst. As Adam tried to sleep, the words kept going through his mind—twenty-five years to life. That's what Duncan said, maybe even life without parole. He was glad when the nurse finally came in and gave him a sedative, and he began to relax.

Duncan seemed certain that Adam had killed Rosenthal. Caldaron had his doubts, but Duncan intimidated him. Bigbee had better be as good as he said he was. Otherwise, Adam could go to prison.

Light from the hallway washed into the room as someone walked in — a man. Why do these people keep coming in all night? Adam shifted his weight and tried to go to sleep, but the aching in his ribs and shoulder kept him from getting comfortable. The man had squeaky shoes that grated on Adam's nerves as he paced back and forth at the foot of the bed.

Whatever he was doing kept Adam awake. Adam tried to block out the sound, but it was impossible. The squeaking finally stopped, and he thought he might finally be able to get some sleep. But just as he dozed off it started again. Then he heard the shoes moving slowly toward him. The squeaking stopped next to his bed.

A pillow went over his face. He couldn't breathe. His arms flailed against the man, but had no effect. He kicked at his blankets. They barely moved. The intruder's weight pressed the pillow tighter — no way to breathe.

Panic — don't panic. Adam continued pushing out with his feet. The blankets loosened. One foot was free. He kicked out, a glancing blow. He tried to shake his head free. The weight on the pillow held him fast. His fist had no effect against the man's solid stomach. He swung wildly — a lucky blow. The pillow loosened. Adam gulped some air. A fist slammed into the side of his head. His ears rang. "Help!" he yelled. The pillow was back over his face.

Adam continued to flail. He grabbed the man's shirt, tried to shove him away — no leverage. He pushed the man against a table. Something clattered to the floor. A woman screamed.

The pillow was released, and Adam filled his lungs. He pulled the pillow from his face to see a tall figure dash from the room.

"Somebody stop that man," a nurse yelled down the hall from the open doorway. She returned to Adam. "Oh my God. Are you all right?" She snapped on the light over his bed.

It was a moment before Adam could speak. "I think so." Then a searing pain shot through his rib cage and shoulder, and he felt a warm sensation where he'd been punched in the face. He was exhausted.

The door burst open, and a uniformed officer came in with his pistol drawn. After glancing around for an instant, he returned it to its holster, said something into his two-way radio and left as quickly as he'd entered.

"That cop was supposed to be guarding my room," Adam said. "Where was he?"

The nurse straightened Adam's blankets. "I don't know. He wasn't at his station when I came in." She whisked out the door.

Why wasn't anyone watching out for him? It seemed as if half the world had conspired to kill him. He couldn't just hang around until someone came back and finished the job. If the police couldn't or wouldn't protect him, he'd be better off on the street. At least there, he wouldn't be a sitting duck.

As soon as the nurse left, Adam found his clothes in the closet. After dressing, he glanced out the door. People ran up and down the hall like the Keystone Cops. No chance to leave this way.

The window—luckily the windows in this old wing opened. Adam unfastened the latch and lifted. The window appeared to be painted shut. After tapping on it and pulling again, it finally lurched open with a loud crack. His arms jerked upward, sending more pain through his ribs. He sprung the screen out and let it fall to the ground.

The drop to the ground was about six feet. His arm felt a little better, and he hoped he could land unscathed. He had to. He climbed onto a chair and eased through the window, landing on a bush. His ribs and arm hurt, though not as much as he expected.

Adam quickly got to his feet and headed toward the shadows. He couldn't let the cops spot him. Being in bed for two days had sapped his strength and made him feel unsteady. He eased his way along the perimeter of the hospital grounds, being careful to stay away from the lighted parking lot. As several police cars arrived, sirens screaming, he hid in a clump of bushes.

If they found him, he'd probably be back in the hospital bed, or maybe even in jail. No, that wasn't going to happen. He crept through the shadows until he came to a side street. Then he headed into a residential neighborhood.

33

It was freezing out here. Adam had been standing near the eastbound on-ramp for what seemed like an hour. His thin shirt offered little protection, and the muscles around his arm and ribs were beginning to spasm. He supported his injured arm with the good one, wishing that he'd remembered to wear his sling.

The drivers of what few cars came along barely glanced at him as they went past. He didn't know if he could last much longer before giving up.

Carla was probably worried, and he needed to get in touch with her, but he didn't have change for a pay phone. Maybe he could find a way to call from along the road.

Finally! A truck's air brakes hissed, and it rolled to a stop. Adam trotted up and climbed into the cab.

"Where you heading?" the driver asked.

"I don't know. Where are you going?"

"East—Wichita and KC." He stuck the lever in gear and let his foot off the clutch, and the truck rolled toward the freeway.

The heater felt good, and Adam rubbed his arms against the chill and leaned back.

The driver went through a range of gears and finally reached cruising speed. He glanced at Adam. "You look like you got a lot on your mind."

"I suppose." Adam looked out the side window.

"I can pretty much tell. Been driving rigs like this since I got out of 'Nam. I've picked up all kinds of hitchhikers over the years—runaways, adventurers, you name it. Even picked up an escaped criminal once."

Adam's breath caught in his throat. "Really? How did you find *that* out?"

"He just told me. It's surprising how people will open up after being cooped up in a truck for a few hours."

"What happened then?"

"Nothing. I let him off a couple of hundred miles down the road. Don't know what ever happened to him." The driver picked up his CB microphone and asked about road conditions ahead. A reply squawked back.

Adam tried to doze off, but his mind raced. If the police told Carla that someone tried to kill him... she must be frantic. He'd have to call her right away.

The driver downshifted as he started up the Sierra foothills. They passed a sign showing that Reno was 107 miles ahead. "You don't look like the hitchhiking type."

Adam closed his eyes. If he went to sleep, he wouldn't have to carry on a conversation.

"So what do you do?"

"What do you mean?"

"Your job—what kind of work do you do?"

"I'm a Realtor."

"No shit. You're the first Realtor I ever picked up. That don't make sense. What's a Realtor doing out hitchhiking?"

Adam's mind went blank for a moment. "My car broke down, and I've got to get home."

"Oh." The driver glanced in his mirrors and signaled to change lanes as he crawled past a slow-moving truck. "Where's home?"

"Reno."

"Reno's nice this time of year. I wouldn't give you two cents for it in the winter. Too damned cold for me. Give me Southern California any day."

"You live in Southern Cal?"

"Yeah. Temecula, near San Diego. Don't get to spend much time there, though. Always on the road. Man, I'd give my right arm to be home every night."

"I know what you mean." Maybe Adam should get off at the next town. He could call Carla, and he wouldn't have to put up with any more questions. Had he remembered to bring his calling card? Adam realized that he didn't even have his wallet.

"What's bugging you?"

"Nothing." Man, this guy was nosy.

"Come on, don't bullshit me. Something's gnawing away at your guts. I can tell."

"Look, if you want to play Twenty Questions, you can let me off right here."

"Don't get your ass in an uproar. I'm just trying to be friendly."

"Sorry. I just realized I left my wallet in Sacramento."

"You need a few bucks?"

"Thanks, but I can phone my wife." He still didn't know how, though.

"Well if you contact your bank when you get to Reno they can issue you a new credit card. And it's no big deal to get a new license at the DMV. Here." The driver handed Adam his cellular phone. "Give your wife a call."

"I don't know how to get a hold of her. She's in Sacramento."

"Have a little spat?"

"No!"

"Sorry. I guess it's none of my business. Say, why don't you just call your answering machine at home? That way, if she checks for messages, she'll know."

"Thanks." Adam dialed his home number and waited as the machine kicked on, and he heard his own voice and then a beep. "Hi, Carla, it's me. Sorry I ran out on you so fast. The police took my wallet from me. They said it was in the hospital safe. I'll call later and tell you where to send it."

The driver gave him a side-glance. "You in some kind of trouble?"

"No!" Adam sighed. "Yeah, I guess I am." He started talking as the miles went by, and without thinking, he'd told the entire story. As he finished, they came over a rise, and the lights of Reno opened up before them.

"You still want off here?"

"I might as well."

"Look, if you want, you can stay with me. You can crash in the sleeper. I'll be coming back through in a few days."

"Thanks, but I should really get off here."

The driver took the 395 off-ramp near downtown and stopped.

"This is as good a place as any. The center of town is just a few blocks that way. Good luck to you."

Adam opened the door. "Thanks."

"Oh, before you leave, here." The driver held out a fifty.

"I can't take that." Adam felt his face flush.

"Sure you can. Just send it back when you get squared away." He pulled out a business card and handed it to Adam, along with the bill. They shook hands.

Did angels drive big rigs? Adam watched as the truck climbed back on the freeway, heading toward Wichita.

34

RENO: THE BIGGEST LITTLE CITY IN THE WORLD: The sign loomed above Adam as he walked down Virginia Street, surrounded by the clinking and clanging of the gaming business. Though it was barely sunup, people stood in front of slot machines, dropping coins into one-armed bandits. He wandered through a casino until he found a restaurant, and ordered breakfast.

As he sipped coffee, he grabbed a newspaper from a nearby table. A headline on page three caught his attention. *ABANDONED MINE YIELDS BODIES*. Adam read that police had found a body at the bottom of a mineshaft in California's Santa Cruz Mountains. The article mentioned that police had also found the bodies of two other men on the property. It indicated that they all had police records and had ties to a white supremacy group. Now maybe Lieutenant Duncan would believe him. He had to call Bigbee.

Bigbee was out of the office, but his receptionist transferred the call to his cellular phone.

"Where the hell are you?" Bigbee said. His voice had an edge.

"Reno."

"I don't know what your problem is, but you get your ass back here pronto!"

"Someone tried to kill me last night."

"I know all that. They caught the guy. Now I want you to go to the airport and look up a guy named Wes James at Sierra Aviation. He'll fly you back here. I'll call him right now and set everything up. Just go on out to the airport."

"I can't chance it. How do I know someone isn't still trying to kill me?"

"Look, if you aren't in my office in four hours, I'll kill you myself." The line went dead.

Adam hung up and headed for a nearby taxi stand.

"Mr. Bigbee is expecting you." A bleached-blonde receptionist in a mid-length black-and-white dress escorted Adam down a hallway and opened the door to Bigbee's office.

Carla jumped up and rushed to Adam, crushing him with a hug. "Oh, Adam. I've been frantic."

"Ow! My ribs."

"Sorry, sweetie. I forgot. You okay? When they told me you weren't in the hospital, I was afraid I'd never see you again." She pulled a Kleenex from a box on Bigbee's desk and blew her nose.

"I'm fine." Adam reached for Carla's hand, and they sat in the two chairs in front of the desk.

In a few moments, Bigbee waltzed in. "Well, it looks like you're off the hook with the SFPD," he said as he dropped into a well-worn leather chair. "Duncan called about an hour ago and told me they're dropping the charges."

Adam breathed a heavy sigh and squeezed Carla's hand tighter.

"We're gonna have to hide you out until we can put this thing away. A friend of mine has a place in a gated community up at Wildwood Lake. You can stay there until you're safe."

"How long before it all comes down?"

"Shouldn't be much longer. The SFPD has handed off to the FBI. Looks like they're getting ready to raid the coastal compound. They told me they'd like to get some info on the layout from you before they go in."

"When do they want to see me?"

"ASAP. I just made an executive decision to have you talk to their guy right here. He ought to be arriving PDQ. You okay?"

"I'm fine."

"Good." Bigbee stood and grabbed his jacket from the clothes tree behind his desk. "Look, I've got to run an errand. You two lovebirds can stay here and fool around until the FBI gets here. Just remember that sometimes people walk in without knocking."

Man, this was the life. Adam sat in a lawn chair on the end of a private dock. He held a fishing pole in his right hand and a bottle of Sierra Nevada in his left. A stringer of large-mouth bass rested in a five-gallon bucket of water at his feet. He inhaled the crisp air of the Sierra foothills and realized that his ribs no longer hurt.

Carla came out wearing a gauzy white maternity smock. She set a tray of cold cuts and crackers on the table next to Adam's chair.

Adam looked up and smiled. "You're sure looking sexy lately."

"Stop that." She blushed.

Adam caressed her thigh just above her knee. "No, really. When I see you like this, I just want to ravage and pillage your body." He pulled her into his lap.

This was their third week at Lake Wildwood, and Adam had gotten into a comfortable routine. The FBI had told him that they were close to raiding the Weatherly compound, and it wouldn't be much longer before he and Carla could go home.

The cordless phone rang, and Adam picked it up.

"Are you sitting down, kiddo?"

"Yeah." It was Bigbee.

"Well, they raided the Confederacy's compound at the crack of dawn. They went in with about twenty Federal agents and a couple of hundred National Guard. Hauled in sixteen people and found a database with the names of about two hundred militia members. Not only that, it showed their master plan for robbing armored trucks. The county sheriff's right in the middle of it. He's sitting in his own slammer right now. And they confiscated enough ammonium nitrate to level a big city."

"That's great." Now he and Carla could go home.

"And hold on to your hat. They found some Russian at the compound. The guy couldn't even speak English. Had to fly a translator up from Berkley to interrogate him."

"CCCP."

"Say again?"

"CCCP. That's the initials for USSR in the Russian alphabet."

"Yeah, the Cyrillic alphabet. What's that got to do with the price of scotch in China?"

"There was a crate in Weatherly's barn that said CCCP. I didn't think much about it at the time, but there was writing on the box I couldn't make out. Must have been in Russian. What do you think the Confederacy got from Russia?"

"We'll find out soon enough. These FBI guys are pretty good at getting to the bottom of things. One other thing you need to know, though. Your friend, Weatherly—he wasn't there."

35

Adam placed a call to Herk Bigbee's office and waited as the receptionist connected him.

"This is Bigbee."

"Hi, Herk. It's Adam. Carla and I want to go home. It's been three weeks since the raid, and they still haven't found Weatherly. He's not coming back. Besides, Carla needs to get settled before the baby comes. It's been over two months since she's seen her own doctor."

"Is anything wrong?"

"No, but she's due in less than a month, and she wants to go back to her regular doctor and her regular routine."

"Let me call the FBI and see what they say. I want you to go home, too."

"Bigbee here. I called the FBI and talked to their head guy in San Fran. He doesn't think Weatherly's going to chance coming out in the open. Says he didn't know you were still laying low. I'll have a limo up there by noon tomorrow to pick you up."

The banner jumped out from a block away as the driver turned onto their cul-de-sac: *WELCOME HOME.* As the limousine pulled into their driveway, Al and Dixie dashed out the front door, followed by several neighbors. It felt great to be back.

People converged as Adam helped Carla out of the car, and he found himself being hugged, slapped on the back and jostled. He glanced at Carla, who showed the strain of the four-hour trip. Though she was pleasant to everyone, he could tell she was tired.

"I hate to break this up," he said, "but Carla needs her rest."

The neighbors dispersed, leaving only Dixie and Al.

Adam grabbed a suitcase in each hand and headed up the front porch steps into the entryway.

"Hello, Adam."

"Cindy!" She stood in the doorway to the living room, smiling with a self-assured look. Adam rushed to embrace her. This was the first time he'd seen her since the funeral, and it was all he could do to keep from breaking down.

Carla came in moments later, squealed and hugged Cindy. They went to the family room where Carla settled into a straight-back chair.

"Where's Justin?" Carla asked.

Cindy left the room and returned with a carrier containing a sleeping baby.

"He's adorable," Carla said. "I can't get over how much he's grown."

Al came to the doorway. "If everything's okay here, we're going home. I'll call you tomorrow."

Cindy looked good, for all she'd been through. "How long has it been?" Adam asked. "Six months?"

"Just about. I left for my brother's two days after the funeral and just got home last week. It was hard at first, but I'm doing better. I can go through Craig's things without crying, now."

"They still say it was an accident."

"Maybe it was."

"No way. I think Craig found out about the armored truck robberies and all the white supremacy stuff, and they just got rid of a witness. I hear they're all in jail now — all except Weatherly. He just disappeared. But the FBI seems to have everything under control. They'll catch him."

What a week — all that catching up. Adam had surprisingly little to do at work. He'd been gone for over three months, and other people in the office had handled all of his pending work. His activity was zero, almost as if he were starting over. He spent most of the week catching up on what was new on the market and what had sold in his absence, and calling his clients to let them know he was back. Now that he was no longer after Weatherly, he was surprised at how relaxed he felt.

With nothing to do for the afternoon, he decided to drive out to the Kinneys'. He'd had Jack's belt sander for so long Jack had probably bought a new one. He could drive out, visit with Jack and Elsa for a while and be back in time to help Carla fix dinner.

The drive to the coast brought back all the memories. As he rounded a familiar curve, Adam slowed and pulled onto the shoulder.

He walked onto the bridge and gazed into the creek bed, so far below. There was no sign of Craig's accident now, except some scraped concrete on the bridge abutment. The railing had been repaired long ago. Adam thought of Craig, of finding him trapped in his truck and the panic of not being able to save him. Even though it had happened months earlier, it still choked him up.

Craig had been so happy for him when he'd sold the property to Weatherly. But if neither of them had ever met Weatherly, Craig would still be alive. Adam couldn't stay here a moment longer.

As he continued toward the coast, he thought back to the days when he really enjoyed making this trip — to the days before all the bad memories. Maybe someday, he'd get those good feelings back. He hoped so.

Bruno trotted toward the car, barking and wagging his tail as Adam drove down the Kinneys' driveway and stopped. Where were Jack and Elsa? Normally, one or both of them would be out in front. He stepped up to the porch and rang the bell.

The yard looked almost perfect, as it always did, with deep brown mulch surrounding the plants. The lawn had been recently mowed, and bright blue flowers bordered the sidewalks. Adam had almost forgotten how much he enjoyed coming here. He rang the bell again.

The gate to the chain-link fence sat open, and the shed door was ajar. Maybe that's where Jack and Elsa were. He looked around the yard for a time and then headed toward the small outbuilding.

The door to the shed swung open, and Jack emerged. "Well for crying out loud. When did you get back?" He closed the door. "It's sure good to see you." Jack shook Adam's hand.

"Been back a few days. Sorry to barge in. I just wanted to return your belt sander."

"You've got to come in for a minute. If I let you get away before saying hi to the missus, I'll be sleeping in the doghouse for sure."

Elsa came out the front door. "I was out in back and didn't know you were here. Come in and have some hot tea." She shot a glance at Jack.

"I really can't stay," Adam said.

"Nonsense. You've got time to come in for a few minutes."

Adam followed Jack and Elsa into the house. The dark living room still gave him the creeps. As they headed through, Adam saw a flag draped over the back of a chair. He could make out the design through the folds—red background, large white circle in the center and a swastika. "A Nazi flag?"

"Oh, that. My uncle brought it home from the war. We just decided to get it out and look at it."

"Why would you even want it?"

"I don't know. Criminy, it's just a war souvenir." Jack's voice had an edge that Adam had never heard before.

"Piping-hot tea, coming up," Elsa said from the kitchen.

Jack regained his composure, and he and Adam headed toward the sunroom.

"Here you are." Elsa set Adam's tea on the near side of the coffee table, facing the window.

"Honey, why don't you put him on the other side," Jack said. "My knee's acting up, and I need to stretch it out."

Adam sat down with his back to the window.

Jack dropped into a chair across the table and propped his leg on a footstool. "So when's your missus due?"

"Thirteen more days. She's so excited and nervous she can hardly stand it."

"Well, Elsa and I wish the two of you the best, don't we, honey?"

Elsa nodded. "We're so happy for you."

Jack shifted his weight in the chair. "So what have you been doing besides what I read in the paper?"

"Just trying to get back into the groove. I've been gone from work so long I have to practically start over."

"You shouldn't have any problems. From all the free advertising you're getting from being on TV and getting your picture in the paper, you ought to do real well. You know, they say all publicity is good."

"I hope you're right."

Jack seemed almost to be looking through Adam and out the window, and appeared to be following something outside. Adam started to turn around.

Jack stood and walked to the window. "Do you mind if I close the drapes?" He pulled the drawstring. "My eyes are real sensitive today."

Jack was sure jumpy. And Elsa didn't seem to be her normal self either. "I really can't stay," Adam said. "I just came by to return your sander."

"Well I'm glad you came," Jack said, rising slowly. "We need to have you and your missus out for dinner after the baby is born."

Elsa went to the hallway closet and returned with a box wrapped in pink foil paper with a blue bow. "I was going to drop it by the next time I went to town. I hope this is appropriate. I didn't know whether you were expecting a boy or a girl."

"We don't know either. We didn't get an ultrasound, so we'll be surprised like everyone else."

Jack and Adam headed toward the front door, followed by Elsa. When they got outside, Adam glanced toward the carport. It must be nice to have all that room. There must be six cars in there, awaiting restoration. Adam noticed Jack's refurbished Corvette and went to give it a closer inspection. The finish looked as if it had been done at the factory.

"Here, Adam. Let me show you something." Jack headed toward the vegetable garden. He opened the gate for Adam and walked to an area where several cabbages, all over a foot in diameter, were growing. "You ever see one this huge?"

"No. How do you do it?"

"Mulch and good old-fashioned chicken manure. Works wonders." He took out his pocketknife and cut off a head. "Honey, grab a bag out of the carport, would you."

"I can get it."

"No, that's okay. She knows right where they are."

Elsa returned with a plastic grocery bag. Jack dropped the cabbage in, then cut several heads of broccoli. He placed them on top of the cabbage and handed the bag to Adam.

"Thanks," Adam said. "I have to be going." He stepped toward his car, glancing at the Corvette once more as he opened the door. It was then that he noticed a vehicle parked in the darkest part of the carport. It couldn't be possible—or could it? Even from this distance there was no doubt. It was a silver Hummer.

36

Could it have been Weatherly's car? There weren't that many silver Hummers on the road. The forest shadows closed in as Adam wended his way toward home. Weatherly wouldn't be *that* stupid. With the whole world looking for him, he was probably in Brazil or the Cayman Islands by now.

But how many silver Hummers could there be? Was it a coincidence that Jack had one just like his neighbor's?

Jack wouldn't be involved with Weatherly. He was too nice a guy for that. Maybe he bought it from Weatherly before he disappeared. Besides, it probably wasn't even a Hummer. But it had to be. No other car even came close in looks.

How well did Adam really know Jack? Adam had only been to his house a few times. When he thought about it, he really didn't know Jack at all. And what about that Nazi flag? Jack sure got defensive when Adam mentioned it.

It was probably none of Adam's business. But if Jack were involved with the Confederacy, being right next door when the property came on the market would have worked to their advantage. And Weatherly might have just been a front man. Jack could act as though he didn't know the guy, but he could still be right in the middle of it. Adam had better call the FBI when he got home. If they said it was nothing, he'd forget about it.

But he couldn't just drop it. That would be an insult to Craig's memory. Adam knew that with the baby coming and everything, he'd need to concentrate on that. But for now, he could at least try to find out if Jack and Weatherly were collaborating. The FBI wouldn't act on it until tomorrow. That might be too late.

By the time he approached town, Adam knew what he had to do. He didn't want to leave Carla alone tonight, but this was important. He phoned her. "I have to run an errand. I might be a couple of hours late." Then he called Cindy. "Could you go over and keep Carla company until I get home?" She said she would.

Adam felt guilty. Sure, Carla was almost due. But if he didn't follow up on this lead, he'd feel even worse. At least in the unlikely possibility that Carla went into labor tonight, Cindy would be with her. He knew Carla would understand after the people who killed Craig were behind bars. Besides, Dixie said the first baby was always late.

Adam looked at his watch. First he'd stop at the grocery store. Then he'd drive back to the coast. He should arrive at Kinney's just after dark.

"Come here, Bruno." Adam called quietly to Kinney's barking dog.

Bruno trotted up and accepted a Milk Bone and then another. After a few more barks, he stopped.

Adam clicked on his penlight and started through the redwoods bordering Kinney's yard. Bruno tagged quietly along. When he reached a good vantage point, Adam checked the carport with his binoculars. It was so dark inside he couldn't see a thing. But with several yard lights around the carport, there was no way he could go in right now.

Bruno nuzzled Adam's hand and got another treat. The wind picked up, and Adam folded his arms against the cold. He should have worn a jacket over his sweater. The weather report predicted a chance of rain, but he'd just have to put up with it. For now, he would just wait until he could get into the carport undetected.

As he got closer to the shed, he saw that the door was ajar, and a light glowed from inside. He'd love to know what Jack did in that small, windowless building so much of the time.

He continued to the area behind the house. Elsa busied herself in the kitchen, and he felt a little uneasy spying on her. Soon, she spoke on the phone for a moment and then set the table.

After several minutes, Jack emerged from the shed and headed toward the house.

Adam stared at the shed. The door was closed, but the gate remained open. He walked in the shadows until he reached the chain-link fence. The shed had no outside light, and Adam felt comfortable approaching it, feeling certain he wouldn't be seen. He crept through the gate, listening for sounds, then reached for the knob on the shed door. It turned.

Light from a small overhead bulb washed over him as he pulled the door open, slipped inside and eased the door closed.

Bruno scratched from outside, and Adam let him in. He didn't want the dog giving him away.

The shed was a lot smaller than it looked from outside. There was nothing in here—just a few cardboard boxes on shelves against one wall. Adam opened the first one, which appeared to be tax records. The second box looked about the same. He couldn't imagine why Jack spent so much time here. The place was practically empty. And where was the ham radio? There was no mistaking that antenna.

Bruno sniffed the floor and followed a scent to a section of shelving in the middle of the wall. He was so focused that Adam checked to see what held his attention.

"What are you looking at, boy?" He glanced at the bottom shelf, but it was empty. Then he noticed a sliver of light coming from a crack between the two sections of shelving where Bruno sniffed. When he checked closer, he saw that one section rested at a slight angle. He grabbed a shelf and pulled. It swung out, revealing a concrete stairway bathed in the glow of sodium vapor lights. At the bottom, a steel security door with a deadbolt lock sat slightly ajar.

Adam stood at the top of the stairway, undecided on whether to check it out or leave. Bruno trotted down to the bottom and looked back at Adam, as if asking him to follow. The dog scratched his ear, and the tags around his neck jingled.

Adam held his breath. If someone came out, he'd just say he was looking for Jack. Yeah, that's what he'd do. If that didn't work, he was screwed.

Bruno was becoming a nuisance, and Adam wished he hadn't let him come along. He watched helplessly as the dog stuck his nose into the crack, pushed the door open and trotted inside.

Adam ducked back into the shed and waited, expecting someone to come out. No one did so he tiptoed down the steps and stuck his head through the doorway.

In the dim light he saw a large room full of electronics, at least twice what he'd seen in Weatherly's barn. He stepped inside and closed the door.

A ham radio sat at one end of a desk-height counter, and two sets of reel-to-reel tapes slowly turned. Two computer monitors, on opposite sides of the room, displayed the random twirling of screen-save patterns. He switched on the light.

The entire room, including the ceiling, was made of concrete. There were three closed doors, one on each wall, and a small kitchen with no door. Adam opened the closest door, which led to two others with restroom symbols on them. He opened the door to the men's room and flipped the switch. Fluorescent lighting reflected off the sparkling tile walls and floor. There was a large common shower area, two toilet stalls and three urinals.

He opened the second door off the main room. This looked like a dormitory, with five sets of bunk beds. The walls were a neutral off-white color, and the floor had a covering of plush cobalt blue carpet. A landscape painting hung on the far wall. It appeared that Jack had tried to make it seem homey, but Adam felt claustrophobic.

He looked at his watch. Jack probably wouldn't be back until he finished dinner. That should give Adam a few minutes to nose around. He tried the third door, but found it locked.

After a quick look around the main room, he went to the closest computer terminal and tapped the keyboard. A menu display appeared.

Adam wasn't a hacker—didn't know much about it. But he had enough computer knowledge that he hoped he might be able to somehow get in.

He clicked "A" at the top of the menu and hit "ENTER."

The screen jumped to life. He couldn't believe that they hadn't protected the computer with a password. As Adam scanned the screen, Bruno went to the door, barked softly and wagged his tail.

"Quiet, Bruno." Then he realized why the dog had perked up.

Adam hit the escape button and dashed for the restrooms. He heard the door open just as he closed his.

"Bruno! How in the world did you get in here? Git! Go on, now! Outside!"

Adam held his breath, waiting for Jack to search for him. He knew he could overpower the old man, but would it be possible without Jack seeing him? He couldn't let Jack know that he was on to him.

He heard a door open, and guessed that Jack had gone into the dormitory and would check the restrooms next. He slipped into the men's room and into a stall. The only way he could think of not being conspicuous was to crouch up on the seat. Then he waited.

Jack mumbled something that Adam couldn't understand. It sounded as though he was on the telephone. He spoke inaudibly for a few minutes.

Adam opened the door a crack and listened as Jack continued talking. Then the light went off, and Adam heard the door close. There was another unmistakable sound: that of a deadbolt being locked.

37

Adam tried the knob. It turned, but the door wouldn't budge. The double cylinder lock had to be opened with a key, and unless he found one, he'd be here when Jack returned.

He flipped a light switch on and began pulling drawers open and rummaging through them. He had no idea where to look for a key.

There had to be something, maybe a screwdriver that he could use to remove the hinge pins. He reopened a drawer, this time searching carefully. There was a box of pistol ammunition, but nothing of use. He tried the second drawer with the same results. The center drawer had a key in one of the trays. Adam inspected it for a moment. It was small, for a desk or a toolbox, not a high-security deadbolt.

His hands shook, and he found it hard to control them. He had to stay calm. What if he were still here the next morning when Jack came in? What would he say? What would Jack do?

He went into the dorm and pulled open each dresser drawer to find that they were empty. Carla must be getting frantic. He'd heard about how weird women get when they near the end of their term. All he could do was hope to find a way out. He switched off the light and closed the door behind him.

A filing cabinet stood in the corner next to a desk. As he passed the desk, his foot caught on the telephone cord, and he momentarily lost his balance. Why wasn't it behind the desk instead of out where people could trip over it? He reached the filing cabinet and slid the thumb latch on the top drawer—locked. He realized he was hyperventilating—no time to panic.

Slow controlled breathing—take regular breaths. The best way to get through this was to use common sense. There had to be a way out.

Think rationally. Search systematically. Stay calm. If he checked the hinge pins, they might be loose enough to remove by hand. Adam wiped his sweaty fingers on his pants and reached for the top pin. It didn't budge.

Maybe he could get them started with a coin. He tried to force a dime under the pinhead. It slipped, bending his thumbnail back. He watched as the nail instantly turned red.

He dashed to the bathroom for some toilet paper to stem the flow of blood. He took several deep breaths and tried to stop shaking as he pressed the tissue against his thumbnail. For the moment at least, he felt better. Five minutes to nine. A light on the telephone blinked on. Jack must be calling someone from inside the house. He'd like to phone Carla, but that would only alert Jack to his presence.

The portrait on the far wall caught Adam's attention, a picture of the same man whose picture hung in Jack's living room. On the bottom of the frame, an engraved brass plate read, *George Lincoln Rockwell, 1918-1967.* Adam had never heard of him.

Adam tried to lift the picture, but found it hinged to the wall. He swung it out, revealing a safe embedded in the concrete. It was locked.

The key that would get him out was probably inside. Couldn't anything go right? Adam slumped into a chair at the closest terminal. The telephone light went off.

He couldn't just sit here and wait for Jack to arrive the next morning. Pulling open the center desk drawer, he saw the small key again. He looked at the filing cabinet and back at the key. It was worth a try.

The lock popped out when Adam inserted the key and turned. He snapped the latch and pulled. The drawer slid smoothly out.

It was half-full of folders, each tab labeled in handwritten block letters. Adam scanned through and stopped when he saw his name. He removed the folder and began reading. How could they know so much about him? They had information on his parents and how they died, on Carla's family, and so many facts on him that it scared him. They even had his mother's maiden name.

He found a folder for Craig, too, but it was empty. No need to keep a file on a dead man.

Adam read on as it listed what they thought he knew about their operation. Much of it was true. The conclusion gave him goose bumps. It read, *TERMINATE*. That was lined out, with one word scribbled next to it: *NO*.

He wanted to read on, but he had more pressing things to do. He closed the top drawer and went to the second one. It was half full of folders. Adam thumbed through them and discovered that most were empty. In the back of the drawer he found a pistol in a shoulder holster. He pulled it out—a Colt Python .357 Magnum, covered with a thin coat of oil that reflected the overhead fluorescents. This thing could make a hole big enough to put a fist through and would come in handy for protection.

But where was the ammunition? There was none in this drawer. He opened the third drawer, which held an assortment of stuff— computer cords, packages of electronic parts and office supplies, but no ammunition.

The cartridges in the desk—Adam opened the drawer. Damn— 38 caliber. He returned to the filing cabinet and pulled everything out as he searched. A key—there was a key at the bottom. He grabbed it and rushed toward the door. The telephone cord: Adam caught it with his foot as he went past.

The phone crashed to the floor. The sound reverberated through the room. How could he be such a klutz? Could the sound travel to the outside? Adam picked up the telephone, the receiver a cord length away on the floor. The phone button shone brightly enough that Jack would see it if he were near an extension. If he came out to check, all Adam could hope for was a little compassion. It probably wouldn't help, but he was out of ideas.

This key had to work. Adam's hand shook so much that he couldn't get it into the slot. He held the key in both hands—tried to slide it in. It caught halfway. His hopes were dashed as he realized that it didn't fit.

Back to the filing cabinet, he checked the bottom drawer as he listened for approaching footsteps. His heart pounded so hard he wasn't sure he would hear them. At least fifteen or twenty keys lay in a box in the back of the drawer, and a dozen or so looked like door keys. He had to hurry. It might already be too late.

Just in case, he turned off all but the overhead light. Next he closed the filing cabinet and returned the phone to its proper place. It might gain him an extra few seconds should Jack show up.

He inserted the first key into the slot as he listened for footsteps on the stairway. It slid in, but would not turn. It was the same for the second and third. Some keys went completely in. Others caught partway. He stuck the next-to-last key in, and surprisingly, it spun completely around, and Adam felt the precision bolt click open.

Finally! He opened the door a crack. A sound filtered down from above — probably Jack coming. Adam immediately locked the door and turned off the light. He went into the dorm and slid under a bed. The old feelings of claustrophobia returned as he wedged himself in the few inches between the mattress and the floor.

Spiders had taken over the cramped space, and Adam found the sticky webs clinging to his arms and face. He hated spiders and imagined black widows crawling all over him. He waited for Jack, using every ounce of willpower he could muster to suppress his fears.

And the dust: before Adam could react, he sneezed, then again. If Jack were coming in, he'd have heard it for sure.

How long had he been under the bed — five minutes, ten possibly? Maybe Jack wasn't coming. Adam slid out and brushed the webs and dust off. It made him want to take a shower.

After checking the room to make sure nothing had changed, he opened the door a crack. The sodium vapor lights still illuminated the stairway, and he didn't see a switch to turn them off. The thought that someone might be waiting for him at the top of the steps — why did he let his mind dwell on stuff like that? If someone were here, he'd probably have known by now.

It wouldn't help to overanalyze. It was beyond his control at this point. All he could do was to make a swift exit and hope for the best. He locked the deadbolt behind him, crept up the steps, pushed the section of shelving aside and felt a rush of cold air as he entered the pitch-black shed.

He clicked on his penlight, quickly swinging it around, then turning it off. The shed was empty. He reached for the knob.

This door was also locked. He glanced over his shoulder as he slid the key into the slot, still half expecting someone to emerge from the shadows he'd just checked. He turned the key. A soft click came from the door as it unlatched, and Adam felt it push out. He pulled his collar up as he stepped into the dampness of the autumn night.

He'd forgotten about the gate. Damn! Adam stared at the padlock. It was huge. There was no way out without a key, unless he climbed the fence. And as much noise as this would make, plus dealing with the barbed wire at the top, he didn't want to chance it. There had to be a key in the filing cabinet — there had to! He slipped back into the shed and down the steps, wishing he were home with Carla.

He unlocked the filing cabinet and stared at the box of keys. Which one would it be? He picked through them, having no idea which of them might work. His eye caught a glimpse of one particular key. *MASTER* was embossed on its head. He knew of Master padlocks, and this appeared to be the only Master key in the box. Hopefully, it would fit.

Adam trotted up the steps and into the shed. If this key didn't work, he was going over the fence, barbed wire or not. He unlocked the shed door, slipped out and re-locked it for what he hoped was the last time. As he reached the gate, he whispered a quick appeal to Craig and stuck the key into the padlock.

A metallic click came from the lock as it popped open. Adam exhaled the breath he had been holding. He removed the key and lifted the latch.

The hinges groaned as he pushed the gate. He stopped and listened. All he heard was the breeze going through the trees. He leaned against the gate once again. Just a little more and he could squeeze out. Gritting his teeth against the sound, he pushed. The gate noisily inched out, and he slipped through the opening, afraid that he'd probably awakened Jack. He pushed it closed and snapped the lock back in place. Now to get the hell out of here.

That sound — what was it? Adam's heart skipped a beat, and he almost cried out. Someone moved in the dark. Then he recognized the familiar jingle of Bruno's tags as the dog scratched. "Bruno! You scared the hell out of me!" he whispered.

Bruno nuzzled Adam's hand and received another Milk Bone.

Adam slipped behind the shed and kept in the shadows on the way to his car. He started the engine and crept away, using just his parking lights. When he was safely down the road, he clicked his headlights on. That's when he realized he hadn't checked the carport to see if the Hummer was there.

God, it was almost 9:30, and Carla was probably frantic. Hopefully his cell phone would work. He'd tell her he was with a client, and that he'd be home late. Even if he pushed it, he wouldn't get there until after eleven. He hoped she'd understand.

Adam had been worried for nothing. When he phoned, Cindy told him that Carla had gone to bed at a little past eight. Adam finally relaxed and arrived home about 11:15. He sent Cindy home and grabbed some leftovers from the fridge. Then it was time to do some research on the Internet.

Adam typed *George Lincoln Rockwell* into the keyboard and clicked *SEARCH*.

The screen went blank for a moment, and then reappeared. He scrolled past the advertising down to the first selection. *Hate: George Lincoln Rockwell and the American Nazi Party, Book by William Schmaltz. Founded American Nazi Party in '59, ran for governor of Virginia in '65, planned to be president in '72, assassinated in '67...American Nazi Party Leader — George Lincoln Rockwell.*

Adam clicked onto that site and read about the book. Next he was directed to the Web site for the American Nazi Party. He clicked the box marked *Rockwell's Works* and read the quote on the monitor. *"We must have an all-White America; an America in which our children and our grandchildren will play and go to school with other White children; an America in which they will date and marry other young people of our own race; an America in which all their offspring will be beautiful, healthy White babies – never raceless mongrels. We must have an America without swarming black filth in our schools, on our buses and in our places of work; an America in which our cultural, social, business and political life is free of alien, Jewish influence; an America in which White people are the sole masters of our own destiny." – George Lincoln Rockwell*

Another site held tributes to George Lincoln Rockwell. Adam read one written by a J. L. Kinney. No need to wonder who J. L. Kinney was.

This was obviously what Jack and Weatherly stood for. Adam searched through related Web sites that expounded the beliefs of the Nazi Party and the Ku Klux Klan, then to sites for fringe whacko groups. There were several on Timothy McVeigh and the Oklahoma City bombing. These guys were all nutcases, and Jack Kinney was a part of it. It almost made him sick that he'd thought of Jack as his friend.

It all seemed so logical. Weatherly and Jack Kinney belonged to a white supremacy group modeled after the Nazi Party. One or both of them were involved in Craig's death, and he was certain that the computer held the evidence. He looked at his watch and decided that he'd better go to bed. Tomorrow night he'd return to the underground bunker.

38

B runo, come here, boy." Adam snapped his fingers.

The black Lab silently trotted up and took a Milk Bone from Adam's hand.

Adam cut through the stand of trees, past the back of the house and up to the shed as a light drizzle fell. Through the window, he saw Jack and Elsa seated at the table, eating dinner.

Adam had told Carla he was working late and had gotten Cindy to stay with her again. Carla shouldn't go into labor this early, but at least with Cindy there, it would be one less thing on his mind.

This time Adam had remembered to wear dark clothing and dress warmly. And he also brought a small can of WD-40 and drenched the gate hinges with it. Then he pulled out the two keys he had copied, stuck one into the padlock and turned. The lock clicked open and the gate swung out with a barely perceptible creak.

He'd also brought something else: several Zip disks on which to copy Jack's files.

This morning he'd called Agent Botelli at the FBI, to clue him in. All Botelli did was chew him out for taking the law into his own hands. With his pompous attitude, you'd think the case was closed. He did thank Adam for the information, though, and said he'd get some resources right on it.

Adam inserted the new key into the locked shed door, slowly turned it and felt the door unlatch. He quickly slipped inside and re-locked the door.

Bruno whined from outside, but Adam couldn't chance letting him tag along again. Had Jack been more perceptive the previous night, he would have figured out that someone had let the dog in.

Adam pulled the shelving aside and stepped onto the stairway landing, pausing to return the shelves to the opening. As he stopped to listen, it seemed eerily quiet—too quiet. He waited a moment and finally decided his brain was playing tricks on him. He continued downward.

When he reached the landing at the bottom, he tried the doorknob, but it held. He put his ear to the door and listened for a moment before deciding that no one was there. Then he inserted the key and unlocked the door.

He switched on the light. There was so much to do. First he had to copy Jack's files. He inserted a disk. Hopefully it was compatible with this computer. He held his breath until the computer's drive groaned into action. Next, he secured the door and then returned the original keys to their box in the filing cabinet.

The locked door at the far end of the room drew his attention. He slipped the key to the main door into the cylinder and turned it. The door unlatched, and he stepped inside.

A bench of wooden planks ran the full length of one wall, with fluorescent lighting directly above. He flipped on the switch. A set of tools lay in a neat row near the middle, along with a notepad with some kind of unfamiliar writing. And blasting caps—dozens of them—stood upright in a heavy cardboard box.

Adam noticed the wooden crate in the corner, the same one he'd seen in Weatherly's barn. This was the first time he'd had a chance to study it in the light. It measured about a foot-and-a-half square and three feet long, and was built solidly, with two padlocked steel bands encircling it in each direction. The stenciling on the side definitely looked Russian. He tried lifting one end of the crate. It wouldn't budge. For something this small, it weighed a ton.

It seemed that before Weatherly's compound was raided, he had just moved their operation here. Adam wondered if someone had tipped him off. It seemed unlikely, since so many of their people were captured. Hopefully the computer would hold all the answers. Why was it taking so long to copy the files?

Adam sat down at the second terminal and flipped the switch on. While he waited, he might be able to learn something. When the menu appeared, he clicked "A." A small hourglass replaced the menu, and a new picture blinked onto the screen.

The other computer terminal beeped, and Adam inserted the second disk. God, it was taking forever to copy the files. He figured that Jack would come back at any moment, so he'd better be prepared for that possibility. But he had to find out everything he could, and do it fast. He scrolled through different menus, without a clue as to what he saw. Pictures of several well-known landmarks popped onto the screen, including Seattle's Space Needle and the Golden Gate Bridge.

A beep came from the terminal across the room, and Adam saw that it had finally finished. After placing the disks in the inside pocket of his jacket, he returned that terminal to its main menu, then continued searching files on the other.

He wanted to take some notes, but there seemed to be no writing pads here. He pulled a business card from his wallet and quickly jotted his thoughts.

That sound — Adam thought he heard a creak, but concrete bunkers don't creak. He listened. The computer's humming was all he heard. Was it his imagination? It was insane to look through the files with Jack likely to return at any moment. He'd better get out of here.

The sound of keys being inserted in the lock filtered through the door. Adam hit *ESCAPE* several times on the keyboard, then ducked into the dorm and back under the bunk bed. No time to turn off the light.

His claustrophobia returned as he slid into the tight space, but there was nowhere else to hide. At least he'd gotten rid of most of the cobwebs the night before. If he had to, he could tough it out under here, as long as he didn't have to stay very long. He inhaled the dust under the bed and stifled a sneeze. That's all he needed.

His business card — where was it? He prayed that he hadn't left it on the desk.

Two voices filtered in. "What in the world is the light doing on?" Jack said. "I know I shut it off."

"You sure?" It was Weatherly's voice.

"I think I'm sure. Jeez, I've got to be more careful. Must be getting old-timer's disease." Jack's voice trailed off.

The door burst open, and Bruno's nose was under the bed, sniffing Adam's face, his tags jingling in Adam's ear.

"Get out," Adam whispered, pushing the dog away. "Go." Bruno wanted to lick Adam. God, no.

"Bruno, what in tarnation are you doing in there?" Jack called from the next room. "Get out of there! Go on!" The dog followed Jack out. "You know, sometimes I think this mutt's more trouble than he's worth. Hang on just a second while I put him outside."

Adam heard the main door open, and the jingle of Bruno's tags faded. Weatherly slowly entered the dorm. Adam saw his feet head to the wall in front of the picture, pause for a moment, then turn and face the bunk bed.

His business card—Adam saw it on the floor within easy arm's reach. He couldn't move, or even breathe, much less reach out for it. If Weatherly didn't turn on the light, maybe he wouldn't see the card. Yet, something that white on a blue carpet would surely stand out.

Weatherly sauntered slowly around the room. Adam heard a drawer slide open and close. Then the feet turned toward Adam and stopped right in front of the card.

"Well, that's done," Jack said. The light came on. "Sorry it's so austere in here."

"No problem. We all need to make sacrifices."

"True. The whole place is yours for now. Just pick any bunk. The missus will bring your meals down. You know, you're gonna love her cooking."

Jack continued. "Now when you come in, remember to park around behind the shed. I got a scare the other day when Adam showed up. Good thing he didn't notice your car. I'm glad you're finally driving something a little less conspicuous."

Weatherly took another step forward, the tip of his foot touching the card. "We should have finished him off when we had the chance."

"Darn it, you can't just go knocking people off this close to home," Jack said. "That's what's causing all our trouble right now. You knocked off the other kid, and now we've got all those people nosing around here."

The two men walked into the next room, leaving the door open. Then the light went off. Adam grabbed the business card as Weatherly spoke. "I had no idea it was this elaborate."

"I built it a couple of years ago, figuring we could run all the operations from here," Jack said. "When the place next door came on the market, I couldn't believe our good luck. If that kid hadn't gotten nosy, we'd still be in business there. Anyway, it'll take the Jew-boys a while to find this place."

"Yeah. If we didn't have it, we'd be out of business."

"Probably. Now that Boris is gone, it'll be up to you to get this thing up and running. We can't let up, you know. The Mexicans are breeding like rabbits, and if we don't do something fast, they'll be running the whole darn country before long."

"We won't let that happen," Weatherly said.

Adam could hear only muffled voices. They grew louder as Jack and Weatherly stood near the doorway to the dorm. "What will happen to Boris?" Weatherly asked.

"He'll probably spend some time in prison and then be deported. I thought you knew that."

"Too bad."

"Yeah, good man. But you have to expect casualties in a war. We lost some good people. Besides you and me, I don't think we have any trained soldiers left. But we just have to cinch up our belts and get out there and recruit some more forces.

"As soon as you finish up in San Francisco, I want you to go down to Southern California. They got some real problems down there. You know, they got this Mexican Congresswoman in Orange County that's gonna give the whole state over to the wetbacks if she gets half a chance. You're probably going to have to dispatch her. Might be good to do it when she's got some of her greasy friends around — kill a whole bunch of birds with one stone. And oh, I almost forgot to tell you about Boris's notes. It's all in the computer."

"Hopefully it's been translated to English."

"It has. Here. I'll show you how to work everything."

Adam's neck began to cramp. Jack and Weatherly could be working here all night. Adam could see himself hiding under the bed for days.

"You got a key for me?" Weatherly asked.

"A key? Oh. I almost forgot." Adam listened to what sounded like a desk drawer opening. Then he heard a drawer in the filing cabinet being opened and someone fumbling though some keys.

"This doesn't look right," Jack said.

"What?"

"I'm not sure, but I wouldn't have left this drawer looking like this. It's like someone was rummaging around in here."

"Who?"

"I don't know, but I aim to find out." Adam saw Jack's feet in the doorway as the light went on. After a moment, he turned it off. "This bothers me," Jack said.

"Nobody's been here," Weatherly said. "How could they?"

"Yeah, you're probably right."

Soon Adam heard the filing cabinet drawer close. "Here's the keys," Jack said. "This one fits the shed and all the doors down here. This other one goes to the padlock on the gate. Oh, before you settle in, let me get the missus to bring you some of her apple strudel. It's out of this world."

Jack spoke on the phone, and Adam soon heard Elsa's voice as she came in. The conversation went on for a time and Jack said, "We'll be getting out of your hair now. Just make yourself at home, and call me if you need anything."

"Okay. I'll probably stay here until I finish. Shouldn't be more than a day or two."

A day or two? Oh, God. What would Adam do?

"Let us know the minute you finish," Jack said. "Everything else is in place."

Adam heard the main door latch. Weatherly came into the dorm and undressed, dropping his clothes on the floor. He walked out, and soon Adam heard the sound of water going through pipes. He waited, not sure of what he should do. After a time, he slipped from under the bunk and peeked out the door into an empty room. He heard the sound from the shower. This might be his only chance.

39

As Adam tiptoed toward the door, the sound of the shower abruptly stopped. He turned the doorknob and pulled. It didn't budge.

He expected the bathroom door to open at any moment as he dug in his pocket for the key. It wasn't there. That's where he'd put it. He was certain. He frantically checked his other pockets. There was no way he could have lost the key. It had to be here.

Soon the muffled buzz of an electric razor came from the bathroom. This would buy him some time. He shined his flashlight under the bottom bunk — nothing. He fumbled through his pockets once again — completely emptied them one at a time.

There it was, in a clump of coins in the first pocket he'd checked. He felt stupid as he stuck the key in the lock. It wouldn't turn. Now, what? This had to be the one.

The sound of the razor stopped. Adam glanced toward the bathroom. One more time — he wiggled the key in and out, and turned it. The latch slid open, and Adam made a quick exit. He couldn't lose concentration like this if he expected to survive. He eased the door closed, being careful not to click the latch, then trotted up the steps, through the shed and into the nighttime chill.

"Get away, Bruno." As he opened the gate, Adam had to shove the big Lab away.

Bruno backed up several steps, woofed softly and crouched. Then he barked again, this time louder.

"Shut up, damn it," Adam whispered as loud as he dared. Why did this mutt want to play in the middle of the night?

Bruno nuzzled Adam's hand and received a head pat. There were no more treats. He followed Adam away from the shed, toward the shadows. Water dripped from the redwoods, and Adam pulled his collar up.

The patio light came on, and Jack, wearing a bathrobe, stepped out. Adam slipped into the darkness, with Bruno coming alongside. "Get out of here." He slapped the dog hard on the rump.

"What's the matter, boy?" Jack's voice came from just a few feet away. Adam saw a flashlight beam swing his way and stepped deeper into the shadows. Bruno trotted toward Jack. If dogs could talk, he'd be toast.

Adam hurried through the trees along the driveway, toward the road. A U-Haul truck he hadn't noticed when he arrived was parked near the carport. In the faint light, he noticed a Howard Dean-for-President bumper sticker in the middle of the roll-up door, no doubt put there by someone other than Jack or Weatherly. He crossed the road, went behind the stand of redwoods and continued toward his car, using those trees to shield him as he passed Jack's driveway.

He was afraid to turn on his flashlight and could hardly see a thing in the dense cover. He stepped carefully. Soon the moon peeked from behind the clouds, and he caught a reflection off his car's windshield. He broke into a trot, wanting to get away as fast as he could. He doubted that anyone was trailing him, but just the same, he drove to the first curve with his headlights off.

After driving a few miles, Adam pulled off the road to dial the FBI, but couldn't get a good signal. Their office would be closed now anyhow. Besides, from the conversation he'd heard between Weatherly and Jack Kinney, neither of them were going anywhere for now. He'd call the FBI the first thing tomorrow morning.

"FBI. This is Agent Botelli."

"This is Adam Knight. I've just seen Weatherly." Adam sat at the kitchen counter, sipping coffee.

"Where?"

"At the Kinneys'. Jack and his wife are in on it, too. Their whole operation is set up in an underground bunker." Adam gave the agent the details and answered several questions.

"Good news," Botelli said.

"When will you pick them up?"

"We're already working on it. Thanks for the information."
"Don't let him get away."
"We won't. Thanks. I'll keep you posted."

Adam checked his calendar. He had almost two hours until his first appointment and couldn't wait to see what information Jack's computer held. He sat down at his terminal and loaded the first disk. He should have told Botelli about copying Jack's files, but it slipped his mind. He'd check it out first and then call Botelli back.

At the top of the menu was a box marked HEADQUARTERS. Below were listed several cities: Boise, Las Vegas, San Francisco and Seattle. San Francisco was enclosed in a box and had a flashing red arrow pointing at it from each side. Adam clicked on the box, and a new screen with two pictures, one of the Golden Gate Bridge and the other, the Transamerica Building, appeared. There was also a photo of what appeared to be a train station with BART in logo form in the background. The next screen again showed the BART logo. Underneath was printed, Embarcadero, Montgomery, Powell, Civic Center, each on a separate line.

He clicked the photo of the Golden Gate Bridge. The screen shifted to a close-up of the tower in the middle of the channel. Following pictures showed the bridge from several different angles, from the water line to the roadway. Another screen had the water current patterns around the bridge. The next picture showed the base of the tower. The one after that had a photo of where the tower intersected with the road.

Next Adam clicked the Transamerica Building and looked at several different screens of the structure. Cross sections showing the elevator shafts, the underground area and the peak of the building flashed onto the screen.

"What are you looking at?" Carla rolled a desk chair beside Adam and eased into it.

"You won't believe this stuff. Take a look." Adam clicked another box.

"What is it?" she asked.

"A bomb. Check this out."

The next screen showed how to make a bomb from ammonium

nitrate and motor oil. "In large enough quantity, this type of explosive can take down a skyscraper. It's the same stuff they used in the Oklahoma City bombing. I wonder if they plan to set it off in the Transamerica building?" Adam searched through the entire file, but could not find a plan for smuggling a bomb inside.

"See this?" He pointed with the cursor. "They use a cheap digital wristwatch for a timer. The wires connect to a detonator. The way it's hooked up, if someone cuts a wire to disarm it, it'll go off."

"You're not in the army anymore. I hope you're not planning to disarm any bombs."

"You kidding? I'm not that crazy."

Adam pulled into the driveway, clicked the transmitter and waited as the garage door slowly rolled up. He'd wanted to get home earlier, but a client had come in late in the afternoon, staying for almost two hours.

The *Jeopardy* jingle played on the family-room television and that's where Adam headed. The room was empty.

"Carla, where are you?"

"In the baby's bedroom."

Adam found her rearranging baby clothes and blankets. "How you doing?"

"Junior's kicking up a storm." She placed Adam's hand on her stomach. "Feel."

Adam felt something push against his hand. "Whoa! He seems ready to pop out."

"Mom says it'll be another week or two, but we're getting close."

"Want me to fix dinner?"

"You've been working all day. Let's order pizza."

Adam phoned the pizza parlor and then placed a call to Agent Botelli. "Just calling to see if you picked them up."

"We're still coordinating it."

"What are you waiting for? They're going to get away."

"We won't let that happen. Trust me on this, Mr. Knight. We can't go in until we have all our ducks in a row."

Adam sighed. "I hope you know what you're doing." He prayed that this wasn't just another botched FBI job.

Adam could scarcely believe what he read in Jack Kinney's files. It was almost one a.m., and he could not stop. A newspaper editorial stated that some members of the Russian military were selling nuclear components to anyone with enough money, and that it was just a matter of time before somebody exploded a bomb in the U.S. Many Russians were so destitute they'd do just about anything for cash. According to this article, it was fairly easy to buy off some military officers and nuclear physicists.

He scrolled through the files and stopped at a picture of the Transamerica Building. Superimposed over it was an exploded firecracker surrounded by a star burst. Above it in block print, *SEND THEM A MESSAGE THEY WON'T FORGET*, almost jumped off the screen at Adam. It showed a cross-section of the Transamerica Building with a bomb at the base of an elevator shaft. The next several screens showed photos of other San Francisco landmarks with the same graphics and message superimposed over them: the Golden Gate Bridge, the Bay Bridge and the Mark Hopkins Hotel. He had to notify Botelli.

He checked his watch as he punched in the phone number — almost two a.m. An answering machine came on. *"You have reached the Santa Rosa office of the FBI. Business hours are Monday through Friday, eight to five. If this is an emergency, call our San Francisco office."*

Adam jotted down the number and then dialed.

"FBI."

"My name is Adam Knight. I've been working with Agent Botelli in Santa Rosa."

"Yes sir, how can I help you?"

"Are you familiar with the Righteous Confederacy?"

"The supremacy group?"

"Yes. I have information that they're planning to bomb an important San Francisco landmark."

"How do you know?"

"I copied their computer files."

"Did it say when or where?"

"No. It could be at any time, though, based on the conversation I overheard."

"We'll need to pick up the files as soon as possible."

Adam checked his watch. "If you tell me where to deliver them,

I can be there with the disks by eight a.m."

"That would save us considerable time." The agent gave Adam the address.

"Thanks. I'll be there in a few hours."

What an idiot he was. Adam crept ahead in bumper-to-bumper traffic as he approached the Golden Gate Bridge.

Had he been thinking, he would have realized there would be a traffic problem at this time of day. It seemed especially bad this morning.

He woke Carla from a sound sleep and told her he was going on this trip. She was so sleepy she didn't even protest. He'd drop off the file and be home by noon.

As he rounded a bend, the bridge loomed straight ahead, emerging from the fog and then fading back into it. Five miles an hour and stop. Adam was glad he didn't have to commute to work like this every day. He crept forward.

Finally on the bridge, he felt the wind pressing against the side of his car, and watched as billows of fog sped across in front of him. How could people stand to do this every day?

As he eased toward the first tower, he finally saw the apparent cause of the bottleneck. A U-Haul truck sat stalled in the slow lane and cars funneled around it. On the back of the truck, in the middle of the roll-up door, was a Howard Dean-for-President bumper sticker.

40

Adam speed-dialed Botelli's office. Would someone be there this early? He counted the rings: four... five... six...

"FBI. Agent Botelli."

"It's Adam. There's a truck stalled on the Golden Gate Bridge with the driver missing. I think it belongs to the Righteous Confederacy."

"Where are you?"

"I'm on the bridge, standing beside the truck. I think it's full of explosives."

"I'll call the bomb squad and have the CHP close it off. You get the hell out of there!" Adam heard the phone click.

His thoughts flashed back to Oklahoma City as he checked the padlock on the rollup door — one of those huge, high-security types. If he had his toolbox he could probably break in. Better to leave it for the bomb squad, though. They were better equipped to handle it.

It was time to put some distance between him and this truck. If Carla knew he was here, she'd freak. He got behind the wheel and started the car.

That padlock — it looked like a duplicate to the one on Jack Kinney's gate. Adam had the key to *that* lock in the car. If he could open it, he would save the bomb squad valuable time.

But this thing could blow at any second. He couldn't make Carla a widow.

But what about all the people crossing the bridge? Hundreds, maybe thousands of innocent people — men, women and especially children — would be killed. If it blew during the morning commute, it could be worse than 9-11. He grabbed the key ring from his glove compartment.

Cars passed inches from him as he returned to the back of the truck. He realized that his hands were shaking. He could hardly hold the key as he reached for the padlock.

Wait—booby traps. He almost forgot to check—could be a fatal mistake. He looked in the crack around the door. No wires. That didn't mean there weren't any. His brain shouted to get the hell out of there. No way. He had to try. He took a deep breath. His shaking hand stuck the key in the lock and turned. It popped open.

The wind whipped up, sending puffs of fog past. Adam shivered, more from his fear than from the cold, as he unfastened the latch. He slowly lifted the handle. The door rolled up.

The truck looked almost empty. Maybe it had just run out of gas. Adam felt a little foolish, thinking he'd caused all this commotion over nothing. He'd better call Botelli back.

As he looked closely, he recognized the wooden box in the darkest corner of the truck and climbed in to get a better look. It was the crate that had been at Kinney's. The top and front were off, and he could finally see inside.

He recognized it instantly—the bomb. Adam stared at the nuclear bomb pictured on Kinney's computer.

His senses went numb as he inspected the metal and plastic device. This couldn't be happening.

A pair of tie wraps attached a digital wristwatch to the front. Two strands of bell wire emerged from the back of the watch and went through a hole in the plastic housing—nothing fancy. Most of the stuff for the timer probably came from Radio Shack.

Adam looked it over. When would the timer go off? He wanted to run, but his feet wouldn't move.

It was too dark to see the timer's digital readout. If he could slide the crate to the doorway, the light would be better. Adam grabbed each side and pulled. It wouldn't budge. He had to find some other way to read it.

Why was he still here? Whatever the reason, he felt compelled to stay.

Where was the bomb squad? It had been almost three years since he'd disarmed any explosives. And he sure as hell had never worked with anything like this. He didn't even know if it gave off radiation.

If he could disable the detonator—yes—disable the detonator.

That would take care of the immediate problem. Adam returned to his car and sifted through the computer printouts. He skimmed each sheet and discarded it. Several pages down he finally found the right papers.

He studied the wiring diagram in the light and then climbed into the bed of the truck. He could barely see the connections. And unless he could read the timer, it might not make any difference.

He pulled out his key ring and clicked on the penlight. A faint glow whimpered out, not nearly enough.

The flashlight in the glove compartment: no, he remembered taking it out of the car when he returned from the Kinneys'. He went to check, just to make sure.

Gone. He looked in the glove compartment and under the seats. It wasn't there. That meant the penlight on his key ring was his only hope.

He pressed the switch. A faint glow eked its way out—not enough. He tapped the light against his palm. It went out. His hands shook. Sweat blurred his vision. Damn. He had to get control—too easy to make a mistake. It had been so long since he'd disarmed any explosives that he'd forgotten how.

He held the penlight with both hands and pressed his thumb on the switch. This time the light glowed a little brighter. If he kept his thumb in this position, it might be enough.

Adam directed the faint beam toward the digital display. Finally he could make out the numbers. He watched, almost mesmerized, as the timer clicked down, one precious second at a time—just over nine minutes and counting. He had to get out of here.

Cars crawled past. A school bus with about a dozen small kids crept forward. In a few years his child would be that age. He couldn't let this thing blow them away. Where was the CHP? They should have been here by now. If they weren't going to come, he would have to stop traffic himself.

But Carla and his baby had to come first. It wouldn't help them a bit if he were a dead hero. He had to be there for his wife and to watch his baby grow to adulthood. It wouldn't be fair to deprive them of a husband and father.

Traffic came to a stop in both directions and then began to ease ahead. There was no way he could get off this bridge in time, as much as he wanted to.

This was wasting precious time. He looked back at the bomb. If he couldn't disarm it —

"Stop right there." That voice was unmistakable — Weatherly. He had a pistol. It pointed at Adam.

41

Maybe Adam could reason with Weatherly. "If this thing blows, it'll take you, too."

"Then I'll be a martyr, like Tim McVeigh was."

Adam had to get the gun. Weatherly was bigger, but Adam was at least twenty-five years younger. Adam knew he could take him. If only Weatherly weren't holding the pistol. It didn't make any difference, though. He had to try. He took a step toward Weatherly.

Weatherly squeezed the trigger.

Adam cringed as he heard a click.

Weatherly looked surprised as he glanced down, quickly cocking the pistol.

Adam lunged, knocking Weatherly down. The pistol fell from his hand. As Weatherly grabbed for the weapon, Adam kicked his hand. The gun slid away.

"You son-of-a-bitch." Weatherly swung as he rose from a crouch, landing a solid blow to Adam's jaw.

Adam hit the floor, his ears ringing. Maybe he'd underestimated the old man. He shook the fuzziness from his head. The pistol—he saw it just as Weatherly reached for it.

Adam connected with an uppercut to Weatherly's jaw, slamming him against the wall of the truck. He couldn't waste precious time like this.

Weatherly rubbed his mouth with the back of his hand and glared as Adam closed in. Without warning, Weatherly thrust a foot forward, catching Adam full in the groin. Adam collapsed.

He struggled to his knees, almost paralyzed as Weatherly picked up the sidearm. Adam couldn't give him a chance to use it.

He lunged as a shot fired off. Both men went out the back of the truck and onto the pavement. Adam landed on top of Weatherly. The air rushed from Adam's chest. He tried to breathe, but his lungs would not cooperate.

He gasped several times and struggled to his feet. His legs barely held him. Weatherly scarcely moved. As much as the fall hurt Adam, Weatherly got the worst of it, landing on his back. This might be Adam's only chance to get the upper hand. He lunged for the pistol, which rested a few feet away, and clenched it in his fist.

The timer: how much time was left? Adam had to get back to the bomb. He should just shoot Weatherly to save time. No, he couldn't. He struggled to his feet and pulled Weatherly up. It took all his remaining strength.

Weatherly hunched over, holding his arm. It was broken for sure. Blood dripped from a bump on the back of his head. He offered no resistance as Adam took him to the back of his car and opened the trunk. "Get in."

"Like hell." The words grimaced out.

Weatherly cried out as Adam pulled on his injured arm. "Get in the goddamned trunk."

"What are you doing?"

Adam glanced up to see a stranger standing there. "This man's wanted by the FBI."

"Don't believe him," Weatherly said. "He's got a bomb in the back of that truck."

The man stepped forward. "You're hurting him."

"Get out of my face, man."

"Let go of him," the man said, coming uncomfortably close.

No time to argue. Adam turned toward the man, pointing the pistol at his head. "One more step and I'll blow your fucking head off."

The man's breath caught when he saw the pistol. He wheeled about and sprinted to his car. Adam shoved Weatherly into the trunk. Weatherly yelled and then whimpered as he landed on his arm.

Weatherly slid his pants leg up. God, his leg holster: Adam had forgotten about the other pistol Weatherly carried. "Touch it and you're dead," Adam said, pointing his pistol at Weatherly's head.

Weatherly went limp. Adam removed the weapon from the leg holster and slammed the trunk lid.

He climbed back into the truck, tossing the pistol into the corner. Almost four more minutes had elapsed — time he didn't have. With trembling hands, he tried to read the schematics. He steadied his hands against the wall to keep them from shaking. As dark as it was in here this penlight was worthless. He walked to the back of the truck and leaned into the light — much better.

A gust snatched the pages from his hand. He jumped down and chased them across the roadway.

A horn blast, inches away, startled Adam. "Asshole," the driver yelled.

Adam dashed toward the floating pages, grabbing some. But there were too many. He could only watch as the instructions for his survival drifted off and over the edge of the span.

He returned to the bomb. It was different than any he'd ever studied. He didn't have any idea if he could pull it off. He looked at the timer. It ticked off the seconds — less than four minutes and counting.

His cell phone rang. It had to be Botelli. "Where the hell's the bomb squad?"

"Bomb squad?" Carla said. "Adam, what's going on?"

"Nothing. I'm real busy. I'll call you back."

"Wait. Adam..." Carla paused.

"What? Hurry up."

"Honey, I'm having contractions."

"Call your mom. I'm busy." Adam closed his phone and checked the timer — three minutes, fifteen seconds.

Carla was in labor — no time to think about it. He had to stay focused. Should he cut one of the wires? No. Too easy and too obvious — probably blow the whole thing off the map. But he couldn't think of anything else. "Do something, idiot," he mumbled. But what?

His nail clippers — he pulled them from his pocket. With two snips, the tie wraps that held the timer dropped away. The watch had a hole drilled in the back, with two wires coming out. Should he cut one? No, that would set it off.

Three minutes... two minutes, fifty — he had to try something. It would either work or it wouldn't. Was he going to die on the day his baby was born? He couldn't think about that. Two minutes, thirty.

He traced the strands of red and white bell wire to where they disappeared inside the bomb. What he wouldn't give for a screwdriver.

Two minutes, ten. "Just cut the goddamned wire," he heard himself say. Two minutes.

The battery—if he could take it out of the watch. Yes. That might work.

He pried at the back of the watch with the blade of his nail clippers—too thick. One minute, forty. He tried again. Nothing. One minute, twenty—In just over sixty seconds this thing would blow.

His Swiss Army knife—did he have it in the car? He rushed to the front seat and found it in the center console. He dashed back to the bomb—forty seconds.

The largest blade snapped open as Adam pulled it out. Less than twenty seconds—enough time? Adam dug the blade into the crack on the back of the watch—almost. Once again he tried. It snapped open. The back dropped into his hand. He tapped the watch onto his palm. The battery fell out, rolling off his hand and onto the floor.

The display went blank. If another timer were working in tandem—Adam didn't want to think about it. But he couldn't help it. He counted off the seconds in his mind. Ten, nine, eight, seven, six—his cell phone rang—four, three, two, one.

He cringed. The phone rang again and again. "Hello." It didn't go off. Would it? No!

"Adam, what's wrong with you? Did you hear anything I just said?"

Adam sighed and slumped to the floor. "Oh, sorry honey, what was that?"

"Where are you? I'm in labor. I can't get a hold of Mom, and I need you here right now."

Adam took a deep breath and slowly expelled the air from his lungs. "I'm in San Francisco. I'll be there as fast as I can. See if Cindy can help for now. How are you doing?"

"The contractions are about five minutes apart."

"Five minutes? Oh, God. Don't forget your breathing exercises. I'm on my way."

42

A step van, with *SFPD Bomb Squad* emblazoned on the side, finally arrived, and men dressed in bulky protective gear waddled toward the back of the truck. That stuff would be worthless if this thing blew. Then Adam noticed that the bridge was almost empty. The CHP must have finally arrived.

Three black-and-whites pulled up from the San Francisco side. Several officers got out and began milling about. Soon a Marin County Sheriff's Department car arrived from the other side of the bridge.

"Over here," Adam said as he opened his trunk.

Weatherly lay curled in a fetal position. His face was scrunched into a pained expression, and his hand clutched his broken arm.

"This is the guy who's responsible for the bomb." Adam almost laughed as the officers and deputies struggled to get Weatherly out without causing him more pain. Weatherly screamed and cursed at each movement.

An ambulance arrived about five minutes later, loaded Weatherly inside and screamed away with an escort of several police cars. Adam had done all he could here. Now Carla needed him.

He headed for his car as a black sedan zoomed up with siren blaring and red light flashing. The siren stopped abruptly and Agent Botelli emerged from the car.

Adam looked at his watch as he shifted from one foot to the other. He couldn't wait any longer. "My wife's in labor. I'm out of here," he said.

"Wait a minute. We need to debrief you."

"No way. I'm going home."

"This won't take long."

"Sorry. My wife needs me more than you do."

"Before you go, let me make a call."

"You can't keep me here if I don't want to stay."

"I know, but how would you like to fly home?"

"Now? Sure."

"Let me call my supervisor." Botelli returned to his car and spoke on his cell phone.

Adam couldn't hear the conversation, but it was long. It sounded like Botelli had a hard sell on his hands. When he finally returned Adam was waiting in his car, ready to leave.

"My boss says he can have a plane at Marin County Airport in a half hour. I can debrief you on the way home."

"That should work."

"Okay, follow me." Botelli climbed in his car, hit the siren and peeled away.

It seemed as though the cab driver hit every stop light between the airport and the hospital, but Adam finally made it. He tossed a twenty over the seat to the driver, jumped out of the cab and raced to the main entrance.

The door slid open, and he dashed to the receptionist. "Which way to maternity?"

"Right down the hall."

Adam sprinted down a long corridor and burst through double swinging doors.

A lone nurse sat behind the counter halfway down the hall, engrossed in a computer screen. "I'm looking for Carla Knight," Adam said.

"Oh," she said, giving him the once-over, "you must be the father."

"Where is she?"

"Second door on the right."

Adam trotted down the hall. What if there had been complications when he wasn't here? He'd carry that guilt around for the rest of his life. He rushed into the room and almost ran into Dixie, who was heading out.

"Oh, Adam. You made it. I'm going to find the nurse."

"What's wrong?"

"Nothing. Carla's water just broke." Dixie whisked out the door.

"Adam. You're here," Carla said after a long grimace. She seemed to be in a lot of pain.

"Sorry I'm late." Adam elbowed Al out of the way and kissed Carla on the cheek. Cindy stood on the opposite side of the bed.

A nurse came in, followed by Dixie. "How you doing, hon?"

"My water just broke."

"So I heard." The nurse's jaws worked furiously on a wad of gum as she looked at Adam. "You the father?"

"Yes."

"Glad you could make it." She looked at the monitors and then checked Carla's progress. "Okay, hon, on your next contraction, remember, short bursts of breath. And whatever you do, don't push. Think you can handle it?"

Carla nodded.

"Where's Dr. Malone?" Adam said.

"Out of town. Dr. Rydell is on call."

"Well then, where's Dr. Rydell?"

"He's down in the cafeteria, putting some pollen on the new emergency room nurse. Should be along in a minute or two." She pulled back Carla's sheet. "Let's see how much you're dilated." The gum snapped between her teeth. "Holy shit," she mumbled.

"What's wrong?"

"Nothing, hon, you're about to become a daddy." She reached for the phone. "Hi, Emily. Is Lover-Boy still there? Well tell him to get his cute little butt to Room 104 before he misses the whole show."

"Oh." Carla clenched her teeth. She began a rhythmic blowing in short bursts. Adam was sorry he'd missed most of the Lamaze classes.

The nurse checked the monitors. "Looks good. Keep it up."

The door burst open, and a kid looking barely out of high school walked in. "We about ready?"

"Won't be long, doctor," the nurse said as she chewed.

Carla grimaced as another contraction hit her. They were coming faster now, one on top of the other. Adam felt helpless and wished he could do something for her.

"Okay, honey," the nurse said, "on the next one bear down just as hard as you can."

"Here it comes," the doctor said. He moved in closer. "Give it a good, hard push."

Carla's face turned red as she took a breath and followed instructions.

Adam watched in wonder as first a head, then the rest of a tiny, gray body emerged.

"It's a boy."

The doctor suctioned the baby's mouth, and then tapped his backside. Tears welled in Adam's eyes as he heard his son cry for the first time. The gray color slowly changed to pink.

Adam parked in the hospital's loading zone. After making sure the baby's safety seat was properly fastened, he headed toward the lobby. Carla and the baby were coming home. They'd named him Craig, and Cindy was thrilled.

As Adam walked around the corner to the entrance, he noticed a clutch of people headed his way, three with video cameras and several holding microphones. A flash bulb went off in front of him, then two more in succession. He wanted to run.

"Adam," an attractive brunette said as she thrust a microphone toward him, "tell us how it felt to disarm a nuclear bomb."

"Didn't have time to think about it," he said as he hurried past. He was more interested in seeing Carla.

"You know you're a hero."

"Just doing what had to be done."

"How does it feel to be a father?" a female voice in the crowd shouted.

"Great." He stepped briskly toward the maternity wing, not wanting to look at the reporters. He'd give them a couple of minutes on his way out. They might bug him for a while, but he could handle it. After a few days this would be old news, and then he could get back to a normal life.

Carla sat gently rocking baby Craig. When she saw Adam, she brightened. "Isn't he precious?"

"For sure. Ready to go home?"

"I can't wait."

The reporters crowded around as Adam wheeled Carla, with

their baby in her arms, toward the loading zone. He stopped as photographers snapped dozens of pictures.

"Adam, tell us what went through your mind when you were disarming the nuclear bomb," the brunette reporter said.

Carla's jaw dropped, and she looked up at Adam. "When did you disarm a nuclear bomb?"

"It wasn't anything, honest." He could tell she didn't believe his lie. He'd have a lot of explaining to do.

As he drove slowly down their cul-de-sac, Adam realized how much he'd missed his hometown. The ordeal that began when he met Weatherly was finally over. Weatherly was in jail, and the Righteous Confederacy was gone. Too bad about Jack and Elsa Kinney. Adam really liked them. Agent Botelli told him the FBI found them sitting in their living room under the picture of George Lincoln Rockwell. Each had a bullet in the head, a murder-suicide, they said. How could he have been so wrong about them? They were as much responsible for Craig's death as Weatherly, and now they'd gotten what they deserved.

43

Adam got Carla and little Craig settled in the family room. His mind raced ahead to Little League, shooting hoops in the driveway and taking his son fishing. He was going to be the type of father he always wished he'd had.

"It's feeding time," Carla said as she unbuttoned her blouse. "Need anything?"

"I could use a tall glass of water."

Adam brought Carla's water, settled in beside her and gently touched Craig's cheek with the back of his index finger. "Did I tell you about the reward?"

"No."

"According to Agent Botelli, Morrie Rosenthal's family put up some money. As soon as they wrap up the case, it's ours."

"How much is it?"

"Fifty thousand. I want to put it in a trust fund for Justin. It's going to be hard enough for him without a father. This will help."

"I think we should."

The doorbell rang. "That's probably Mom," Carla said. "Is the door locked?"

"Yeah. I'm trying to train her not to barge in all the time." The bell sounded again as Adam walked toward the front door. "Coming." Dixie wore a little thin at times.

As Adam unlatched the door, it pushed inward, knocking him off balance. He almost cried out as Weatherly barged in, his left arm in a fiberglass cast. He held a nine-millimeter semi-automatic pistol in his right hand, and it pointed at Adam. "Don't be a hero," Weatherly said, motioning Adam toward the family room.

"Let's keep them out of it." Adam took a step toward Weatherly.

"Don't do it." Weatherly's voice sounded almost casual.

"Adam, who is it?"

Adam backed toward the living room, hoping to divert Weatherly away from Carla. "What do you want?"

"You took away the things that meant the most to me, and now it's payback time. At first I was just going to put a bullet in your head. But I decided it will make a better impression if I kill your wife and baby and let you live."

Adam's knees went weak.

"Who's there, Adam?"

"Carla, I want you to take the baby and go out the back door to the neighbors."

"Stay right where you are," Weatherly said. He spun Adam and shoved him toward the family room.

Carla screamed and shielded Craig with her body as Adam stumbled in. He had to do something to distract Weatherly so Carla and the baby could get out. "How did you escape?"

Weatherly smirked. "I staged my own hanging. When they found me, they thought I was unconscious. It wasn't hard to overpower the incompetents who took me to the hospital."

Adam could hardly breathe. His heart pounded as Weatherly backed him against the wall. He'd do anything to keep this lunatic from harming Carla and their baby, even if it meant his own death. "Let them go," he said.

"Not a chance."

Carla started crying and rolled into a ball to shield Craig. Craig also began to cry.

"I won't let you hurt them," Adam said. The strength of his voice surprised him.

Weatherly took a step toward Adam. "You should have stuck with real estate."

"You killed my best friend. I couldn't let you get away with it."

"Not me, one of my soldiers did. He beat him with a tire iron and ran his truck off the bridge. It would have worked if you had stayed out of it."

"You killed Henry Battles, too, didn't you?"

"He knew too much."

"Rosenthal?"

"He was undermining our cause."

"You bastard." If he could keep Weatherly talking, maybe he could buy some time. He had to get the drop on Weatherly before he harmed anyone, but he didn't have a clue how to do it.

The front door swung open. "Hello, hello. Where's that baby?" Dixie walked in, her arms full of brightly wrapped packages.

Weatherly wheeled about. Adam grabbed his wrist, and the gun discharged. Someone screamed. Adam banged Weatherly's hand against the fireplace mantle. The pistol held fast as another round fired off.

"Get out of here," Adam said. Carla wrapped herself around Craig and dashed from the room.

Weatherly swung his broken arm. Adam felt the cast connect with the side of his head and heard Weatherly scream from the pain of the contact. Adam's knees buckled, but he didn't dare let go of the hand holding the gun.

He shoved Weatherly against the wall and brought a knee hard into his groin Weatherly groaned and slumped.

The lamp: Adam grabbed Carla's Tiffany lamp. He swung wildly, and the heavy brass base found its mark, the shade shattering as it made contact. The gun dropped from Weatherly's hand, and he fell to the floor.

Blood oozed from the side of his head. He began to stir, first lifting his head and then rolling to a sitting position.

Adam quickly picked up the sidearm. "Don't move," he said, training it on Weatherly. He pulled out his cell phone, glanced down and dialed 9-1-1. As he looked up, Weatherly reached behind his body and pulled out a pistol. Adam fired three rounds into his chest. Weatherly collapsed.

"Adam!" Carla screamed from outside

"Go next door!" Adam yelled. He turned back to Weatherly. Blood gurgled from the wounds and onto the carpet. Adam wilted into a chair.

"Sir, speak to me," the voice on the telephone pleaded. "What is your emergency?"

"I just shot a man."

The sounds of sirens wailed in the distance, their volume rising as they grew closer. Soon, several helmeted officers burst through the back door with rifles at the ready. "Drop the gun," the first officer said, training his rifle on Adam. Adam let the pistol fall from his hand.

Two more policemen entered from the front. One of them checked Weatherly's pulse, looked at the other officer and shook his head.

The first officer helped Adam to his feet and steadied him as he stumbled out the front door, where several police cars, their lights flashing, were parked at odd angles. Carla dashed to him as he came down the steps.

Adam reached out to his wife and baby and held them close. They were safe. That was all that mattered.

44

The sounds of barking filled the air as Adam pulled into the parking lot at County Animal Services. He glanced through the chain-link fence on his way toward the entrance, hoping to catch a glimpse of the animal he'd come to adopt.

When he opened the door to the reception area and approached a counter, a woman looked up from her desk and smiled. "May I help you?"

"Yes. My name is Adam Knight. I called about claiming a dog."

"Oh, yes, the Labrador retriever."

"That's right."

The woman carried a sheet of paper to the counter. "Just complete this form, and I'll have someone bring him in." She slid it in front of Adam.

He began filling in the blanks as the woman picked up the phone and punched two numbers. "The new owner is here for 2410." She hung up and began typing into a keyboard. Moments later she looked up from her computer monitor. "I see that all his shots are up to date, so it will be just a twenty dollar transfer fee."

Adam pulled a bill from his wallet and handed it to the woman as a side door opened, and a man came in holding the end of a leash attached to a Labrador retriever.

"Bruno!"

The dog barked and lunged against the leash toward Adam, pulling the man along.

Adam crouched and stroked Bruno's head and ears. He received a lick in return. Bruno's tail thumped loudly against the front of the counter. He barked again.

"He certainly seems happy to see you," the woman said.

"Yes, he does. And the feeling is mutual."

"Well, you're lucky to have each other."

"I know. He'll be a great dog for my son." Adam took the leash from the man and patted Bruno's head once again. "Come on, boy, let's go home."